ROUND ONE

Braddock leaped out of his corner, lean and determined, a lunging predator. Before Baer even made it to the center of the ring, Jim was on him, a light tap with his left followed by a stiff right to Baer's body.

The Cinderella Man's no-fear ferocity lifted the audience out of their seats.

But Baer recovered quickly and came back at Braddock with a short uppercut that missed Jim's chin by less than an inch. Braddock stepped away, circled Baer until he spied an opening in the champ's defenses, then closed on him again with a twisting hook—right into Baer's side.

Spun by the blow, Baer dropped his fists, leaving himself wide open for a combination. Braddock let him have a long, stinging right to the face. Baer grunted, sneered. Braddock let fly with another right, then a left, and a final terrific right that bounced off the champ's iron jaw.

Novelizations by Marc Cerasini

CINDERELLA MAN
AVP: ALIEN VS. PREDATOR

Cinderella Man

WRITTEN BY
MARC CERASINI

BASED ON THE
MOTION PICTURE SCREENPLAY BY
CLIFF HOLLINGSWORTH
AND
AKIVA GOLDSMAN

MOTION PICTURE STORY BY
CLIFF HOLLINGSWORTH

HarperEntertainment
An Imprint of HarperCollinsPublishers

HARPERENTERTAINMENT
An Imprint of HarperCollins*Publishers*
10 East 53rd Street
New York, New York 10022-5299

ISBN: 0-06-077958-6

HarperCollins®, 🔥®, and HarperEntertainment™ are trademarks of HarperCollins Publishers Inc.

First HarperEntertainment paperback printing: May 2005

Printed in the United States of America

Visit HarperEntertainment on the World Wide Web at
www.harpercollins.com

10 9 8 7 6 5 4 3 2 1

This book is dedicated to
Antonio A. Alfonsi
&
John F. Cerasini
and all of our Depression-era
parents and grandparents, who never
stopped fighting, no matter the odds . . .

ACKNOWLEDGMENTS

The author would like to thank Cindy Chang at Universal and Josh Behar at HarperCollins for their support on this project. Most particularly, the author would like to thank Alice Alfonsi for her invaluable help in the research and in the preparation of this manuscript. Without her assistance, this novel would not exist.

In my experience, I have found that the toughest game is the game of life, and when a man can do in that game what Jim has done, what does a fight mean, or a punch on the chin?

—Joe Gould,
manager of James J. Braddock

In no list that you will ever see will he be listed among the ten greatest, but . . . [because] others see themselves in him and read their own struggles into his, he may have belonged to more people than any other champion who ever lived.

—W. C. Heinz,
boxing writer and novelist

He is a great fellow, and he has a great story.

—Damon Runyon,
legendary journalist who first called
James J. Braddock "The Cinderella Man"

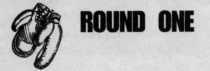 **ROUND ONE**

When the bell rings, you're in there to win.

—James J. Braddock,
as quoted by Peter Heller in *In This Corner*

Madison Square Garden
November 30, 1928

Boxing is a game of half steps and half inches, of timing, nerve, pain, endurance, and sometimes chance. Around the center ring of the Garden arena, nineteen thousand fight fans rose in a spiraling incline—too far to notice inches, too removed to notice chance. Most spectators simply waited for one gladiator to murder the other, in tonight's case, for the wiry Jim Braddock to be flattened by Gerald "Tuffy" Griffiths, the "Terror from out West."

With round one's clang, the bulked-up, corn-fed Griffiths roared out of his corner like an unstoppable cyclone. Under the broiling hot lights, Braddock stood firm and watched him come. Tuffy had blown into town claiming more than fifty consecutive wins, the last with a stunning first-round knockout. Seven-to-one Braddock was just another Tuffy KO. A sacrificial lamb. Everyone knew it—the promoters, the oddsmakers, the sportswriters. Everyone knew it except Braddock himself and Joe Gould, his excitable little round-faced manager, punching the smoky air in Jim's corner.

Whenever a reporter asked Gould why he thought his fighter was worth a plug nickel, he'd grab the man's lapels and bark, "What do you know about Braddock? What? Were you on that Jersey Hillside when Jimmy was just a scrawny teenager, forcing his older, bigger, golden gloves-winning brother to eat punch after punch? Did you watch him rise through one hundred amateur bouts to win his own pair of golden gloves against Frank Zavita—a giant stovemaker who'd outweighed him by fifty-three pounds? Were you with me that day in Joe Jeannette's gym when I offered some kid, a total nobody, five dollars to get smacked around by my top-ranked welterweight, never expecting it would be the kid, Jimmy Braddock, who'd do the smacking?"

Tonight, like every night, Joe Gould stood in Braddock's corner, close enough to see the half steps and half inches. Close enough to know that when Tuffy Griffiths launched himself across the ring, Jim was never more ready.

Braddock's sharp, solid jab surprised the charging Griffiths, sending the confident hulk back on his heels. The boxers advanced and retreated, hooking, blocking, and counterpunching, as they slipped and pivoted across the springy canvas. When Griffiths saw an opening, he launched again. His shoulders rippled through a flurry of combinations—jabs, hooks, body shots. These same fistic flurries had taken out Tony Marullo in Chicago, Jon Anderson in Detroit, Jim Mahoney in Sioux City, Jackie Williams in Davenport, even Mike McTigue, the former world's light heavyweight champion.

Blood flowed and sweat streamed, soaking Jim's brow, burning his eyes. Blows felt like thunderclaps and lightning together, exposing Jim's guard, splitting his head. But Braddock failed to hit the deck as Griffiths' other opponents had. Jim stayed on his feet, weathered the storm.

At ringside, reporters in straw boaters and fedoras sat chomping cigars, their fingers pounding the stiff keys of heavy typewriters. Every blow of the first round's action was recorded, and nobody thought the New Jersey boxer would last a second round.

But by round two, Braddock had timed his rival's rushes, and inside of a minute his power punch detonated—Jim's golden right cross. Griffiths went down. The crowd rose up. A deafening din.

On three, the Terror was up again. The count didn't stick.

By now Jim's adrenaline-rich world had turned hyper-real. Colors exploded, sounds spiked, awareness was dagger sharp. Time stretched for Jim, as it does for all good fighters, slowing in the face of violence. Inside the ropes, the slightest movement of his opponent's arm swept bigger than an Atlantic wave.

Jim blotted out everything then: the wild screams of the crowd, the contemptuous stares of the sports writers, the shooting pain in his injured and taped ankle, the hysterical yells from his corner. All Braddock knew was this chance to put away the great Griffiths. He cocked his right again, timed it just right, and let fly. Tuffy reeled.

"One . . . Two . . . Three . . . Four . . ."

Glassy-eyed, Griffiths rose once more, shutting down the ref's ten count.

Braddock was ready. He vaulted close and hurled a nonstop bombardment to his opponent's face. Shoulder muscles, slick with sweat, were primed and loaded. Leather slammed forward at breakneck speed, then came the jab, jab, cross, and Braddock's famous right connected for the last time, smashing into Griffiths' chin like an Irish freight train.

The fighter's jaw distended at an impossible angle, his eyes rolled back. Listing like a torpedoed ship, Griffiths sank a third time to the canvas. On three, Tuffy tried to stand with rubber legs. He staggered, and without another glove on him hit the deck for the last time.

"And from the great State of New Jersey, by technical knockout, tonight's light heavyweight winner . . . Jim Braddock!"

The announcer's bellow brought the capacity crowd to its feet. The hometown boy had done it—and just a stone's throw from the Hell's Kitchen tenement where he'd been born. Sweat dripping from his shock of black hair, Braddock pumped his fist in the smoky air, his bulky leather glove threatening to KO the Garden's high, steel-trussed ceiling. With an explosion of insane screaming, thousands of fight-mad fans cheered the "Bulldog of Bergen."

Jim took in the hooting, hollering faces—clerks and

tycoons alike sporting double-breasted suits and diamond tiepins; flappers and floozies with bobbed hair and fox furs. It was Friday night, the world was throwing a party, and Jersey Jim's victory was one more reason to celebrate.

Griffiths was Jim's eighteenth knockout since he'd turned pro in 1926. His twenty-seventh win. And that's how Braddock wanted to see himself—as a winner—not a Catholic-school dropout or punk kid scraper, not a Western Union messenger, printer's devil, or silk mill errand boy. Tonight those former lives had sloughed off Jim like dead skin.

Braddock knew that promoters had held high hopes for Griffiths' big Eastern debut. Tonight's upset in the Garden, the very mecca of this sport, would ink Braddock's name into headlines across the country and—if the right men said so—get him a shot at the heavyweight championship. Then Jim would be more than a winner. He'd be on his way to joining Gene Tunney and Jack Dempsey, to becoming what every boxer dreamed of, what every red-blooded man respected: the champ.

Inside the ring, hands grabbed Braddock's slick shoulders, then came the familiar jolt. Joe Gould had burst out of their corner with a big yahoo, leaping onto the boxer's back like one of Jim's kids. Drenched in sweat, the little guy looked like he could have fought this one for Jimmy all by himself.

Gould hopped down and hugged his boxer's neck. The Griffiths match hadn't lasted more than five minutes; just the same, it had been a long, hard fight for the both of them. With bright, quick eyes, the manager took in the stomping, whistling, adoring horde, met his boxer's steady gaze, and gave a huge grin. In reply, quiet Jim's lips twisted up wryly.

To come against something you can see and beat back. That's what the ring was for Jim Braddock: the right to give as good as he got. Tonight, the underdog had showed them. "Plain Jim," the nice guy, the humble man . . . the *winner*.

In the swarming street, a parade of cabs had already whisked most of the golden throng away—to Times Square with its music halls, burlesque shows, and talking pictures, or all the way up to Harlem's jazz joints, the Cotton Club and Paradise. A good hundred or so still lingered beneath a fire escape near the Garden's side entrance, where an illuminated billboard announced tonight's Jersey boy matchup against Tuffy the Terror from out West.

The door swung wide, banging against the clean brick wall and releasing a pearl-gray cloud of smoke. A single lightbulb flashed, throwing a split-second spotlight on the lean six-foot-three boxer and his paunchy, cigar-chomping manager as they emerged from the doorway and made their way through the electric knot of dapper fans.

The air was cold, the November whipping off the Hudson a few avenues away, but Braddock's muscles were still warm from his two-round workout. Jim nodded at the tailored overcoats and mink stoles waiting in the chill. He recognized some regulars from his Newark and Jersey City fights—loyal followers who'd come across the river.

"Just give a few, leave 'em wanting," Gould croaked

to his fighter. The manager's voice was usually sharp and resonant, but after a fight, he was hoarse for days from all the yelling.

"You want to sign my name for me too?" Braddock quipped as he stopped in front of a woman in a long overcoat with rabbit cuffs and collar. She held out her program.

"Least then they could *read* it," said Gould.

"Hand it to skill and experience over here."

The woman appeared bewildered, unsure how to respond to the wisecracking men. Jim smiled warmly, took her program. "Better let me," he told her in a mock whisper, "Not so sure he can spell."

When fans saw Jim was stopping to give autographs, they closed in. Programs were thrust forward, sports pages, glossies of himself in a staged boxer's pose, gloves up, expression fierce—Marquis of Queensbury by way of Newark.

Jim signed and signed.

"Gave him a cold meat party, Jim," a guy shouted from the back.

"Way to go, Braddock!"

Jim's brown eyes danced. He liked these people, the fact that they loved him so. A willowy brunette caught his attention—supple and slender, impossibly tall with a spoiled little heartbreaker smile. She opened her coat, lifted her hem. The flapper skirt rose like a Broadway curtain, revealing long legs in white stockings, blue garters at the knee. Then came that glimpse of naked promise—an invitation to a performance not to be missed.

Jim just smiled. Shook his head. Got back to business.

"Hey! Win some, lose some, huh Johnston?"

The hoarse bark of his manager's voice made Jim look up. Who was Gould baiting now? From the smoky side door, a big man had emerged, Jimmy Johnston, the Garden's fight promoter, twice the size and weight of Gould—in more ways than one.

You didn't get in the Garden without Johnston's say so. Men like him and Tex Rickard, mastermind of the first million-dollar gate, set up boxers like bowling pins. Griffiths' star had been rising, and he should have rolled right over Braddock like all the other setups. That's what the bookies had predicted, that's what Johnston had wanted.

Braddock hadn't even been considered for the Gerald Griffiths matchup until the month before. Pete Latzo, the former welterweight champ, had been the man originally chosen to fight Tuffy. Jim Braddock had been selected to serve as nothing more than Latzo's small-time "tune-up." Then Braddock shattered Latzo's jaw in a Newark ring and doctors had to use eleven feet of wire to put the man's face back together. Suddenly Latzo was sipping his meals through a straw, and Griffiths' headlining fight card had a vacancy.

Sure, Braddock was supposed to have been the sacrificial meat, but it was Griffiths who got slaughtered. Now Jimmy Johnston was wearing an imported silk suit and the face of a man who'd lost.

Braddock had seen that look before, on the men he'd sent to the canvas. He'd seen it on other men, too. Men his father's age, working those errand-boy jobs Jim had held through his teens. It was a look that said you'd been beaten but weren't going to show it—even though it did show. It was the rigid mask of pride that couldn't quite cover the shattering embarrassment of being thought a loser. Braddock had never seen that face in his own mirror, and he never intended to. But Jim wasn't a spiteful man, and he had no desire to be a sore winner.

He turned, touched his manager's sleeve. "Leave it be."

Gould nodded, as if he agreed. Then he kept on talking.

"Although you gotta figure this one, you gotta figure maybe you get behind the *wrong* guys." The little manager was now officially squaring off with the big suit. "What's Griffiths favored, six to one and, oh yeah, outweighs my boy by, what, five pounds more than that scale you fixed says, then jab, cross . . ."

"Actually, it was jab, jab, cross—" Braddock corrected. He wasn't keen on watching Gould spar, especially with a man as influential as Johnston, but he couldn't let his manager confront the promoter alone. For the past three years, Gould had been in Braddock's corner every step of the way, collaring sportswriters and singing Jim's praises. The least Jim could do was back his friend up.

"Jab, jab, cross!" the manager repeated, moving his short arms with the hits, punching the air like he always did when Braddock was inside the ropes. "And your boy's hearing highball whistles. Hell, I could hear 'em. You, Jimmy?"

"I heard something."

"So maybe no one's a *bum* after all, huh Johnston . . . ?"

Braddock hated that word. Had heard it before.

Some in the press said his early KOs were pushovers, no-accounts, bums. So what did that make Jim? After tonight . . . after *Griffiths* . . . what could Johnston say? What could anybody say?

Gould cocked his head to one side and fixed a withering glare on the promoter. Johnston held Gould's gaze. The moment hung for a long time, adrenaline soaked and dreamlike. Like the ring, thought Jim, where a second became a minute and a minute became an hour—and when you were taking punches, one three-minute round could last till the end of time.

Finally, Johnston turned. Breaking off, he strode to his waiting car.

"TKO," Gould told Braddock with a smile.

Jim narrowed his eyes. No matter what the Griffiths fight was ruled he knew what he'd done. "I won on a *knockout*, Joe."

The manager smiled. "Not you. Me."

Braddock shook his head. The fans might call him the Bulldog of Bergen, but it was his manager who deserved the title. After years with Gould, Jim knew one thing for certain—his little, obstinate, constantly barking manager had almost no control over his own mouth.

"I'll get a cab."

"A cab, *James*." Gould pointed to the curb where a long, sweet, 1928 Cadillac Imperial limousine waited with shining fenders, polished running boards, and a leather roof.

Braddock's eyebrows rose. He knew his manager favored fawn-colored suits, expensive cigars, and deluxe restaurants, which went right along with Gould's favorite motto: "Gotta keep up appearances." But this seemed over the top.

"Jimmy," said Gould, waving Jim to the limo, "we gotta talk."

A uniformed chauffeur pulled open the back door. Gould nodded to the driver and ducked inside. Braddock copied Gould, nodding and ducking just like his manager. As the car took off, Braddock settled into seats with backs higher than his living room sofa and leather softer than his oldest pair of gloves. There looked to be enough room in this ride for a baseball team, he figured, plus gold trim and fixtures so polished Jim could see his broad nose, square Irish face, and amused brown eyes reflecting back.

Gould grinned. "So I'm saying it."

Braddock glanced out the dark window. "No you don't. You'll jinx it."

"That's ten in a row," Gould said anyway, pulling a small brown bag from a leather pocket in the limo door. "Ten in a goddamned row."

Jim allowed a little smile. Knockouts, like tonight's, were what the fight fans wanted, and Gould knew it. Sure, Jim could outmaneuver a guy for the duration, dance around his opponent all night like a ballerina, but his big right cross, his power punch, was what brought the thunderous roars and the big paydays. Jim had learned fast that pleasing the paying public was what scored dollars for the promoters—and boxers who scored serious dollars were taken seriously.

Gould reached for a glass from a fixed gold tray and opened the fifth in the brown bag. He poured his scotch in silence, not bothering to offer Jim one. The boxer

would just decline it, like he always did. It had nothing
to do with the Volstead Act, or being famously absti-
nent like the current heavyweight champ, Gene Tunney. Braddock would take the occasional glass of beer
or wine. But he performed better off the hard sauce.

Braddock watched Gould knock back a few. Jim
waited. Then waited some more. Finally, he laughed.

"What?" asked Gould.

"Just seeing how long you could stay quiet is all."

Gould shot him an irritated look.

Horns were blowing up ahead, and Jim leaned forward, curious, to peer past the lowered partition. The
driver was trying to crawl through a crowded intersection. The light was green for him, but a tipsy group of
partyers in fedoras, overcoats, and furs were defying
their own red light. While cars honked, a giggling
ruby-cheeked debutante in a headband and full-length
sable began to dance the Charleston in the middle of
the jammed avenue.

As the driver carefully crawled through the crowd,
Jim noticed they were passing the famous 21 Club, a
restaurant and two bars now bursting with swank customers. Braddock had never been inside, but Gould
had. He'd once told Jimmy the owners had created a
secret chute where bottles could be tossed during a
raid. Even Braddock's wife, Mae, knew about it from
one of her favorite gossip columns.

"Behind Twenty-one's doors," she'd read to Jim one
morning in a playful voice, "lovely little heiresses, the
intelligentsia of Wall Street, Broadway, and Fashion
Avenue gather at any hour to discuss the news of the
town. The speakeasy has become the coffeehouse of
our age."

A cop fan of Braddock's once told him that since Prohibition started, almost nine years earlier, thirty thousand illegal bars had opened up in Manhattan. Judging from the way drunken crowds routinely plugged up traffic, Braddock figured that estimate was low.

"You're getting stronger every fight," Gould said as he nursed his scotch. "I been seeing it."

Braddock leaned back. Gould's tone was serious, but Jimmy still quipped, "So you're not blind, after all."

Gould well knew Jimmy had worked long and hard for tonight's upset. Before they'd even dreamed of setting foot in the Garden, before Jim had become a headliner, before he'd even turned *pro*, he'd boxed more than one hundred matches and earned the New Jersey light heavyweight and heavyweight amateur titles—both in the same night.

"You may favor the right, sure, but you got no stage fright or nerves," continued Gould in his assessment. "And you never been knocked out."

Braddock shifted his weight on the luxury seat. Not having a left was a sore spot for him, but he let it go. It hadn't mattered tonight anyway. Like Gould said, he'd never been knocked out—and as far as he was concerned, he never would.

Gould leaned close, took the cigar out of his mouth. The next thing out of it was no joke. "You're in line now, Jimmy. You're gonna get your shot."

Braddock nodded, couldn't help but feel the shiver. He glanced away a moment, saw his reflection in the dark window, confident, prepared. Everything was falling into place.

Outside, crowded sidewalks rolled by, the city's dazzling lights bathing raucous revelers in a golden glow.

Theater marquees shined with a glory that dispelled the night, as if the Strand, the Embassy, and the Globe's Ziegfeld Follies were all bragging, "So who needs the sun anyway?"

Beside the limo, an expensive roadster pulled up. Inside, two well-dressed young men laughed and clinked glasses. They looked more like kids really, playing at drinking scotch and holding fat cigars. Top of the world, they were—and why not? Braddock thought. It was the fifth straight year of the boom. Everything was going up, skyscrapers and stocks alike. The market had been driving upward, punching through records month after month, and everyone seemed to be getting rich. Braddock and Joe had wanted a piece of it, too, so they'd sunk their winnings in deep. Together they'd invested in another venture as well, a taxicab company, and Jim was certain they could only get richer.

That's right, thought Jim, he was a winner in the market and in the ring. More than that, he was going straight to the top of the highest skyscraper in the fight game. With Gould talking up the right promoters, setting up the right opponents, Jim was going to get his shot at knocking them all down, and becoming the Heavyweight Champion of the World—

"We need to get you out, being seen," said Gould. "Flash-flash, bing-bing. Satchmo's playing the Savoy. And there's this new jinny uptown."

So *that's* why the driver had turned north, thought Braddock. Gould was trying to hijack his hide, throw him in with the up-all-night crowd again. Jim had been holding out hope he might be the first passenger to cross the George Washington Bridge. But that crossing was still under construction—and this was one husband and father who wasn't going to any celebration that didn't include his wife.

Braddock shot Gould the usual look. "Home, Joe."

Gould had a comeback. He always did. But Braddock beat him to the punch—

"*Home.*"

With familiar resignation, Gould shook his head. Leaning forward, he called to his driver. "Jersey, Frank. For Mr. Adventure."

They reversed direction and headed downtown to the Holland Tunnel, a feat of engineering that had opened just the year before to become the world's first underwater vehicular roadway. Newspapers said the ventilation system was a model for similar tunnels planned around the world. That's what Jim loved about this city. Like a fighter, it never stood still, even punching under rivers through rocky earth to come out the other side.

Jim's parents had done that, too. Started on one side of an ocean and come out another, emigrating across the Atlantic to make a better life. The year Jim was born, Joseph Braddock and Elizabeth O'Toole Braddock had moved across water again for the same reason. With their six boys and two girls in tow, they traveled over the Hudson to relocate in West New York, New Jersey, once known as Bergen Hills. The peaceful residential township of churches, stores, and small houses, with the occasional outcroppings of the underlying Palisades' prehistoric rock, reminded Jim's parents of the old country—more so than the crowded concrete at 551 West Forty-eighth Street anyway.

In Jersey, Jim had grown up a typical American boy, playing marbles and baseball and hanging around an old swimming hole on the edge of the Hudson or under the Hackensack River Bridge. He'd endured Saint Joseph's Parochial School, where a classroom of thirty-five boys engaged him in constant fistfights. His chief nemesis had been a kid with the same name. Jim and Jimmy had tangled more than thirty times, with Braddock's best friend, Marty McGann, holding his coat and keeping score. Sometimes Jim won, sometimes he lost, but always the fight was interesting.

It was another friend, Elmer, who'd been Braddock's first KO. Some argument over marbles had led to Elmer's going at it with Jim, the kids in the schoolyard running over to look on, eyes wide. Suddenly, Jim landed a terrific right on his pal's chin. The kid went down like he'd been hit by an axe, then his head hit the sidewalk and he lost consciousness.

"Elmer is dead!" some kid yelled and Jim had frozen in terror.

A doctor came and Elmer woke again, but in the time it took, Jim had gone through a sickening scare. He'd never felt he was cut out for school—books, math, history, none of it connected. So a few months after Elmer dropped, Braddock dropped out for good.

At fourteen, he started working a series of unskilled jobs. Along the way, his older brother Joe had started to box and made it all the way from an amateur welterweight championship to a professional rating. One day, he and Jimmy got into a brotherly argument. The fists started flying, and to everyone's astonishment, including Jim himself, the skinny younger brother held his own against the older, more experienced fists. It was the first time Jim thought maybe he could be a winner in the ring.

Finally, on the night of November 27, 1923, at the age of seventeen, he'd climbed through the ropes in Grantwood, New Jersey, using the alias Jimmy Ryan. The alias was necessary for two reasons. His brother Joe had already put a Braddock on the card that night, and Jimmy had been *paid* to enter the bout—a grand total of three dollars. Jim Braddock wanted the chance to prove himself, but he knew a professional match on his record would derail his ability to fight as an amateur. Thus, to prevent the New Jersey state amateur boxing authorities from finding out, he'd used the "Ryan" moniker.

Jim's opponent that night was Tommy Hummell, a member of the Fort Lee police department. During the bout, both boxers went down more than once, but they came back every round. Newspapers wrote about it, calling it the best fight they'd seen that night, which was as good as the church blessing to a young boxer who'd just fought the first professional match of his life.

These days, Braddock lived in Newark, New Jersey, the state's largest city, with a thriving business district, green parks, and neighborhoods that had buildings from the time of the Revolutionary War still standing. To the west, the gently sloping woods of the Watchung Mountains overlooked a city center of skyscrapers, built up among the remnants of an old seaport town. To the east, the city faced the gaunt flatlands of the Hackensack tidal river, with Jersey City and New York visible from taller buildings. The industrial area was also to the east, where freight lines ran from Port Newark's docks past large factories, electric plants, great garbage dumps, and Newark's poorest residential districts.

Braddock and his family lived far from those bleak

industrial areas. His recently purchased home sat in a sedate, old suburb north of the city center, where Victorian and colonials occupied large, well-tended yards. As Frank, the limo driver, turned down Braddock's wide, tree-lined street, Gould dipped into his pocket and pulled out a thick wad of green.

"We've got eight hundred eighty-six for Jeannette," he said counting out bills for Joe Jeannette, the veteran heavyweight who'd opened a gym on Summit Avenue in Union City, the place where Braddock trained and he and Joe Gould had first met. "Two hundred sixty-four each for the two bucket kids; three hundred for the ring fees; my two thousand, six hundred fifty-eight; and your three thousand, two hundred forty-four makes eight thousand, eight hundred and sixty dollars."

Gould handed Jim his share of the prize money.

"You could come in for a drink?" Braddock offered as the car pulled up to a stately white colonial. "The kids would love to see you."

Gould paused a moment. "You still married to the same girl?"

Braddock gave a little smile. "I was this morning."

Gould chomped his cigar. "Maybe a rain check. And tell her I *undercharged* on the gym fees, and no load on the towels, would ya?"

"I'll point it out."

As Braddock climbed out of the limo, he bit his cheek to keep from laughing. Fearless Joe had chased down some of the meanest junkyard dogs in boxing, yet when it came to tangling with the headstrong lady inside Braddock's own home, the man turned his tail-lights and ran. Then again, thought Braddock, watching the limo speed down the road, the way Mae grilled Gould on the splits, Braddock could hardly blame him.

Jim turned toward his house to find the front door swinging wide. Framed in the golden glow of the vestibule light was a woman too lovely to be any man's wife, let alone a big, tongue-tied bastard like him.

From the moment he'd met Mae Theresa Fox, she'd knocked Jim out. It was the only time in his career it had happened—and that was just fine with him. He moved toward her, his gaze traveling over her chestnut hair and slender curves, primly wrapped in a flowered dress with an intricate lace collar—like a gift specially bound with a delicate ribbon only her husband could undo. He took in her serious face and wide-open eyes, full of that unusual combination of good sense and longing, and deep inside his body, Jim felt the familiar stirring, the impulse to touch her more powerful than the need to breathe . . .

 **ROUND TWO**

The bridegroom was a positive picture of health and carried no black eyes. And Mae Theresa was a distinctly lovely bride.

—Ludwig Shabazian, *Relief to Royalty*, James J. Braddock's authorized biography, 1936

When Mae finally saw her husband striding up the fieldstone walkway, her eyes refused to blink. Jimmy was here again. Her lean, strong husband had come back to her on his own two feet, whole and unharmed. Alive. The realization instantly lifted the dark cloud, released the suffocating weight. She could breathe again. Feel again.

Fight nights were always like this for Mae. Jimmy would kiss her good-bye in the afternoon, and half the evening she'd feel paralyzed, whispering prayers, watching the clock. Then he'd come home, and the exhilarating relief would release her from all those hours of fearful numbness.

Men died in the ring. It was not an uncommon occurrence. And if they didn't die they got hurt. Bad. The whole thing was a spectacle of injury and pain, and Mae didn't completely understand it. But she loved her husband, so she tried her best.

It was a cold Saturday in January, at a 9:30 A.M. Mass in West New York's St. Joseph's of the Palisades Roman Catholic Church, that Mae Theresa Fox had vowed to take Jim Braddock in sickness and in health, in good times and in bad.

Mae had been a telephone operator. She'd lived in Guttenberg, New Jersey, close by the Braddocks' home in West New York. Her brother, Howard, had been a friend of Jim's. Next to Marty McGann, the kid who used to hold Jim's coat while Jim fought in the school-yard, Howard was one of Jim's closest pals.

Mae's brother used to bring Jim back to the Foxes' for something to eat, and it was Mae who liked to set the table—mainly because she liked to be around the handsome, shy smiles of one Jimmy Braddock.

Although Jim had loved Mae from the moment he'd met her, he didn't get around to actually telling her so for quite some time. As a suitor, he'd been timid and reserved. Yet Mae had come to understand that although James was a person of few words, he was a considerate and generous man, and when he did have something to say, his wry sense of humor was usually evident, as well as his decency and quiet strength.

It took Jim a great deal of nerve to pop the question. He'd told Mae he'd wanted to wait until he had enough money to set up a nice home. When his boxing winnings had given him a small fortune of $30,000, he presented his case. Some of the money was in the bank, he told her, some in stocks and bonds, and the remainder invested in a West New York taxicab company. The money didn't matter to Mae. She'd have married Jim Braddock no matter the figures on his balance sheet. But he hadn't been certain of her feelings, and as he waited for her answer, she noticed he was shedding nearly as much perspiration as he did during one of his fights. Her yes gave him such obvious relief, she couldn't stop herself from laughing.

After their wedding, a home and family quickly followed. For Mae, she discovered that old saying was true. With each passing day in a good marriage, the love for your spouse grows stronger than the day before. But because of her husband's profession, this meant Mae's fears for him had grown as well.

Her Jimmy was moving closer now, toward the doorway. He paused a moment, just to gaze at her. She searched his wide-set brown eyes, his square, rugged Irish face for any sign of tonight's outcome. Jimmy was a man unaccustomed to losing—only twice in the two and a half years since he'd turned pro. Mae knew tonight's fight had been a long shot for Jim. The fighter named Griffiths had been favored to win. For a moment, she was hopeful, but then Jimmy looked down.

I can't ask him, she thought. *I can't.* She let her eyes do the awkward work of questioning. Jim's answer was a slow shake of his head.

Mae looked away. She couldn't stand to see her husband suffer. Not physically—which was why she no longer went to his fights—and not like this either. Losing to Griffith had to be a terrible blow. But boxing always let men down, sooner or later. For Jimmy, Mae always knew this moment would come—

Just then, a tiny chuckle made her look up again, back into her husband's face. The tragic frown had disappeared. In its place was a roguish grin. The storm had passed. The flood was over. The world was new.

She closed the distance.

"I could *kill* you."

The words were soft in his ear, just so he knew *killing* truly wasn't what she had in mind.

"I like the sound of that."

Jim was already pulling her slight form against his solid frame. His big, callused hands traveled down her slender curves, his mouth moved over hers.

Mae sighed longingly. When they were newlyweds, after his fights, she used to let him carry her right up the staircase and into their bedroom. But they weren't newlyweds anymore. There were kids to be seen to, a guest right behind her.

"Jimmy," Mae whispered, "my sister."

Jim looked at the door to find his sister-in-law Alice, a slightly older version of Mae, walking into the hall. Racing past her were two jackrabbits with bright eyes and light brown hair. They circled Jim's legs, hopping and squealing.

"Daddy, did you win?" cried four-year-old Jay.

Jay understood about Daddy's job. Three-year-old Howard was still too young to comprehend what all the excitement was about, other than Daddy being home. Jim smiled down at his boys. He took hold of the younger one's belt, hoisted him up for a kiss, then bent down to plant another on the older one. *My little men*, thought Jim. His eyes met Mae's. *My little family.*

The Braddocks moved inside after that. Jim gave them a dramatic accounting of his pugilistic performance under the Garden's broiling lights, and then Alice helped Mae settle the boys in to bed—not easy after Jim's big boxing tale. Mae checked on her sleeping baby girl, Rose Marie, said good-bye to her departing sister, then sat down with Jimmy for some food.

Mae didn't eat much, just opened a bottle of wine.

"Was he a real slugger?" Mae's lively eyes were playful. Her face flushed.

Jim's eyebrows rose. His wife had gotten tipsy. "You could come watch," he suggested.

Having Mae see him win as a headliner in the Garden, that would be grand, thought Jim. He considered the nearly empty bottle beside the burned-down candle. Maybe if she had a little wine first, he thought, maybe then she'd come.

But the suggestion didn't go over. Mae's eyes looked away, the playfulness gone. "You get punched. Every time, it feels like I'm getting punched too. And I ain't half as tough as you . . . and anyway . . ." she added, forcing her smile to come back, her fears to recede, "who wants those articles about me running out on a fight again?"

Jim caught her waving hand, brought it to his lips. He knew how much it bothered Mae to see him get hurt. He could still recall the terror-stricken look on her face at ringside during his first ten-round bout.

Jack Stone had sent him sprawling to the canvas at the West New York Playground. Braddock had never been knocked out in his career, but that day had been one of the few times he'd been knocked *down*. Mae had been there to witness it, and she'd been scared senseless.

Jimmy had gotten up again, had even won the fight, but the knockdowns had shaken Mae something awful.

After that, she kept trying to put on a brave face. She even came to a few other fights. Jim never knew how hard it was for her, until the night he stepped in the ring with the "Harlem Harlequin." The fighter was nothing special, but Jim was having a bad night. So pathetic did he look against his opponent—dreadfully awkward and appallingly slow, being forced to eat haymakers round after round—that Mae fled long before the final bell.

Jim had lost on points in ten rounds that night, and he'd lost Mae at ringside forever because some smart aleck sportswriters had seen fit to inform the public about Mae's heartbroken flight from the building.

Jim understood her reluctance to sit at ringside now. But that stuff she claimed about her not being tough? *Malarkey.* He'd seen Mae take on the barking Joe Gould without a moment's pause, seen her corral his wildcat boys into quiet little saints for Father Rorick's Masses. She'd even bossed Jim about their wedding date.

Jim would never forget it. At the last minute, Gould had scheduled an important match in Chicago on January 17, the night before Jim and Mae's wedding. The money was too good to pass up.

"I'll take a plane right back after the fight on Friday night," Braddock had pleaded with Mae, "and I'll be back here in plenty of time for the wedding Saturday."

"Nothing doing," Mae had told him in that firm, pert tone she now used on their two little boys. "Suppose you get a black eye. Do you think I want to walk up the aisle with a bridegroom who has a black eye? I do not. No, Jim. We'll postpone the wedding for a week."

The memory made Jim smile. Yeah, he knew what

tough stuff his wife was made of—even if she didn't. It was one of the reasons he'd married her.

"Tell me about the girls," Mae said suddenly, her eyes narrowing suspiciously at his faraway smile.

"Were there girls?" Jim asked innocently.

"Come on. There was one."

"Yeah. Maybe there was one."

A familiar game was starting.

"Blond?" asked Mae.

"A brunette," answered Jim.

"Tall?"

"Like a gazelle. Don't know how she breathed up there."

Mae rose from her seat, moved around the table.

"Oh, Mr. Braddock," she cooed, her head bowed in mock coyness. "You're so strong. Your hands are so big." She looked up, batted her eyes. "So powerful."

Mae moved in close, her voice suddenly sincere. "I am so proud of you, Jimmy."

Her small hands reached for her husband's solid shoulders and she climbed onto his muscled thighs.

"Introducing two-time state golden gloves title holder . . ."

She rose up, onto her knees.

"In both the light heavyweight and heavyweight divisions . . ."

Now she was standing on his thighs, looking into his eyes.

"Twenty-seven and two with eighteen wins coming by way of knockout . . . the Bulldog of Bergen, the pride of New Jersey, and the hope of the Irish as the future champion of the world . . . James J. Braddock!"

Jimmy rose, catching his wife by her tiny waist. Her

hands moved under his shirt. She was kissing him now. He picked her up, carried her to the stairs and up to the second floor, then softly kicked open the door at the end of the hall. Their colonial was beautiful to start, but Mae had made it a real home. The solid oak four-poster dominated the master bedroom's space. Dressers, night tables, a huge oval mirror, everything matched. Mae had picked it all out, arranged it with care. He laid her down on the soft white quilt, kissed her. She whispered some delightful words, then came a little boy's call. Mae smiled, touched her husband's cheek, left for a moment.

Jim began to undress. Listening to his wife's tender whispers in the next room, he unbuttoned his shirt, took off his gold watch, laid it on the richly polished bureau. He gazed a moment at their wedding picture, framed in thick silver. As he took off his gold cross, he glimpsed himself in the mirror—the face of a man who'd been blessed and knew it. Jim kissed the gold. A lucky man, a winner.

ROUND THREE

If you get the breaks, you're in there, you're up on top, but if you don't, you're on the bottom.

—James J. Braddock,
as quoted by Peter Heller in *In This Corner*

Newark, New Jersey
September 25, 1933

Jim Braddock stood at the same oak bureau where he'd once felt so lucky. Opening one drawer after another, he shifted through the meager pickings of tattered clothes, mended repeatedly by patient fingers. The top of his dresser was scarred now and barren. No watch. No cross. Not even the silver frame to hold his and Mae's wedding picture.

Outside the sooty window, something scampered through the dingy alley. A rat was Jim's guess, part of the wildlife that came with the view from a basement apartment in a rundown tenement near the Newark docks.

Dressing was a quick affair these days. Whatever clothes Mae had patched the night before and dunked in the washtub, he pulled on. No need to spend time winding his expensive watch or kissing his solid gold cross for luck since both had been pawned years before. Besides, by now, everyone's luck had run out—even Jim Braddock's.

Behind him, three hungry kids shared the same mattress in the chilly family bedroom. Steps away hung a worn blanket, Mae's idea of turning one cramped room into two. On the other side of the thin wool, his wife cooked breakfast by the light of a single bare bulb. Jim heard the meat frying, felt his empty stomach clutch at the smell.

A drawer stuck and Jim pushed hard to close it. The once richly polished bureau was part of a set that had been sold off piece by piece: the four-poster bed, the framed oval mirror, the night tables, even the silver lining around their wedding picture—but not the picture inside. Propped for Jim to look at every day, his wedding photo was the last possession left sitting on his chest of drawers.

Jim gazed at the image of Mae in her wedding dress, radiant and rosy cheeked, himself next to her, wearing a suit of clothes he no longer owned. To another man, this blissful couple might appear ridiculous, grinning fools from another time and place, completely oblivious to a future like this one. Another man might have shoved the photo into the deepest recess he could find. But Jim liked seeing the picture every day. It was the singular reminder of what had gone right in his life. The one thing that still made him a lucky man.

Tugging back the hanging blanket, Jim stepped into the kitchen—an old gas stove, a table, and four chairs. A few feet away sat a single shabby sofa. The Braddock parlor. Mae stood at the stove, frying two thin slices of bologna. Since their meals had become spartan, her curves seemed less pronounced, her face more careworn. Shadowy circles now lived beneath her eyes, and her plump, pink cheeks had become sunken and pallid. To Jim, however, she was still a raving beauty.

"Can't find my good socks," he called, buttoning his frayed shirt.

Mae turned from the stove, her voice a scolding whisper. "Jim!"

He winced, lowered his voice. "Sorry. God. Sorry."

"Mama." The sleepy whimper came from the other side of the blanket. Rose Marie, their youngest.

Mae closed her eyes. "Great." The damage had been done. She leaned down, reached into the oven, pulled out his socks—the ones that hadn't gone threadbare yet in the heels and toes.

"Sorry," said Jim again, taking the precious strips of wool like an archeologist handling a rare find.

His wife sighed and turned away. Now that Rosy was awake, the girl would want breakfast too. With resignation, Mae picked up the knife and sawed a third sliver of meat from the meager stump.

"I washed them last night," she said. "I took them right off your feet, remember? You were dead to the world."

Jim shook his head, sat at the table, pulled on his socks. The fabric smelled clean and felt warm—toasty heaven on his freezing toes. He smiled at his wife. "How can I keep 'em this warm?"

Mae might have replied with a quip, or even a smile, but a tiny figure pushed forcefully through the blanket, reminding her of yet another reason she just couldn't.

"Mama, I want to eat too."

Mae hated that her six-year-old was too young to remember what it had been like to live in a spacious, well-heated house with a stocked pantry, to take a drive downtown and blithely purchase a brand-new pair of shoes and a pretty hat at Bamberger's Department Store, to have a sumptuous picnic on a sunny day in Weequahic Park, throwing extra bread to the birds, or spending hours window-shopping on Market Street then refreshing yourself with an ice cream soda at the drug store on the corner.

As Rosy climbed onto her father's lap, Jim smoothed her hair and kissed her head. To him, she was as pretty as her mother, with big, curious eyes and silky, chestnut-colored hair. Yet her face appeared gaunt, and her fingers and toes felt far too cold. Jim hugged her close. Seeing his children grow up like this was harder to take than any beating he'd endured in the ring.

"We got a notice yesterday," Mae told him. "On the gas and electric."

Jim's shoulders sagged a fraction. He didn't know which was worse about the Depression—fighting so hard for so little, or having no real opponent to target, nothing and no one to haul off and punch.

He looked toward a mason jar on the shelf, where they kept their big "rainy day" savings—a better bet for holding his money than his stocks and bonds had proved to be. He reached for the jar, shook it. The few remaining coins jangled against the glass. He set it on the kitchen table, raised an eyebrow.

"It must have been raining lately, more than I noticed."

Mae didn't laugh at the joke. She didn't even smile. She stared at Jim, considering her once golden husband. His eyes appeared hollow now, the circles of fatigue like sooty smudges. His broken nose had healed slightly broader, one ear had gone cauliflower, and his clothes hung off his thinning frame. Even his teasing, boyish sense of humor had faded into recurrent stretches of weary sullenness. Yet Mae knew that beneath his rough morning stubble, his visible exhaustion, James Braddock's square jaw was still firm, his quiet strength still evident. Mae counted on that strength like a tent counted on its center pole in a storm. She could keep herself steady, she told herself, keep the children protected—as long as he held her up, as long as he stayed firm and strong for all of them.

Jim ignored Mae's stony silence and placed Rosy on an empty chair. "I'll get the milk."

At four in the morning, the sun had a few hours left to sleep. Jim didn't have that luxury. The loading dock foreman would be choosing men soon and he had to get down there or he'd miss his chance. Quickly climbing the basement steps, Jim emerged into the predawn gloom of the tenement courtyard.

His charming white colonial with the manicured lawn and two-hundred-year-old tamarack trees felt like the remnants of a dream. The heart of a slum was where he lived now. Filthy bricks stretched eight floors up. Clotheslines crisscrossed the quad, the hanging laundry fluttering above him like raggedy signal flags. Below, rats scavenged through spilled garbage cans, consuming whatever paltry crumbs were left to pilfer.

Jim moved to the spot where the milkman always left his early morning deliveries. Two fat bottles stood empty. A few final drops of white clung to their insides. Pink past-due slips circled their necks like collars of shame.

"Mama, I want to eat too."

That moment Jim knew Rosy's words would haunt him all day long. Every hour. Every minute. He picked up the bottles, went back inside, showed them to Mae. Her face went pale. She held his gaze. Jim looked away. Like a hard tenth round, he felt himself weakening.

"Oh!" said Mae. Something in her voice surprised him. "Some left over, I think."

Jim watched her open the icebox, pull out the last cold milk bottle, barely an eighth full. At the sink, she began to top it off with water. She smiled at Rosy, winked at him. "Who needs a cow?"

Jim didn't laugh at her joke, just sat down heavily at the table. Mae's smile was brittle. He could see the effort she was making, hear the forced brightness in her voice. She went to the stove, picked up three dishes, slid a slice of hot bologna onto each one. As she set down the pathetic plates of food in front of them, Jim found himself watching his wife's hands. He remembered Mae's hands from years before, when her brother routinely invited him to dinner at the Foxes' house. He'd become entranced back then, watching such small, dainty hands offering him such large, heaping platters of buttered mashed potatoes, thickly sliced slabs of beef, steaming heads of cabbage, corned beef, and soda bread. He remembered how her looks, her eyes, had distinctly offered him more.

"Rosy," Jim said, turning to his daughter. "Your fork, please."

The meat may have been thin, but as he cut his little girl's portion with the fork's edge, the scent of sizzling fat made his mouth water. Maybe it was the idea of hot food that revived Jim, maybe the memory of that young, flirtatious Mae, or the sight of her now, trying so hard to appear happy for the sake of her husband and daughter. Whatever it was, when he spoke again, he did his best to sound more than cheerful—he sounded downright hopeful.

"I got Feldman tonight."

Abe Feldman. Eighteen wins, one loss, no draws. A better record than his these days, but Jim wasn't telling Mae that.

"That's half a C," he said instead. And half a hundred was better pay than a week's worth of sweat on the loading dock, which he seldom got anyway. Well worth a few rounds of physical punishment.

"I beat him, maybe I can get back up to seventy-five."

Mae looked up from her plate. The old fear in her eyes was better hidden than the doubt in his, but the familiar dread shuddered through her anyway. It had been two months since her husband's last fight, and well over a year since she'd started actively praying that he'd give up the gloves for good. In the past, for his sake, she'd tolerated the sport. But as the Depression began to take its toll on her family, Mae had grown to hate the ring, its punishments—and all its empty promises.

"Mama, I want some more."

"I'm sorry, honey. We need to save some for the boys."

Jim looked at Mae and Rosy. Both their plates were

empty now. His still held that mouth-watering slice of greasy meat.

"Mae, you know what I dreamed about last night," Jim said, rising from the table. "I dreamed I was having dinner at the Ritz . . ." He pulled on his old coat, his mended gloves, his frayed hat ". . . and I had a big, thick steak . . ." He spread his thumb and finger. "This thick, Rosy, and so much mashed potatoes and ice cream, I'm just not hungry anymore."

Rosy studied her father with lips pursed, eyebrows skeptically knitted together. Even at six, she was no pushover. Jim could see there was more scamming to be done—

"Can you help me out?" he asked his daughter. "Mommy cooked and I don't want it to go to waste."

When Rosy continued to hesitate, Jim picked up her fork again, this time to stab his own slice and deposit it on her plate. Eyes wide, stomach still hungry, the child immediately began to eat.

"Jimmy—" Mae tried to object, but his mouth covered hers, halting the debate.

When the kiss ended, Mae's gaze found his. *You can't work on an empty stomach*, her eyes protested. *What are you thinking?*

Jim's answer was simple. "You're my girls."

When Jim thought he and his family had it bad, he just walked around the block. What he saw on the street made him count his blessings, few as they were. Near the tenement where he and Mae rented their one room, junker cars lay next to trashcan fires in an abandoned lot. Every day, Jim passed by the line of them on his way to the docks, rusted out and broken down, their cold glass windows steamed opaque with warm breath. Homes on wheels for the unemployed.

One car's door suddenly swung open. A mother climbed out, pushing her two little boys in front of her. Bleary-eyed, they stumbled across the dirt to the side of the nearest building and began to urinate against its wall.

Jim walked on.

He'd come a long way from the stately, old neighborhood north of the city, where large frame and brick houses sat comfortably spaced and attractively landscaped. Here on the southeast edge of the business district, not far from the Port of Newark, cracked concrete sidewalks lined long stretches of store windows, every one boarded up. Buildings were a monotonous brown and gray, many of them crumbling with paint peeling, windows broken, gutters hanging loose because no one had the money to fix them. Soot and coal dust dirtied streets that the city could no longer afford to clean. Garbage cans lay on their sides, rummaged through, empty. These days, people threw almost nothing away, and whenever anyone did, another worse-off soul would find a use for it. Just like that, it was out of the can before a truck could haul it away.

Of the twenty-nine thousand factories in the New York City area, ten thousand had shut down. And the plight was no better across the river. By now, the Depression had gone well beyond factory workers. College graduates, professional men, people who'd thought of themselves as middle class, were out of work too. Hundreds of brokers and bankers had been fired, small businesses had gone bust, a third of the doctors in Brooklyn had been forced to close their practices, and six out of seven architects were now idle.

Men in four-year-old suits and frayed ties wandered like ghosts, nowhere to go, glad to clean a yard to make a dollar. Teachers, lawyers, accountants, businessmen were still leaving home every morning with empty attaché cases, ashamed to admit they had no work. Others sat on benches and bus stops in tattered coats, heads bowed like defeated rag dolls.

Everywhere Jim looked, he saw part of the army of unemployed, selling apples on Manhattan street corners, standing on line at employment offices from morning till night, waiting at bakery back doors for day-old bread.

Black Tuesday, the Crash, the worst day in stock market history, the end of the Roaring Twenties, the beginning of the Great Depression, whatever they wanted to call October 29, 1929, didn't matter. What mattered was the country had been hit by a thousand-foot tidal wave, smashed by the power punch of a raging financial Goliath. In one day, sixteen million shares of stock had been dumped and the country lost more capital than it had spent in all of World War I. The entire week's losses added up to 30 billion dollars, ten times more than the annual budget of the federal government.

Much of the nation was on its knees, knocked into a stunned stupor. At first, people told themselves it would all be over in a month or two, then a year or two. At first, Jim believed it too, even though he'd been among the group worst hit—short-run investors, small guys who believed that everyone could be rich. In a matter of hours, his stock investments had gone to zero. Then his bank failed, wiping out much of the money he'd put there. Finally, his taxicab company went under, but not before he'd sunk even more money into it. By 1932, the Braddocks had lost every cent of the $30,000 Jim had earned during his rise in the ring. Jim had borrowed from friends and relatives, but nobody was in any better shape. The Braddocks were only one drop in a desolate ocean of families who'd lost their homes, their life savings, and in some cases even more.

Within days of the Crash, the president of the Country Trust Savings Bank had taken a pistol from the teller's cage at work, returned to his town house on West Twelfth Street, and blown his brains out. Everyone had heard stories like that, of men jumping out of windows. Less talked about were the ones who went into insane asylums and nursing homes, the ones who'd broke down mentally and physically, as well as financially. Others took their lives hoping to at least leave their wives and children some insurance money.

Fathers deserted their families, ashamed at not being able to support them, feeling what was happening to them was a consequence of their own personal failure. They'd just wandered off in disgrace.

The newspapers talked about overspeculation being the cause, how everyone had ignored the signs of economic downturn in the months before—rising unemployment, the fall off in automobile sales and department store revenues, farms failing in record numbers. The market just climbed higher and higher. Then the waves of panic hit, brokers ruthlessly unloaded margin accounts, banks withdrew their funds, and the market completely collapsed.

New York's dazzling lights and frolicking revelers of the Twenties gradually faded, a vanishing mirage. Appearing in its place was a gray, raggedy throng of desperate down-and-outers rounding the block at relief offices, waiting on breadlines, freezing on street corners, their faces creased with want, looking everywhere for work and finding none. Hungry, empty, hopeless, defeated.

Jim's only hope had been boxing. Although the prizes had gone down with the ticket prices, prizefighting was still a popular sport, mainly because it was a relatively cheap good time and a side bet might double a fan's pocket. But after the crash, Jim's career had gone into a tailspin. He'd racked up more losses than wins in 1930, '31, '32 . . . and, thus far, 1933 wasn't bucking that trend. As his fight record sank, he had a harder time getting on decent cards. Jimmy Johnston had Gould touring him on a low-rent circuit, Cauliflower Alley, and for over a year, Jim had been forced to take on any sort of work he could find.

With so many factories closed, the docks had been his best shot. Port Newark, on Newark Bay, was one of the country's largest cargo ports. Inside of thirty years it had been transformed from a desolate marsh to a seaport terminal with twelve thousand feet of docks including space for large warehouses and twenty freight steamers. Shipments were constantly being unloaded here and then transferred to the many railroads and truck lines that ran through the area. So every morning before dawn, Jim rose and hiked down to the water, hoping to beat the odds among a horde of others just as desperate for work.

Shoving his cold hands into his pockets, Jim moved across a gravel lot and toward the small group of men already waiting by the locked gate of the high fence. The weather was cold for this time of year, even colder by the water, but the two-hour wait in the predawn mist earned him a valuable spot at the front of the swelling crowd.

When dawn finally hit Newark Bay, New York Bay, and the Atlantic Ocean beyond, Jim barely noticed. The sky was so overcast little sunlight could penetrate the gloomy mist. To the north, the Hudson remained slate gray under cement clouds, and across its churning currents, the great skyscrapers of Manhattan looked more like tombstones in a crowded cemetery.

The sudden rattling of metal drew Jim's attention to the gate. The gaunt, middle-aged foreman stood on the other side. Jim straightened and glanced around at the murmuring crowd. Most of the men were huddled against the biting, wet chill, hands buried deep in the pockets of their old coats, faces stoned by sleeplessness. There were more than usual today, sixty at least.

With his clipboard under an arm, the foreman finished fumbling with the lock, then pulled the gate open and stepped up to the waiting swarm of unemployed. This man had the power over life and death, the power to change the fortunes of Jim and his family—of every man here.

"I need nine men and nine men only."

The jostling began immediately. *Me! Pick me!*

"One, two, three . . ." The foreman was pointing out men far too fast. "Six, seven, eight . . ."

Jim could feel the panic around him, the fear, as the

foreman's joyless expression continued to scan the crowd. *Me! Pick me!* Jim prodded his way closer, trying to be seen.

"Nine."

Jim closed his eyes. All that waiting, hours in the cold, and it was over in less than thirty seconds. He hadn't been chosen.

"I been here since four."

Jim opened his eyes. The crowd was dispersing around him, men were already heading off to look for work elsewhere. One man from the crowd had stepped up to complain. Jim recognized him from a short chat they'd had a few weeks before. His name was Ben and he had remembered Jim from one of his old boxing matches in Jersey City, in the days when Jim had had no trouble rolling over opponents. Like Jim, Ben had a wife and three kids—two were sick.

"Sorry brother," the foreman told Ben, turning away. "Luck of the draw."

Ben's gun came out of nowhere. A pocket, a waistband, Jim didn't know, but everyone knew where Ben's revolver was aimed—point-blank at the foreman's heart.

"I was here first." Ben's eyes were wild, desperate. The hand that held the gun began shaking. The foreman stared at it and began shaking too.

"What about it?" Ben asked.

The foreman lifted his eyes from the gun to Ben's face. Time went perfectly still, then the foreman spoke, "My mistake, pal. I need ten."

Still stunned, Jim's gaze followed Ben as he stepped through the gate. Jim wanted to look away, but just couldn't, simply watched and waited without breathing. Then it happened. Ben had barely put the gun back into his pocket when a few of the guys inside jumped him, wrestled him to the ground.

It was over for Ben now, thought Jim. Prison. How could the man help his wife and kids now? How?

Jim's eyes looked away, down to the broken concrete. Beneath his ratty shoes, he saw the front page of today's paper. The two-inch headline was no news to him:

UNEMPLOYED REACHES 15,000,000

"No shifts today, Dad?"

Hours later, Jim had finally returned to his tenement courtyard to find his eight-year-old, Howard, playing on the fire escape landing above the basement steps. One in four working people were now unemployed in America. One in four. But an eight-year-old didn't need to know that. An eight-year-old couldn't even fathom 15 million.

Giving his son a smile, Jim shrugged. *Win some, lose some*, he tried to say, even though he'd lost for hours, walking and hitching rides for miles, looking for work everywhere, finding it nowhere—not in Newark, Bayonne, or Jersey City.

"What're you doing, son?" The boy appeared to be jumping on a mattress spring.

"I'm being good," answered Howard. "I'm being quiet. I'm being *hayve*."

Jim recognized Mae's don't-mess-with-me warning list—which told him something was up. He raised an eyebrow. "Good?" he asked, but before he could get more out of him, a tiny wide-eyed rocket fired itself down the alley and into his arms.

"Daddy, Daddy, Daddy!"

Rosy hugged her father's neck, then the six-year-old grinned brighter than Times Square's lights used to shine.

"What, sweetheart?"

"Jay stole!"

With a sigh, Jim carried Rosy down the steps and into their basement apartment. He found Mae standing over their eldest. Jay's ten-year-old face was red. He was staring at the floor.

Jim set his daughter down. "What's this all about?"

The little girl pointed at the table with a proud tattle-tale grin. "See? It's a salami!"

Mae replied sharply. "Your brother is in enough trouble without you telling, young lady."

Jim looked questioningly. Mae pointed. It was a salami, all right, and it was a beauty, fat and marbled and laced with garlic, and the way Mae slivered the meat these days, Jim figured it could surrender enough slices to feed the whole Braddock family for a week.

"From the butcher's," said Mae. "He won't say a word about it, will you Jay?"

Mae's stare moved from her son's furious face to Jim's questioning eyes. She held her husband's gaze—a silent handoff.

"Okay," said Jim. "Pick it up. Let's go."

For the first time, Jay raised his eyes to look at his father. The boy's expression was pleading, desperate, angry—and full of fear. *Don't make me do this. Can't you see we need it? Can't you?*

"Right now!"

The front door banged open. Jim was on his way, his son, salami in hand, dragging slowly behind. As Jim strode down the street, he said nothing. Jay followed on his heels, eyes downcast. When they reached the butcher, Jim opened the door, waved his boy inside.

A quick explanation, an apology, and the stolen property was presented to the victim. The butcher glanced from son to father. Braddock met the man's eyes. *I am not raising my son to be a thief.*

No more words were needed. The butcher nodded approvingly, returned the fat, greasy salami to his meat case, then Jim and Jay left the shop. The two walked down the street, side by side. The embarrassment had been endured, the lesson was now over, and Jim couldn't help recalling his own boyhood lessons at the hands of his stern father—after one of those lessons, Jim usually couldn't sit down for hours.

Joseph Braddock was a massive figure of a man, with snow white hair and a thick Irish brogue. He believed in God, hard work, and doing right by your fellow man, and he'd instilled these lessons in every one of his sons.

Once, before one of Jimmy's fights, his dad had said, "May the best man win." The words weren't really about winning. They were about being a certain kind of man—the kind who kept his dignity by fighting fair and respecting the rules. In Joseph Braddock's view, only this kind of man truly deserved to win, to be admired, to be hailed a winner. Jim agreed. Being the best kind of man was not an easy thing, but it was the most important thing. His father had instilled that in him. Now it was Jim's turn to do the same for his own son.

Jim walked beside his ten-year-old in silence, waiting, giving his boy time. Jay was a quiet kid, just like his father, and Jim knew why: It wasn't always easy to find the right words.

"Marty Johnson," Jay finally blurted out after a few blocks. "Marty Johnson had to go away to Delaware and live with his uncle."

Jim frowned, but said nothing.

"His parents didn't have enough money for them to eat," Jay added.

Jim stopped on the street, turned toward his son. The boy's anger was gone now. The shame and desperation were gone too. Only one thing was left in that young face . . . the same thing Jim felt earlier today, and almost every day since the Crash.

"You got scared," Jim told his boy. "I can understand it. But we don't steal. No matter what happens. Not ever. Got me?"

Jay swallowed, managed a nod.

"Are you giving me your word?" asked Jim.

"Yes."

"Go on."

"I promise."

"Things aren't so good right now, Jay, you're right. But Daddy's doing his best." Jim touched his son's cheek. Soon enough, the boy's skin wouldn't be peach smooth anymore, thought Jim, he'd be shaving—he'd be a young man. Now was the time to make the boy understand what kind of man his father wanted him to be.

"There's a lot of other people a lot less fortunate than us. And if you take something, somebody else goes without." Jim crouched down so he could look at his ten-year-old eye to eye. "Here's my word, good as wheat in the bin. We're never going to send you away, son."

Jay's small lips were already trembling, his eyes desperate. *You promise?*

"I promise," said Jim.

Finally, the tears came, spilling from the little boy's eyes. Jim pulled Jay into his arms. He held onto his child as tight as he could.

ROUND FOUR

A man hanging on the ropes in a helpless state, with his toes off the ground, shall be considered down.

—*The Queensbury Rules,*
Number 5

Mount Vernon, New York
September 23, 1933

The locker room was a dump. Bins with broken doors, a filthy concrete floor, half-plugged drains, and rank air polluted with the charming smells of dried sweat and stale urine.

"He's a slow guy. He plants himself. Keep him in the middle. And dance around him. You know what to do. Guy's a bum."

The weary routine had begun. Joe Gould, sporting one of his usual dapper-looking fawn-colored suits, taped up Jim's hands while trying to brace his spirits.

Almost everybody Jim knew had been ruined by the Crash—except Joe Gould. The little fast-talker always

did have something going on the side, and he appeared
to have done okay for himself, still showing smart in-
dications of wealth and a fiercely sunny disposition.
Braddock had borrowed money more than once from
his manager. The sunny disposition, however, didn't
lend. To Jim, it made about as much sense as a summer
day in the middle of the Ice Age.

"I know two bits will buy a guy a seat," Jim muttered, "a guy who gets to watch you bleed and call you
a bum. I know that because he's a paying customer, I
have to take it from him."

"I see. Well. Pardon me. Let me restate." Gould narrowed his eyes on Braddock. "Mr. Abraham Feldman
is a novice fighter whose ass you should gently kick
until it's humped up between his shoulders. If, of
course, it doesn't offend your overly sensitive nature."

Gould finished taping Jim's left, dropped it and
grabbed the right. Jim winced. Gould looked down. He
played with the hand. Jim winced again.

"This break's still a couple weeks away," said
Gould, examining Braddock's knuckles. "Why didn't
you tell me, Jim?"

Jim didn't look up from the grimy floor.

Back in March, Braddock had gone ahead with a
Philadelphia bout against Al Ettore, even though his
badly hurt hand hadn't completely healed from his
January fight with Hans Birkie. Ettore would have been
a hard man to box even with a good hand. Trying to do
it with a bum paw made Jimmy look like he had no
business being in the ring. By the fourth round, the referee had halted the fight.

Still Braddock wouldn't stop. He couldn't. His family badly needed the purses, so he'd gone up against Al

Stillman in St. Louis. In the ninth round, Jim laid a terrific right to the young man's jaw. Braddock won the
match, but had reinjured his hand.

Braddock kept fighting: Martin Levandowski in
April, Al Stillman again in May, Les Kennedy in June,
and Chester Matan in July. For those last battles, he'd
managed to use painkillers, smashing the right again
and again, never giving it enough time to fully heal.

Gould rubbed the back of his neck. Letting an injured fighter climb into the ring was strictly illegal.
Braddock had pushed the envelope in Pennsylvania
and Missouri, but now that they were back in New
York, Gould was worried. Jimmy Johnston was in the
audience tonight, along with two other state boxing
commissioners. Anything went wrong in the ring, it
could finish them both.

"Can't get any shifts," Jim finally admitted. "We
owe everybody."

The weak, desperate voice Gould heard wasn't
Braddock's—not the one he knew anyway. With a
sigh, Gould considered the state of his friend's
patched-up street clothes and ratty shoes, thought of
Mae and the kids.

"Screw it," said Gould. "I'll tape it double."

Double taping was just as illegal. Gould knew it. He
kept wrapping.

"So, this extraordinary opponent of yours who my
grandma could beat with her breath, you keep your left
in his face and when his head pops up like a little
bunny rabbit . . . boom! One shot. Make it good. Finish
early, I'll buy you an egg cream."

As Gould wrapped, Braddock considered the idea of
winning. His record hadn't been *all* bad since the night

he'd KO'd Tuffy Griffiths at the Garden and everyone had started ranking him a world title contender. On the other hand, the very next fight after Tuffy had been a helluva disappointment.

Just two months after Griffiths, Braddock had climbed into Madison Square Garden's ring again, this time to fight Leo Lomski. In the very first round, Jim had walloped Lomski with a dizzying right. But instead of finishing him off, Jim had shuffled around and hesitated, squandering his opportunities long enough to give Lomski time to recover.

After that, Lomski never let Braddock get close again. With Lomski constantly standing off and jabbing, Braddock couldn't get enough leverage to use his right cross. He'd swung and swung his right all night, but Lomski's left had dominated and Braddock had lost on decision.

It wasn't over for Jim that night, however, not by a long shot. One month later, in February of 1929, he'd KO'd George Gemas in one round at the Newark Armory. A month after that, he'd taken on Jimmy Slattery, the "Buffalo Adonis," in Madison Square Garden. An eight to five favorite, Slattery was a brilliant boxer—a flickering, flitting, dancing ghost whose opponents found impossible to tag. Amazing his fans and astonishing his critics, Braddock's terrific right hand had caught and smashed the ghost by the end of the eighth round. By the ninth, Jim had KO'd him.

Now, as Braddock prepared to face Feldman, he tried to keep that ninth-round Slattery KO in mind. Anything was better than remembering his disastrous match against Tommy Loughran.

July 18, 1929, one year after Braddock had defeated Griffiths—and three months before the stock market sent the country's economy from the canvas to the morgue—promoters had finally consented to let Braddock take a shot at the world light heavyweight title by fighting the champ. In fifteen harrowing rounds in Yankee Stadium, Tommy Loughran, one of the best boxers in the history of the game, had crushed Jim's hopes for a world title.

Braddock should have learned a lot from that humiliating match against Loughran, it just wasn't a memory he was keen on recalling before he had to step into the ring one more time . . .

"Let's go," said Gould.

He'd finished double-taping Braddock's bum right and lacing on his gloves. Now it was time for the stout little manager to lead his six-three boxer down the main aisle of the Mount Vernon Armory, past the wooden bleachers and into the ring.

The crowd was an anemic crew compared to Jim's Madison Square Garden days—and not just in volume. Leaner in face and shabbier in attire, there was a desperate look about them, as if the bets they'd made tonight were going to pay the grocery bills tomorrow. They sat murmuring beyond the ring's hot lights, a sea of fedoras and caps sending up clouds of smoke.

Closer to the action sat a small cadre of flashy gamblers with glossy-lipped companions. A long ringside table held tonight's three official judges, the sports reporters leaning on their black typewriters, a few photographers with flashbulbs ready to pop, and a single radio commentator prattling into a heavy steel microphone—

"Jim Braddock, just five years ago, was considered first in line for the world championship. But in the last year, he's lost ten fights and hasn't managed a single KO."

Tell me something I don't know, Jim muttered to himself as he climbed through the ropes and began to shadowbox in his corner. Gould massaged his shoulders, told him to relax.

The hall's low buzz began to rise, swelling into yelling and whistling. Braddock turned to see Abe Feldman making his way down the crowded aisle with a vigorous gait and high-spirited punches.

"Now Braddock faces Abe Feldman," the radio man continued, "an up-and-comer with seventeen wins, one draw, and one loss. In less than two years he has recorded nine KOs."

Jim froze. *This* was the "bum" Joe's grandma could beat?

Under his hands, Gould felt Jim's shoulders go completely rigid. "Who whipped Latzo?" Gould barked to his boxer.

"I did." Jim's voice was barely there.

"Who KO'd Slattery in the ninth when everybody said he didn't have a rainmaker's chance in hell?!"

"I did."

"That's right. But we should pucker our assholes over Feldman?"

"No."

The spectators clapped and whistled as Feldman climbed into the ring. Abe was the crowd favorite, young and golden like Braddock used to be with an untouched nose and two pretty ears. Jim felt his gloves begin to sink.

"Jimmy, Jimmy, look at me!" Gould grabbed Jim's gloves, brought them back up. "Is there someplace else you'd rather be?"

"No."

"Good. So what are you going to do?"

Braddock closed his eyes. Everything went away: the crowd's hoots, the locker room stench, Mae's weary sighs, Ben's pulled gun, Jay's silent tears, all the mistakes and missteps of the last four years. He reminded himself the "underdog" crown was no new hat. Then he opened his eyes.

"I'm gonna get an egg cream."

"There you go. That's the spirit!"

The punch was a leather hammer to Braddock's face. Jim moved for the counter, but Feldman blocked his drive.

"C'mon Jimmy, let's put on a show!"

From the corner, Gould was sweating nearly as much as Braddock as he jabbed the air, mimicking every move his fighter made.

"Let's open him up for the folks!"

Gould's bulldog voice hadn't yet gone hoarse from all the yelling, but it made no difference. The only things getting through to Braddock were the booming bursts of pain inflicted by Feldman's targeted blows.

Every boxer's hits were different. Some felt like *rat-a-tat* tommy-gun bullets, others like beer bottles breaking over your face, cutting your nose and lips. Feldman's jabs felt like he'd picked up a butcher's cleaver—the strikes weren't big, but they were solid and hard and hit squarely with practiced aim.

The first round had been spent in feeling each other

out, but by the second, the young comer had rushed Braddock, layering him with jabs, hooks, uppercuts, forcing him to eat leather. Jim tried to counter, but he just couldn't get a break. Everywhere Feldman threw, Jim was. Everywhere Braddock threw, Feldman wasn't.

Jim looked slow and awkward compared to his young opponent, who lightly danced around him on the canvas, pivoting and punching like some gangland ballerina. Suddenly, Feldman saw an opening, laid into Braddock's ribs with a combination that sent Jimmy back into the ropes.

The crowd began to boo, their jeers rising with the smoke through the armory's musty air. In the corner, Gould bobbed and weaved, willing his fighter to break out, counter, find an opening—do anything but stand there and let himself get pounded into dog food.

"You got to be first, Jimmy! Don't let him get set!"

Jim saw a break in Feldman's guard and threw a hard cross. He smashed Feldman's jaw and sent him reeling. Jim pivoted in fast, cocked again for the finish, but Feldman lowered his head as Jim let go. Braddock's lethal right connected with the top of Feldman's skull. Abe's helmet of a cranium refused to give, but Jimmy's half-healed, double-taped hand did—

Jim grimaced as the horrible crack of bone against bone echoed in his cauliflower ear. Knife-sharp blades of agony sliced through Jim's fingers, and he fell into a clinch with Feldman. The bell ended the round but not the clinch, because Feldman was hurting too. The Ref stepped in to break it up, sending both fighters back to their corners.

While the cutman toweled the sweat and blood from

Braddock's face, Gould unlaced his glove. Even beneath the heavy tape job, the manager could see that Jim's knuckles were out of alignment, and his fingers had swelled into purple sausages. Gould's lightest touch made Jim shudder. His boxer could no longer hide the pain.

"It's broken proper, Jimmy. I'm calling it."

Jim swallowed and thought of the purse, Mae, and the kids, the empty milk bottles. *Mama, I want to eat too.*

"I can use my left."

Rounds were three minutes long. Breaks between them only one.

"Stay inside." Joe quickly replaced the glove, laced it back up. "Don't let him crowd you. Do what you can with the left."

The bell clanged and Jim was up and into the ring. Gould shook his head. "I wish he could find his goddamned left," he muttered to the cutman, then the manager lifted his voice to the rafters. "Shut him down!"

But Jim couldn't. His opponent rushed him, raining solid punches in stinging one-two rhythms. Jim tried to counter, but Gould was right—he just didn't have a left-hand punch. Worse, his right couldn't even block anymore, and his boxing shoes felt like they'd been dipped in lead. As Feldman landed blow after blow, Braddock was practically standing still, a defenseless six-three bag of sand for Feldman to punch at will.

Time usually slowed for Jim under the broiling hot lights, but now it was hurtling forward in a violent frenzy, a breakneck merry-go-round that turned Feldman into a blur of unpredictable movement.

Desperate, Braddock began to throw out his left again and again. His wild jabs missed, but he managed to send one serious uppercut to Feldman's chin. Abe was still hurting from the right cross Braddock had fed him in the last round, and the uppercut did some damage.

Both boxers fell into another clinch. They swayed in a drunken dance, back and forth across the canvas, and the gallery began to jeer again, hurling insults and catcalls.

"Pay attention!" Gould shouted.

The faces in the irate crowd were a whirling blur in Jim's pain-racked vision—

"You stink!"

"Go home!"

"No good—"

Suddenly Jim decided maybe he had *one* more right cross in him.

"Bum!"

Yeah, thought Jim, *one more*—

Jim cocked back and let fly. He struck Feldman on the sweet spot, and the boxer reeled, but beneath Jim's glove, beneath his tape, his broken hand had completely shattered.

As Jim braced against white-hot convulsive spasms, Feldman counterpunched with a vicious right. Jim's head snapped back. He staggered, pulling Feldman into yet another pitiful clinch, holding onto his opponent like the intoxicated host of a party, desperately trying not to pass out. Feldman didn't look much better. His arms wrapped around Braddock, and once again the two waltzed across the canvas.

Gould barely heard the bell over the booing.

* * *

"An embarrassment! That's what it was. An embarrassment."

Gritting his teeth, Joe Gould forced himself to stand quietly and listen to the rantings of Jimmy Johnston, the big-suit promoter whose balls he'd squeezed to get Braddock that Tuffy Griffiths shot, not to mention the world title match against Tommy Loughran in Yankee Stadium.

Barely thirty minutes ago, the referee had stopped the fight. Announcing "enough was enough," he'd declared it a "no contest," and threw any further rulings into the hands of the state boxing commissioners, which meant Joe Gould's worst-case scenario had just come true.

"Where's the purse?" asked Gould, trying like hell to hold his temper in front of this makeshift tribunal, which included Johnston, the ref from tonight's bout, and two state commissioners who'd been in the audience.

"I wouldn't have to tell you that if you gave a shit about your fighter," Johnston said.

Sitting behind the table with his fellow commissioners, Johnston sucked on his cigar and blew out a fat white puff, like Zeus making clouds for the mortals below him. It joined the smoke already hanging in the armory's backroom office. Mount Olympus on the cheap.

"Okay," said Gould. Time to beg. He opened his fists, held his palms to the gods. "So he's fighting hurt. Maybe you got fighters who can afford to rest a month between fights."

"Christ, he hardly gets a punch in anymore. Fights getting stopped by referees . . . He's pathetic."

Gould closed his open palms, made two angry fists. Johnston had always thought Braddock was a bum, that he'd never amount to much. Now the prick had his validation. With his own eyes, Johnston had witnessed the lowest moment in Jim's career. That still didn't give him the right to call his friend pathetic. Gould was about to tell the promoter to shove the purse right up his ass when Johnston told Gould to wait outside the room for their decision. Ten minutes later, Johnston came out. Gould held his breath.

"He was no draw tonight," said Johnston, walking with Gould down the dingy hallway. "And you watch. Next week the gate will be down by half. A fighter like that keeps people away."

Gould stopped at the door to the locker room. Braddock was inside showering off blood.

"We're revoking his license, Joe," said Johnston, just like that. "Whatever Braddock was gonna do in boxing, I guess he's done it."

Outside the Armory, a single dim lightbulb cast the parking lot in deep shadows. By now, all the jeering fight fans had cleared out and the paved lot was all but abandoned by a few isolated cars. The ref and the two boxing commissioners moved toward those vehicles and climbed inside. Johnston was the last to leave.

With a bang, the amory's weathered back door swung open, bouncing off the dirty brick wall. Jim Braddock strode swiftly across the parking lot, Joe Gould struggling to keep up.

"Mr. Johnston," called Braddock. He stepped up to Johnston and planted himself.

Johnston turned. "Jim."

"What's going on?"

The big man frowned at Braddock then turned his eyes to Gould's round face. "You didn't tell him?"

"Yeah. I told him," said Gould. "But he wanted to hear it from you."

Johnston's eyes went back to Braddock. The boxer looked like a walking bruise, his right hand hanging by his side a sickly purple color, swelled and deformed and probably six months away from being able to open a pickle jar, let alone deliver a professional-level punch. One pathetic look from Johnston said it all. *It's over, Jimmy. Get it through your head.*

But Braddock refused. "I broke my hand, okay? You don't see me crying about it. I don't know what you got to complain about. We did that boondock circuit for you. I didn't quit on you." Braddock's desperate look turned deadly serious. "I didn't always lose. And I won't always lose again."

Johnston said nothing.

"I can still fight."

When Johnston spoke again, his bluster was gone, his voice quiet. "Go home."

"I can still fight."

"Go home to Mae and the kids, Jim."

Then Johnston climbed into his car and drove away. Braddock stood there and watched, wondering why the parking lot had suddenly turned into quicksand. For some reason, he couldn't move his legs and his lungs had trouble taking in air.

Then a firm hand grasped his shoulder. The usually garrulous Joe Gould guided Jim back inside without a word. The locker room was a stink hole, so Gould led his boxer to the armory's arena, where the low house-

lights cast long shadows over the empty ring. Gould sat
Jim down amid the deserted bleachers and searched for
a sturdy piece of wood. When he found a section of
broken fence board, he sat next to Jim and began taping the board to Jim's smashed and shattered hand.

"We'll splint it with this until you get to the hospital," said Gould.

Jim said nothing, just stared at the floor.

Gould tried to concentrate on the wrapping, but he
couldn't keep his mind from racing—or his mouth
from running. "Maybe I shouldn't have pushed you so
hard," he muttered. "We shouldn't have gone to California that time . . ."

Jim didn't answer. He didn't look up.

Gould kept wrapping, and the memories started
coming, crashing over him in waves . . . all the fights,
all the crowds, all the dreams and hopes . . .

*"Joe Gould, you listen now, I am going to hold you
responsible for the development of this fighter . . ."*

William Muldoon, 1928. His words had come with a
sternly pointed finger. The distinguished, gray-haired
boxing commissioner had seen Braddock knock Griffiths out in two at the Garden and had ordered Gould to
appear before him with Jimmy in tow.

*"He must not be rushed along too rapidly. But with
a little weight on him, I predict he'll some day win the
world's heavyweight championship . . ."*

The eighty-three-year-old had grabbed Braddock's
hand and shook it vigorously that day. But that day had
been a long time ago. Too long. Muldoon now rested in
a windswept grave in Tarrytown, New York—as dead
and buried as his golden prediction about Braddock's
future.

Gould cleared his hoarse throat. "Jimmy, listen, your legs are heavy, the body lets you know . . ."

"Don't."

Gould's insides twisted. He hated this. The commissioners were forcing him to KO his own fighter, but he knew they were right. He couldn't put a washed-up boxer in the ring with a real contender—not if he wanted his man to come out alive. He had to get Jim to understand—

"We're not fighting for the championship anymore. Hell, we're not even fighting for cash. And now you don't even tell me when your hand's broken before going into a fight. I'm telling *you*, Jim, not them, I'm telling you, you're too slow . . . It's over."

Jim said nothing, so Gould kept talking. "You'd change things, sure, who wouldn't, but sometimes you just can't, you know, end of story."

Joe paused, waited for Jim to say something—to yell, scream, stamp his feet, give some kind of reaction. After a full silent minute, the manager asked, "You waiting to see how long I can keep quiet again?" Gould tried to smile, until Jim looked up. He finally got his boxer's reaction. Jim's cheeks were streaked with tears . . .

"Hey, you! Wanna earn a couple of dollars?"

"Yeah, sure, mister."

For a flashing moment, Gould had gone back to 1926, when he'd called over a lanky kid shadowboxing in a corner of Joe Jeannette's gym.

"Listen, kid, how about you climb into that ring and spar a few with my fighter?"

Gould's top-ranked welterweight, Harry Galfund, was supposed to have knocked the kid's block off—a little pre-sale show for the Hoboken beer barons who'd offered to buy Galfund's contract. Only Galfund couldn't get near the kid, who kept buzzing around the ring like an annoying little bee, landing stinging jabs and crosses that made Gould's welterweight fume.

"You got a manager, kid?" Gould had asked the kid at the end of the humiliating match.

"No. My brother does my business. He's a plumber. Hey, aren't you Joe Gould?"

"Yeah, and if your brother agrees, maybe I can take over the job . . ."

Even now, seven years later, Gould didn't regret taking on the job of managing Jimmy Braddock. Even now, as he looked into Jim's devastated face.

"Get me another one, Joe."

"Jimmy—"

"Got to have it. We're down to our last buck."

"What's done is done."

"Not always."

"No. Not always . . . but this time. I'm sorry, Jimmy."

After all they'd been through together, from that Saturday in 1926 when they'd signed their first contract to getting a shot at the world title; from headlining Madison Square Garden to being jeered at in the stale air of this low-rent dump, Gould really was sorry. They'd weathered the cheers and boos, the praise and accusations in the best possible way—as the best of friends.

That's when it hit Gould. The boxing commissioners hadn't just ended Jim's career, they'd ended a seven-year partnership. Right now. Tonight. It was over. This really was good-bye.

For a few moments, the manager couldn't find his voice. "I'll get the car," he finally said.

Jim didn't even look up as his manager walked off, leaving him on the bleachers beside the dark ring, in a vast, empty space. Alone.

 **ROUND FIVE**

A man can endure a lot if he still has hope.

—Clyde T. Ellis,
as quoted by Studs Terkel in
Hard Times: An Oral History of the Great Depression

"Oh, dear Lord. Baby . . ."

Jim met Mae at the front door. As the scarred plywood creaked open, he glimpsed the tender, attentive expression on his wife's face and knew in an instant how much he was going to miss seeing her look at him this way—like he was some kind of returning soldier who'd been in harm's way, a fighting man who, win or lose, would always come home to steadfast devotion. With his boxing career over, Jim realized, Mae would never have cause to look at him like this again, and he was more than a little uneasy what failing her would do to him. To them.

"I haven't got the money," he told her straight. He was too tired and in too much pain to break it any easier. "They wouldn't pay me. Called it a no contest. Said the fight was an embarrassment."

Mae's fretful gaze went from the blue and purple

bruises on Jim's battered face to his golden right hand, now caged in a fresh white cast. Her small fist reached out, unfurled like a flower. Soft fingers brushed the hardening surface.

"What happened?" she asked.

"Mr. Johnston made a decision . . ." He shrugged. "They decommissioned me."

Fear in Mae's eyes flared to anger. What did she care about boxing commissioners' edicts or violated fight rules? She cared only about her husband. "Jimmy, what *happened* to your *hand*!?"

Jim sighed. "It's broke in three places."

With one blink, Mae's face went blank. Her gaze lost focus. "Mercy . . . I'm so sorry."

Jim stared at his wife. Her words had come out strangely distant, like she'd read them off a Western Union telegram. Deciding she must not have understood what he'd just told her, he tried again—

"Said I'm *through*, is what they said. Said I'm not a boxer anymore."

But Mae Braddock had moved past this already. Chewing the edge of her thumbnail, she began to pace the small front room. "Well, okay," she said, "if you can't work, we ain't gonna be able to pay the electric or the heat—"

With the gas and electric already overdue, Mae had taken to keeping the heat and all the lights off, save a small lamp in the corner. As she walked back and forth, a shadow flickered across the dingy wall, haunting her every step.

"—and we're out of credit at the grocery," she added, "so we need to pack the kids, they can stay at my sister's temporary, I'll take in more sewing—"

"Mae—"

"Then that way we can make two or three breadlines a day and then—"

"I'll get doubles, triple shifts where I can find them," Jim told her. "I'll get work wherever I can."

"Jim, you can't work, your hand's broken—"

She was pacing faster now, her steps going nowhere, just trapped in a repetitive activity in their confined space. Jim could see she was still fretting, her eyes still refusing to look at him.

"Mae!"

The strength in Jim's voice finally broke through. She stopped.

"I can still work," he told her.

Mae swallowed hard, said nothing.

"Get the shoe polish out of the cabinet," he told his wife, clear and firm. "Go on. If they see me lugging this around, they won't pick me will they?"

Mae stifled her response and did as he asked.

"So, we'll cover it up with the shoe polish," Jim continued as he sat down at the table and extended his hard, white liability. Mae sat next to him and looked down at the cast.

"Baby, it's going to be okay," he said, then, for a long minute, he waited. But Mae didn't say a word, and she refused to look at him. Jim sighed. His left hand still worked, didn't it? So he took a deep breath, reached down, and used it to lift her small, pointed chin. He forced himself to see the fear reflected in his wife's eyes, forced his wife to see the truth in his own.

"We still haven't seen anything we can't face down," he reminded her. Tonight, people had told Jim that he was through as a boxer, but he'd be damned if he let anyone tell him he was done fighting.

Finally, Mae saw it, right there in her husband's eyes—Jim's resolve as a man to never give up, never let himself be beaten, and her hard doubts began to soften. The world fell away then. Nothing existed, not Mae's bills or Jim's bruises, not the anger or the dread—nothing but Jim and Mae and the one look between them that held their new vow to each other. A vow to stay steady, a pledge to hold fast.

"I'll cut the hem out of your coat sleeve. Fabric will help cover it," Mae finally said, turning her attention to the black shoe polish. She opened the tin and began to spread it over the white.

Jim kissed her head, and she nearly found a laugh.

"All we need now is a nice piece of steak for your face, Jim Braddock, fix you right up."

"That's a good idea." Jim pounded the table with his good hand. "Steak. Get me a steak out of the ice box. Porterhouse!"

Peeking around the hanging blanket's threadbare fabric, a curious pair of eyes widened. While her older brothers Jay and Howard remained asleep on the kids' shared mattress, six-year-old Rose Marie watched her parents with inquisitive interest.

Jim winked at his spying daughter, then touched his wife's cheek, deciding, not for the first time, that having Mae Theresa Fox as his wife made him about the luckiest man there ever was.

Elevated on a landfill, the road Jim walked to the Newark docks before dawn every morning took a straight course through a congested industrial area. Along the route were some of the city's poorer residential districts. Running parallel were the freight tracks of the Pennsylvania Railroad, and on both sides of the road was an old dumping ground that destitute families had taken over.

Homemade huts, built of materials salvaged from junk piles, served as shelters for men, women, and children. Neatly tended garden patches sat beside them. In summer, the huts were brightly decorated with flowers, flags, and latticework. With the cold mist of fall came oil drum fires and a dependence on bread-lines and root vegetables.

Jim moved through the salvage-yard neighborhood and toward the once desolate marsh that had become the complex of warehouses and docks called Port Newark. A chilly wind whipped across the murky water of Newark Bay and Jim braced himself against it as he strode across the gravel lot toward the familiar locked gate.

Doctors had pronounced his right hand useless for many months, and he had no illusions what the fate of his family would be if he got no work today. Keeping the blackened cast low and slightly behind his back, Jim approached the huddling group of sleepy, stone-faced men with rock-hard resolve.

This morning's dawn seemed brighter than days' past. As rays of red-stained gold broke through the horizon's low clouds, Jake, the gaunt-faced, middle-aged foreman, approached the gate from the other side. Jim shoved his shattered hand farther behind him and pushed forward, holding onto hope.

"One, two, three . . ."

Jake walked along the group, looking over the men, moving his finger one way then another. Half steps and half inches, thought Jim, just like the ring, nerve and chance determining life-changing outcomes.

". . . five, six, seven . . ."

Jim straightened his boxer's built-up shoulders, focused on Jake with a fighter's eyes, willing himself to be seen.

". . . eight . . ."

Jake's appraising gaze fell on Jim. Braddock moved a half step closer. The foreman's finger moved a half inch. He pointed directly at Jim.

"Nine."

A win. With profound relief, Jim's eyes closed, his lungs expelled the air they'd been holding. For a split-second, he almost heard the crazy roar of the crowd, felt the jolt of little Joe Gould jumping on his back.

Behind him, the huddle of men began to break up. Dissipating like ghosts into the gloom, they moved away from the docks, murmuring to each other about where to go next. Jim moved east, toward the rising light of the breaking dawn and the hard physical labor of shift work, counting himself one of the lucky few.

"What the hell happened to you?"

Jim's work partner eyed the black-and-blue bruises on Jim's face with a mixture of curiosity and wariness.

"I got into a fight," Jim told the man.

"What would you go and do that for?"

"Good question."

Jim could easily see why his partner had been chosen for shift work today. The man's handsome face was young and clean-shaven, his bright eyes displayed enough alertness to assure the foreman his orders would be understood and followed, and his lanky body appeared to have the kind of longitudinal strength that could bear a lot of stress before tearing apart.

"Mike Wilson."

"Jim Braddock."

The two had just started moving a mountain of flour sacks from a docked steamer's immense loading net to a line of waiting shipping pallets. The flour sacks had the weight and bulkiness of body bags, and one man alone couldn't lift them. It took two, one on each side, wielding large bailing hooks, to complete the job. It was difficult, awkward labor.

Jim had never before employed his left hand to do much of anything. Trying to operate the hook with it was a struggle, especially while attempting to keep the blackened cast on his broken right hidden behind his back. Sweat broke out on his forehead as he willed his muscles into achieving some kind of workable balance.

"Jim Braddock," Mike repeated. "Used to follow a fighter with that name on the radio."

Jim simply nodded, continuing to manage his clumsy left. He nervously glanced at Jake, hoping the man would keep his distance.

"There's another guy going around using that name now," Mike continued. "Can't fight for shit. A gambling man could lose a lot of money on him. *Twice.*"

Jim wasn't sure how to take that last comment until he saw the amused expression on Mike's face. The man's smile was so infectious, Jim almost laughed. Suddenly the bag of flour they were carrying slipped from his hook. Jim's end dropped to the weathered planks of the dock and the jolt of it caused Mike to lose his grip, too. As Jim bent quickly toward his end, he forgot about his right coming forward.

"Jesus," said Mike, spying the cast. "This ain't gonna work. You're a cripple. You can't slow me down. I need this job."

"Look," said Jim, spearing Mike with an expression sharper than the iron bailing hook. "I can hold up my end."

Before Mike could respond, another voice interrupted. "What the hell is this?" The foreman had come up behind them. Now he stood glowering at Jim's casted hand.

Jim didn't bother explaining. What good were words anyway, when actions got the job done? With a sweeping arc, his left hand sunk the heavy hook into the flour sack. Jim stilled and waited. His gesture was meaningless unless his partner did the same.

Mike Wilson glanced from the foreman to Jim. After a terrible few seconds, Mike followed Jim's lead, sinking his own hook into his end of the sack. With a determined heave, the two men lifted the dead weight together.

They carried the bulk across the dock and pitched it onto the pallet, then they moved to the loading net for another. Working together the two quickly speared and moved a second sack.

"You see us falling behind, Jake?" asked Mike. They hoisted a third and a fourth onto the pallet. "He's all right."

They continued hooking and hauling, bag after bag. Jake stood there with arms crossed, watching every move. Finally, the foreman uncrossed his arms, shook his head, and walked away.

Sweat burning his eyes, Braddock lifted his face to Mike.

"Appreciate it."

Two simple words. A life span of gratitude.

The bright dawn didn't last. By midday, clouds had moved in to drench the city of Newark in sheets of stinging rain. Five years ago, Mae Braddock would have run squealing from the wet, holding her pocketbook over her head as she sought shelter in a corner drugstore, where she'd sit at the counter and warm up with a nice, hot cup of tea.

But this wasn't five years ago, and her place on the endless, snaking soup line was too precious. Her children were hungry and they had no food. So Mae wasn't moving for anything, least of all a little water.

At the head of the line, women in raincoats ladled soup and handed out soaked bread from the open back of a truck. Ahead of Mae were hundreds of men, women, and children. Some were sad, some embarrassed, some just hollowed-out shells, emptied by the relentless years of numbing loss.

While the rain fell, Mae held her six-year-old daughter close to her body. She tried her best to curl around the little girl and keep her dry, but it did no good. Rose Marie ended up as soaking wet as all of them.

After the downpour finally subsided, Mae continued to cradle her daughter in her exhausted arms. Her two boys, bored with all the waiting, began to race around her, shooting finger guns.

"Got you!" shouted Jay.

"No, you don't! Got you!" cried Howard.

For the life of her, Mae didn't know where they got

the energy. "Boys, settle down please." Mae's voice sounded as drained as she felt.

The boys listened and stopped shooting, but less than a minute later they found a pair of puddles—and a whole new form of ammunition.

"Got you!" shouted Jay, splashing his brother.

"No, you don't! Got you!"

"Lady, watch your kids!" complained a man behind them after Jay splashed him with a reckless volley.

"Boys, come here now!" Mae cried. She turned to the man. "I'm so sorry." Then she looked down at the six-year-old in her arms. "You need to stand for a little while, honey."

Mae lowered Rosy to the street's cracked concrete. She hated to do it, but her arms were about to fall off.

"I don't want to," cried Rosy. Her shoes were old, with holes, and as they hit the pavement, the dampness seeped through her socks. "It's wet."

Mae sighed. "Are you a big girl or a little girl?"

"Little!"

Not the answer Mae wanted. "Rosy—"

But Rose Marie was too cold, wet, and tired to listen to any form of parental reasoning. With a scowling face, she began to yowl.

"Who's making all that racket? Sounds like a trombone."

Instantly, the tantrum stopped. Rosy's father had appeared beside her, big and strong and making strange sounds with his lips as he moved one hand out and back from his face.

Rosy blinked wide eyes. "What's a turmone?"

"Trombone, honey," said Jim, smiling down. "It's a musical instrument."

As the little girl's arms stretched toward her daddy, Mae's eyes questioned her husband.

"I got a shift," said Jim, lifting Rosy into his arms. "Foreman says tomorrow maybe a double."

As Jim adjusted his daughter's weight in his arms Mae noticed her husband moving something from inside his coat to his casted hand.

His boxing shoes.

Mae wasn't surprised. Jim had been boxing too long to let a couple of big suits keep him from the ring.

"Are you training today?" she asked.

"I was thinking of selling them."

Jim word's hung between them. Mae didn't know what to feel, what to say.

"Oh," she finally replied.

"I figure the three shifts and what I get for these, by the end of the week, we can pay off the grocer."

Mae looked at the shoes: long laces to support the ankles, leather soles still sturdy. They'd carried her husband across countless rings, buoyed him against every kind of opponent. They'd taken him up the ladder and down again, but always en route to a dream.

Mae swallowed with difficulty. She wanted to say a dozen things to her husband, but all that came out was, "Don't take less than a dollar, Jim."

Jim Braddock saw the tears pooling in his wife's gaze. He gave her a weak smile. "You go home now. I'll stand."

Mae gestured to Jay and Howard in their soggy clothes, her fingers brushing Rosy's damp hair. "I got to turn on the heat, Jimmy," she whispered. "They're chilled through."

He nodded.

"Got ya!"

Howard had jumped in another puddle, launching a giant splash at his older brother. As Mae sighed, Jim put Rosy down then spun and grabbed Howard, lifting the eight-year-old high in the air.

"You know what happens to little monkeys who don't listen to their mother?"

Howard squealed.

"They get . . . the boot!"

As Jim dangled one of his boxing shoes into Howard's face, Jay pointed and shrieked with laughter. Howard stuck his tongue out at his older brother, then Jim set the little boy down.

"Go on, now," Jim told his family.

Mae handed her husband the empty soup pot. She gathered the children together and towed them along, heading toward home.

Jim's gaze followed his wife and children, and then he turned forward again. The back end of the truck seemed as far away as anything in his life, but since the Crash, Jim had mastered the frustrating art of waiting.

Snapping up his collar against the biting wind, he watched the endless line, impossible in number, move forward. Silently, slowly, by half steps and half inches.

Hours later, Jim entered the building on Summit Avenue and Twenty-seventh Street, an area once called West Hoboken but now part of Union City. He walked past the garage and through the narrow hallway. As he ascended the creaking wooden steps, the sounds from above flowed over him: the slip-slap of rope against wood, the smack of bag gloves against punch mitts, the grunting exhales that accompanied right-left-rights as taped-up fists dented heavy bags.

Alone on the staircase, Jim stopped for a minute to lean on the banister and compose himself. He was tired and frozen, and his back was sore as hell from the torturous dock work and the long soup line. Still, the exhaustion couldn't stop the old adrenaline from rising, or the inveterate craving to pull out the boxing shoes tucked in his coat, slip between the ropes, and begin to throw.

It was the perfect moment for Jim to feel sorry for himself. But he didn't have that luxury, not with his family depending on him, and not with his trainer, Joe Jeannette, just a stone's throw away. *After all*, Braddock lectured himself, *what do I have to complain about? I got my day at the stadium, didn't I? I got my shot at a title. More than Jeannette ever got.*

Joe Jeannette had never been a champion, but he'd always been a hero to Jim. The former coal truck driver and son of a blacksmith had started boxing before Jim had even been born. In his day, Jeanette had displayed extraordinary endurance in the ring. His forty-nine-round fight against Sam McVey in 1909 was the stuff of legends. Jeanette had overcome twenty-two knockdowns in three hours. and twelve minutes to win on technical knockout when McVey simply went to his corner and collapsed, exhausted, on his stool.

On offense, Jeanette had displayed quicksilver hand speed and dangerous inside punches. On defense, he'd been slippery and elusive. Nobody could catch him. Within two years of turning pro, back in 1904, the sculpted, strikingly handsome Jeanette had become one of the best heavyweights in the nation.

If Joe had been white, he would have been given a

shot at the heavyweight title. But Jeanette was a black boxer. Few white fighters would consent to enter the ring with him. Even Jack Johnson, a white opponent whom Joe had fought seven times before, drew the color line after he'd won the heavyweight title.

Jeannette never got over Jack Johnson's denying him a shot at the championship, but he sure as hell didn't quit. Instead, Jeannette took on the other great black heavyweights of his time, and in his long career fought, officially and unofficially, more than four hundred bouts—from Paris, London, and Montreal to Baltimore, Philly, and New York.

By 1919, at the age of forty, Joe Jeannette had made the decision to retire without ever getting his shot at being the heavyweight champion of the world, but even now, fourteen years later, Joe was far from out of the fight game. A respected New Jersey referee, Jeannette had made his Summit Avenue boxing gym one of the most popular around. The man was never too busy to give pointers to a young boxer, and Jim had relished the hours he'd spent here. It was a place where he'd always felt a genuine camaraderie. It was the gym where'd he'd first met Joe Gould.

As Jim crested the narrow staircase, the familiar smell of leather and sweat hit him, along with that slight whiff of motor oil from the garage below. Jim stood unmoving at the gym's entrance, his eyes skimming the main floor, taking in the shadowboxers and sparring partners, the slick shoulders working heavy bags. At the far end of the room, a scrawny rookie was dancing around a muscled veteran. The rookie's moves were lightning quick, and the kid landed more than a few jabs on his heavier, more experienced opponent.

The scene looked so familiar, Jim could almost hear his old friend asking . . .

"You got a manager, kid?"

"No. My brother does my business. He's a plumber. Hey, aren't you Joe Gould?"

"Yeah, and if your brother agrees, maybe I can take over the job . . ."

"Jimmy Braddock, what's going on? You come to spar?"

Across the room, Joe Jeannette tossed a friendly wave. Jim tried to return the man's smile, but he couldn't quite manage it. Woodenly, he walked toward the practice ring. He set his soup pot on the floor, set the wet bread on the soup pot, then reached into his coat with his casted hand. It took a moment's struggling to pull his boxing shoes free.

Joe Gould stepped out of the bathroom and into the corridor. Checking his watch, he headed toward the gym floor. Jeannette had promised him a look at a young comer, and Gould didn't have all night. But when he reached the main doorway, he suddenly stopped.

Jim Braddock was here. He was standing beside Jeannette. Next to them stood a young, leanly muscled black boxer. As Gould watched, Jim handed his boxing shoes to the younger man, who paid Jim two bits.

Few words were exchanged, and whatever they'd said, Gould couldn't hear. He simply watched Jim stiffly bend down, pick up his soup pot and bread, then turn toward the front entrance.

That's when Joe Jeannette's gaze lifted and he spotted Gould standing in the rear doorway. Jeannette's eyes met Gould's expectantly, but Gould shook his head and stepped back, behind the door.

Better for us both if Jim doesn't see me, Gould decided. *Better for us both if I just let him go.*

ROUND SIX

So first of all let me assert my firm
belief that the only thing we have to
fear is fear itself. Nameless, un-
reasoning, unjustified terror, which
paralyzes needed efforts to convert
retreat into advance.

Values have shrunken to fantastic
levels: taxes have risen, our ability to pay has fallen, government of
all kinds is faced by serious cur-
tailment of income.

The means of exchange are frozen in
the currents of trade, the withered
leaves of industrial enterprise lie
on every side, farmers find no market
for their produce, the savings of
many years in thousands of families

are gone. More important, a host of
unemployed citizens face the grim
problem of existence and an equal
number toil with little return.

These dark days will be worth all
they cost us if they teach us that
our true destiny is not to be minis-
tered unto but to minister to our-
selves and our fellow men . . .

The people of the United States
have not failed. In their need they
have registered a mandate that they
want direct, vigorous action. In
this dedication of a nation, we
humbly ask the blessing of God. May
he protect each and every one of us.

Jim sat at the rickety kitchen table in his basement
apartment, reading President Franklin Delano Roosevelt's speech aloud from the paper, trying hard to find
inspiration from the words. Beside him, Mae counted
coins from the rainy-day mason jar, trying equally hard
to keep the gas and electric going.

By late fall, Jim's weeks had become an unending
string of dismal gray mornings and sweaty afternoons
of manual labor. At the dock, Jim and Mike were
paired for strenuous unloading jobs day after day: bar-
rels of molasses, bags of rice or sugar or coffee, boxes
of bananas. Jim had learned to ignore the ache beneath
his plaster-encased right, forced his left to do the work
of two hands.

One afternoon, at the close of a morning shift, Jim
was just clearing the dock's gate when somebody's
daughter ran up to the group.

"They're hiring extra at the coal yards!"

Jim took off with the others in a sprint.

Now, after his dock shift had ended, Jim shoveled coal—with his left arm, of course. It was another new exercise, another new struggle, but eventually he found a rhythm and a balance to make the one-handed shoveling work.

Every night, Mae waited up for Jim on the lumpy cushions of the family's worn sofa. She was usually dozing by the time he crept through the door, past midnight. Tonight was no different.

The sound of two quarters clinking into the mason jar stirred Mae from her sleepy state. She glimpsed her husband, black with coal dust, stumbling through the hanging blanket and toward their bed.

Jim wanted nothing more than to fall into the crisp sheets that Mae had turned back for the two of them. The kids were asleep on their own small mattress, and Jim blinked at the sheets on his and Mae's bed. The flat expanse looked so very white, so very clean, a cloud from heaven. He glanced down at his filthy self, covered with coal dust and dried sweat from head to toe.

He sunk down and lay on the floor.

"Jimmy," whispered Mae, pushing through the hanging blanket. "We can wash the sheets."

But Jim was out, already snoring. Mae sighed and pulled the covers off their bed to lay beside her husband on the bare floorboards.

The winter of 1933–34 was one of the coldest in recent memory, with an average temperature hovering around eleven degrees Fahrenheit in the Northeast. The Braddocks hung on to their meager apartment, but just barely.

As the world turned white one morning with a fine dusting of snow, Mae emerged from the basement of their old tenement building. Tramping past closed storefronts and abandoned lots, she traveled to the next neighborhood and dropped off her boys at school.

"Why can't I go to school yet?" asked Rosy, walking home with Mae. "Is it because I'm a girl?"

"Maybe," said Mae, struggling to hold her footing on the icy cracks in the broken sidewalk. "I hadn't thought of that."

They plodded in silence for a time, through the wet, snowy lots, when Mae was distracted by a brand-new car blasting its radio. It was a rare sight, seeing such a shiny new luxury. Nobody she knew had one.

"Mama, who's the man at our house?"

Mae followed Rosy's pointing finger. A man in a public utilities uniform stood at the side of their building, near their electric meter. With her daughter in tow, Mae doubled her strides until she reached the gas and electric man. "Can I help you, sir?"

"I'm sorry, ma'am. You're past due."

The man was probably in his mid thirties, but his eyes looked much older. They were sad and tired, and Mae looked into them with naked panic as his words sunk in.

"You can't," she said. Maybe if she begged? "There's kids. Please."

"I don't, they'll let me go. They let two guys go for it already."

He tried to turn away, but Mae wouldn't let him. She

forced him to stand there and look at her, stand there and hear her. "This apartment, it's what we got left that keeps us hanging on."

"Lady. Lady, I got kids too."

Jim and Mike had been let go early from their Newark dockwork, fifteen cents in their pockets for the six hours of backbreaking labor. As they often did with half days or less, they walked and hitched to nearby towns, trying to find other work—cleaning out lots, shoveling coal, loading and unloading ties at the railroad yards of Weehawken—but there was nothing today. Exhausted, chilled to the bone, they headed home.

"Hey . . . we got until tomorrow!" cried a loud voice.

Jim's heavy steps slowed. Across the street, a young man was arguing with two city marshals. The man wore a double-breasted pinstriped suit, tastefully tailored for the 1920s, its sheen dulled by excessive wear, the buttons mismatched, one sleeve slightly unraveling at the shoulder. His wife stood beside him, fighting back tears in a frayed black coat, its thick wool patched with strips of red and blue cloth, its once elegant fur collar in tatters. On the sidewalk around the couple, their furniture was scattered—a mahogany table, matching chairs, a dresser spilling clothes, night table, bed board, mattress turned on its side, lamps standing erect in the slushy snow next to the end tables meant to hold them.

The marshals were hard to miss on the rundown brick streets of Weehawken. Their uniforms were crisp and neatly pressed—the first really clean clothes Jim

had seen in weeks—and their thick, warm coats were
hardly patched. One officer was young and polite. The
other was a gruff old veteran who had heard it all, and
was tired of listening. While Jim watched, the young
husband caught the edge of an official-looking document the older officer was clutching, tried to yank it
out of the marshal's hand.

"This notice says we got another day," the young
husband insisted.

The older marshal stepped back, stumbling against a
small couch on the curb, spilling embroidered pillows
onto the stained snow.

"Sons-a-bitches," the young man cried. "Sons-
a-goddamned bitches." He glanced across the street
and exchanged a brief look with Jim.

"Come on," said Mike, tugging on Jim's sleeve,
steering him toward home. But Jim was already moving
across the street, a strange light in his eyes. Mike
shrugged, caught up with his partner, then took the lead.

"You can't do this." The young woman's voice was
edged with hysteria. "Once we're out, we'll never get
back in. We'll never get back on our feet, you see?"

Her husband jumped in front of the marshals as they
moved to fit a padlock to the brownstone's front door.
"Please, I got a factory spot I can get next week . . ."

The officers thrust the young man aside and snapped
the padlock in place. The woman winced at the harsh
sound. "The notice said we got another day," she whispered, her tone defeated despite her words. "We're
gonna talk to the landlord tonight. He'll be okay with us
when he finds out we got something coming up. Please,
if we make it until next week, we'll be okay . . ."

"Excuse me," Mike said politely. He stood at the curb, tattered hat in hand, Jim Braddock at his shoulder. When nobody paid attention, he spoke again, much louder. "Excuse me!"

The marshals turned to face him, the young officer reaching for the nightstick on his belt. Mike smiled deferentially. "City marshals, right? How are you boys doing?"

Neither officer spoke. The older man just glared.

"Would you mind, Marshal, if I had a quick look at that eviction notice?" Mike asked, stepping closer. "See, eviction notices are public record. *Tabulae communium*, as it were. And though each is specifically dated, city marshals have been known to try and complete a week's worth of evictions on a Monday, so they don't have to keep coming back and forth to shit little towns like Weehawken."

The older officer's attention strayed from Mike to Jim Braddock with a mixture of recognition and wariness. The former boxer's physical presence was hard to ignore, even though his clothes hung from a frame hollowed from too much work and not enough nourishment.

"So," said Mike. "How about I take a look at the date on that paperwork? The order's legit, we'll just walk on."

Now the younger officer rested one hand on his nightstick. "Or else what?"

Mike just grinned, then turned to his partner. "Hey, Jim, I bet you'd like to see it too, wouldn't you?" Now both marshals were looking past Mike to the man at his side. "You guys know Jim Braddock, don't you?"

"Jeez," said the older officer, suddenly respectful. "I thought it was him. I seen you fight, Jim."

Mike eased a little closer, glancing at the crinkled

document in the older man's hand. "So what do you say, fellas? Honest mistakes happen all the time."

The older marshal lowered his eyes. "Maybe we got our days mixed up."

Mike nodded, his smile forced. "Sure glad we could work this one out. You want to help us move their furniture back in?"

The young officer's expression hardened. "Don't push your luck, pal."

The older man unlatched the padlock and hooked it to his belt. With a respectful nod to Jim, he led his partner away. The young man and woman stood in awe of their rescuers. Mike grabbed a corner of the dresser, then gestured to Jim to grab the other side.

As they lifted the heavy piece, Mike's grin was sincere. "You know, Braddock, a fellow like you could come in handy."

The interior of Quincy's bar was crude and dim—sawdust blanketing an unfinished plank floor, chipped and stained oak bar, grimy mirror on the wall, naked overhead bulbs, most burned out. But the smoke-filled interior was warm and deliciously heady with the aroma of alcohol.

"I'll get us a cold beer," said Mike.

Braddock met the bartender's eyes. "Water for me please, Quincy."

"All I got today," the bartender grumbled. "Big spenders." Quincy dried his hands, his apron soapy, and grabbed two heavy mugs.

"Beer for him too," said Mike. "I'm buying."

Jim opened his mouth to protest, but Mike raised his hand. "Don't hurt my feelings."

Braddock shrugged, then nodded to Quincy, who filled two glasses to the brim with frothy brew. The two men moved to a table. Braddock raised his glass in salute, then blew off the foam. "So you're a lawyer?"

Mike shook his head. "Stockbroker. But I hired so many of the bastards, might as well been to law school myself." Under his tattered coat, Mike's shoulders fell. "Still, lost it all . . . 'twenty-nine."

Jim nodded, savored more of the golden liquor. "Me too," he said, wiping his lips. "Had just about everything I ever earned in stocks. Even had a little taxi company. I mean who loses money on cabs in New York?"

He opened his upturned hand—*poof*.

"You know," said Mike, "they got people living in Central Park and eating the sheep. Calling it the Hooverville." He set his glass down hard on the hardwood table, sloshing foam. "The government's dropped us flat. We need to organize. Unionize. Fight back."

"Whoa," said Braddock. "Fight what? Bad luck? Drought? No use boxing what you can't see, friend." He sat back. "I like what FDR says. You gotta trust in essential democracy . . ."

"Screw FDR," cried Mike, slapping his palms on the table. "FDR. Hoover. They're all the same. I come home one day and stand in my living room and somewhere between the mortgage and the market and the goddamned lawyer who was supposed to be working for me it stopped being mine. It all stopped being mine. FDR hasn't given me my house back yet!" Mike took another swig of beer, then paused before draining half the glass. "In Russia, right now, they're giving the factories back to the workers."

Jim Braddock replied with a crooked grin. "In Russia, right now, I'm pretty sure they're asleep, Mike."

Mike held up the half-empty mug. "Even this," he grunted. "You know why they finally repealed prohibition? You think it's about freedom? It's about federal revenue collection, plain and simple."

With that, Mike drained his glass, and slammed the empty mug on the table. Heads turned. "How about another one, Jim?"

Braddock licked his lips, tempted by Mike's incredibly generous offer. But he shook his head. "Thanks, Mike. But I gotta go." Jim got to his feet.

"Hey, Braddock, I know I talk too much. But it wasn't just me." Mike's eyes, bright from the booze, met Jim's. "You did some good out there. You have a good night." Then Mike was on his feet, too, walking to the bar to order another mug from Quincy. Jim headed the other way, through the door and home to his family.

The wool blanket that once divided the single-room apartment was now wrapped snugly around the children. While Mae, her slight form bulky in two sweaters and a coat, lit candles at the scuffed table, Jim stood over his sleeping children, watching them blow steamy fog as they snored. The dresser gaped, the coat rack stood empty. Every piece of clothing, every scrap of fabric, covered the children in their bed. But even that was not enough to shut out the wind that swirled through cracks in windows and doors, the cold that crept up from the earth to engulf them.

"You think about it, you gotta go to a swanky joint to eat with candles," said Mae. She lit the single candle on the table, blew out the match, then grabbed the mason jar they used for a bank and sat down, waiting for her husband.

Jim crossed the room to toss a broken scrap of wooden sign—some piece of an advertisement from a failed local business—into the fire in the stove, then warmed his hands for a moment. Mae emptied the contents of the jar onto the table. Nickels and dimes jangled. Jim joined her, added the meager contents of his pockets. They slid the money around for a moment.

"Six bucks seventy," grunted Jim. "How much to turn it back on?"

"Three months. Thirty-three ten," whispered Mae, careful not to wake the children.

"If I work twenty-six out of every twenty-four, it still won't add up. And we got nothing left to sell." Jim's body seemed to weaken, his posture waver. He rested his elbows on the table, rubbed his eyes. "All my busted bones, then a piece of paper changes hands and that's it. It's all for nothing."

Mae reached for his hand. Her flesh was cold, but the sentiment was warm, and Jim smiled despite his weariness.

"All the guys you could have married," he said.

"Yeah," Mae teased. "What happened to those guys?" Jim looked at her and she laughed, squeezed his hand. "I married the man I love."

A wet cough across the room interrupted them. Jim glanced at Mae, the question in his eyes.

"Howard," she told him. "Since this afternoon."

Mae took back her hand, folded both of them over

her heart and began to pray. When she realized she was alone, she paused. "Jim . . . ?"

"I'm all prayed out," he replied.

It only took a stern glance from his wife to set Jim backpeddling. "Anyway, God's too busy for me right now. He already gave me you and the kids. He's answered all my prayers."

Jim rose and crossed the room, face hidden in the shadows. Mae watched his back, trying to read his thoughts.

"He . . . He doesn't owe me anything," Jim added softly.

Next morning, as the first rays of dawn streamed through the streaked basement windows, Mae woke shivering under piles of clothing to find her husband had already ventured out, into the relentless cold.

The giant face on the billboard—a well-groomed gentleman in evening clothes displaying a Gillette razor—grinned down at the grimy winter street. Mae glanced around her to find empty sidewalks, save for two children even more filthy than her own, gamely washing clothes in the cold runoff beside the curb.

With no one to see her, Mae began snapping off pieces of wooden latticework from around the billboard frame, breaking a fingernail in the process. She handed the first pieces off to her sleepy children, then broke off more. Suddenly, shouting voices echoed down the street.

"Where are you going?" A woman hung out the second-story window of one of the faceless brownstones, her features flushed with rage, her words a desperate cross between accusation and heartbreak. On the ground below, a man walked down the street, his back to the ranting woman. His clothes were shabby and he carried a small suitcase double-wrapped with twine.

"Go ahead, you piece of shit," the woman wailed. The man walked on without turning, his spine bowed by shame. "Go on then." She sobbed. "We don't need you."

One of the children in the gutter, a small boy, stared after his father. Then the boy locked eyes with Mae, and she saw a tear cutting a canal through the dirt on his cheek.

Mae swept Jay and Rosy in front of her. "Come on, now, let's go."

She knew this ugly scene was typical. No longer able to earn a living, thousands of husbands and fathers had simply given up trying. Some of them vanished into the homeless hordes of Central Park or rode the rails to oblivion. Mae shuddered at the thought of losing her husband this way. She tried not to imagine a day when Jim Braddock would give up on his family. And though she told herself that he was not like those other men, Mae knew that her husband was only human, and there was only so much a man could do in the face of such overwhelming odds against him.

Back home again, Mae shook away her gloomy thoughts as she fed latticework chips to the stove's fire, its warmth failing to reach beyond the corner. Snow caked the windows, frost glazing both sides of the pane. One window was cracked, and the rag stuffed into the hole did little to stop the chill air that poured through the gap.

Mae turned to her youngest boy, still huddled where she'd left him, under a blanket mere inches from the

stove. His face was flushed with fever, moist with per-
spiration that caused him to shiver uncontrollably
when the blanket was removed, even for a moment.

"Baby, look at Mommy."

Eyes glazed, pupils like pinpricks, he looked up. Her
voice hardly seemed to penetrate the sickness. She
knelt at his side, tucked the blanket tighter around him,
and held a glass of water to his trembling lips.

"Drink up now," she coaxed.

Howard's cracked lips touched the rim and he managed to take in a few small sips, dribbling some. Again
Mae tugged at the blankets, unaware of the tears
spilling from her eyes.

"Mommy?"

It was Jay, standing behind her, his fear of his
mother's distress a palpable thing.

"It's all right, sweetheart," she said, pushing the hair
away from his wide eyes. Suddenly Mae stood. "Mommy'll be right back," she said. Eyes blurred by tears,
unwilling to let her children see her break, Mae hurried
out the door and into the dirty, snow-dusted courtyard,
where she stood crying bitterly.

All that mattered in the world was keeping this family together. Jim was killing himself trying to do it, taking as many jobs as he could find. But it wasn't
working. Every week, no matter how many hours Jim
toiled, they fell further behind. They had lost their heat
and electricity. How long would it be before they were
living in the street?

Mae squared her shoulders, deciding for both of
them what had to be done. Despite all of her husband's
efforts, Howard was getting sicker from the scarcity of
food, the lack of heat. Mae turned and went back inside

to dress her children snugly for the trip across town, then across the river to New York City.

The afternoon sun was bright, but provided no warmth as Jim returned home, squinting against the glare while shivering in the wind. He opened the front door. As usual, no electric power meant the basement apartment was veiled in shadow. No gas meant the temperature inside was almost as cold as the sidewalk. Then it struck him, the wall of silence. No childish voice called out to greet him. No tiny body charged forward with open arms.

By the stove, Mae sat alone in her coat, her limbs drawn tightly against herself, her eyes staring into the fading glow of the dying flames. She would not look up as he walked closer. Wouldn't even meet his eyes.

"Howard's fever was getting worse. And then Rosy started to sneeze," she explained before he could ask.

"Where are they, Mae?"

His eyes frantically scanned the tiny space, as if he refused to hear her, as if he could find them hiding among the meager sticks of furniture or inside the spidery cracks in the dingy walls. Mae finally looked up at him, her expression defiant. "We can't keep them warm, Jim."

"Where are they, Mae?"

"The boys will sleep on the sofa at my father's in Brooklyn. Rosy's going to stay at my sister's. We can't keep them, Jim."

Jim's emotions were almost too overpowering to express—fear, disappointment, rage. He stabbed his finger. "You don't decide what happens to our children without me."

Mae stood, seized his arm with icy hands. "Jimmy,

if they get real sick, we don't have the money for a doctor."

"You send them away, this has all been for nothing."

"It's . . . It's only until we can make enough to get back to even, then we can—"

"If it was that easy, why didn't I just go on relief, get a book and put my feet up?" He was simmering now. His own wife had given up, given in. Hadn't he been out on the street seven days, looking for work? Hadn't he been acting like a man? Doing anything and everything he could to support his family? "Every day, out there, it was so we could stay together. What else was it for? If we can't stay together, it means we lost."

"Baby, no one has any good choices anymore, we'll get them—" Mae had tried to embrace him but he shook her off.

"Mae, I promised him, see? I got on my knees, looked him in his eyes and I promised him I would never send him away." Without another word, Jim turned and strode across the freezing room.

"What are you doing? Where are you going?" Mae demanded, tears falling. But he was already gone, out the door, onto the street. Mae ran after him, suddenly remembering the woman she'd seen earlier, hanging out that brownstone window, sobbing, angry, heartbroken.

"Jimmy, come back!"

But he didn't stop. He didn't even turn for one last look. Mae's steps slowed as her husband continued to walk away, silently, resolutely, down the cold concrete of the broken sidewalk.

At the scarred and battered wooden counter of the Newark relief office, a stern-faced woman counted out twelve dollars and eighty cents, then placed the money in a white envelope with a state seal. Hands shaking, Jim signed the receipt book, trying not to berate himself for what he'd once been, what he'd once believed about himself as a man. He snatched up the cash and thrust it into his coat pocket.

Witnessing his shame, the woman's hardened expression softened a moment. "I would never have expected to see you here, Jim."

The words rang like the closing bell of a fifteen-round defeat. With a red-faced nod, Jim pushed through the miserable crowd, eyes downcast, unable to forget the phrase some newspaper columnist had used to describe these unending relief lines: "Worms that walk like men."

They were professionals and laborers. Teachers and dockworkers, lawyers and janitors, bankers and master builders. Some stood in nothing better than rags, while others were clad in finely tailored suits and overcoats frayed and patched after years of wear. And while some, like Jim, kept their eyes averted in disgrace, others displayed only vacant stares, their faces hollowed by loss and privation. One of the latter had quietly fallen forward the week before, dying on the steps of the very institution set up to provide aid for him. Jim had heard about it on the street. The man either hadn't known where to go, or hadn't been willing to go there until hunger and fatigue had done their work.

Jim hurried out of the office and into the street, taking great swallows of fresh air, steadying himself for what had to come next.

On the ferry to Manhattan, he stood at the rail and

gazed at the skyline as the chill winds whipped his hair, cut through his threadbare clothing. The ferry terminal was nearly deserted, and in the lengthening shadows of the fading day, Jim walked wearily along Eighth Avenue, passing homeless men lurking in alleyways, shopworn prostitutes with desperate eyes.

Jim continued his endless walk, passing a man in a dusty suit, standing tall while selling bruised apples from a rickety wooden cart. As he trudged by a brightly lit theater, a limousine rolled up beside him on the sidewalk. Two children, about the same ages as his sons, burst from the car, laughing excitedly, their well-heeled parents in tow. Jim paused to watch them, wondering how such carefree joy could exist in the middle of so much degrading misery.

During his walk, Jim had seen one employment office after another, the blocks around each wrapped with unending lines of men. *No work to be had. No other way to pay off his debts and reunite his family.* He told himself this, over and over, steeling himself for what he was about to do.

When he reached the streets around Madison Square Garden, he recalled the vibrant, glittering scenes of the past. The dazzling lights were gone now, dim as the gloomy winter twilight. No more fashionable fans, tipsy flappers, or Diamond Jim limousines. In their place, vagrants loomed, a sad collection of shabby humanity scavenging old billboards for scrap. A smoky garbage can burned in the alley. The starving panhandlers huddled around it in moth-eaten coats, stretching filthy hands toward meager flames.

Jim went to the familiar side door, below the fire escape. The once clean brick wall was dingy now, no extra pay for a man with a bucket and a brush. He glanced at the billboard above the door. An upcoming fight was advertised, two brawny bodies, stiffly posed, gloves up. He remembered himself up there, sharing one end of the "vs." with Tuffy Griffiths, remembered the dream of that night, the cheering crowds, the astonished sportswriters, the gleaming bliss of a long-held ambition shimmering within reach.

Then, like a vicious uppercut, a different memory assailed him, shattering the fragile mirage. Yankee Stadium, in the heat of summer. Another fight on another day. It was the bout that had tarnished his golden future, branding him a boxer of "failed promise." It was the match that, once over, he'd only wanted to forget . . .

July 1929, four months before the October crash, life was good. Jim Braddock was about to challenge Philadelphia's Tommy Loughran for the light heavyweight championship of the world.

Although neither boxer was a hometown darling in New York City, where the fight was to take place, Jersey Jim Braddock was the sentimental favorite among local sportswriters, and heavily favored to win.

"Does Braddock not have the kick of the mule with his right hand?" Joe Gould barked at Lud, a sportswriter for Union City's *Hudson Dispatch*, before the fight. "Did he not shatter Pete Latzo's jaw to fragments? Take down Tuffy Griffiths in two rounds and Jimmy Slattery in nine?"

But in the weeks before the opening bell, difficulties plagued both fighters. Loughran and Braddock each had a hard time staying within the weight class—Jim because he couldn't gain pounds fast enough, Loughran because he couldn't shed them. Before the fight, the champ from Philly had tortured his body down to 175 pounds while Jersey Jim's nervous sleeplessness had given him an official weigh-in of 170 pounds, barely enough to qualify.

The fight had hardly begun when Braddock scored with a terrific right. Blood gushed from Loughran's face like water from an opened hydrant. A technical knockout seemed imminent. He tore at Loughran again and again, but Jim could not lay another glove on the man in that first round.

In the second, Loughran laid a basketful of lefts on Braddock's chin while dancing around the ring, ducking and jabbing and making Braddock look like the rawest kind of amateur. Jim swung one right after another, missing every time. By the third round, the champ from Philadelphia had gauged Braddock's major weakness—no left-hand action. He fought accordingly.

In that third round, and in the fourth and fifth, Loughran taunted Braddock, making Jim madder and madder. The angrier he got, the more futile right-hand punches Braddock threw, until he was lurching ludicrously around the ring to boos and catcalls from the capacity crowd. In the opening of the seventh round, however, Braddock was able to connect with a sweeping upward blow that grazed Loughran's nose and forehead and brought another torrent of blood.

But Tommy Loughran was far from defeated. After that staggering blow, he stepped up and delivered a right cross to Jim Braddock that set his knees wobbling. That was the beginning of the end of Jim's hopes. During the rest of the bout, Braddock connected one last time—a right-hand wallop in the twelfth round. Unfortunately, by then Braddock's stamina was at its lowest ebb, and Loughran brushed off the blow and came back swinging.

In the heartbreaking fifteen-round decision, the judges ruled that Jim Braddock had dominated his opponent in only two of them, and champion Tommy Loughran retained his title by unanimous decision. Even worse, Jim Braddock had plodded through the final three rounds, offering one of the worst performances of his career, as taunts and insults were hurled at him from the crowd. Those insults continued in the newspaper accounts the next day, which featured the canonization of Loughran, who was compared to Gene Tunney and would go down in boxing history as one of the greatest, while James J. Braddock was pronounced finished and advised to go back to Cauliflower Alley . . .

"I don't know what went wrong."

Freezing in the shadow of the Garden, Jim whispered the same thoughts he'd confessed to Gould after the Loughran fight.

In Jim's view, fate had conspired to interrupt his meteoric rise as a boxer, but it was the crash of 1929 that had finished him. Maybe all those losses that came after Loughran would have been wins if those fights hadn't come in the midst of his losing everything—all his hard-earned savings, his taxicab business, his security, his home. The crash had robbed Jim of more than money; it had robbed him of his optimism and confidence. It had sent his family into poverty and stolen his ability to see himself as golden, to fight like a winner.

Using his good left hand, Jim yanked open the side

door of the arena and moved through its deserted corridors. His casted hand ached as he trudged slowly up the flight of stairs. It was the longest, hardest climb of his life.

The boxing club occupied a large private space inside the Garden. Its walls comprised dark wood covered with black-and-white photographs of prominent fighters from the last three decades posed in a variety of stances. Drinks were served from a rich mahogany bar, leather chairs and heavy tables topped with Tiffany lamps were scattered about the polished oak floor, and all of it was burnished by the bloody-gold flames from a massive fireplace.

Two dozen well-dressed managers, promoters, and professional oddsmakers drank, talked, and played cards in the rarified air of this enclave, only a few stories above the street but miles above the ravages of the ongoing Depression. Here they wheeled and dealed, sipped aged scotch, and angled to close prime matchups for their most promising fighters. The tall tales and good-natured insults were flying as thick as the cigar smoke, and at first no one noticed Jim Braddock willing himself to walk to the center of the room.

As two promoters burst into loud guffaws, Jim stepped up to them. "Mr. Allen . . . Phil . . ."

The men stared, taking in Braddock's bedraggled appearance without comment. Others noticed his presence and the conversations slowly died. The once great fighter cleared his throat and said, "Thing is, I can't afford to pay the heat. Had to farm out my kids . . ."

Jim's voice broke just then. He looked down at the floor and swallowed hard.

"They keep cutting shifts at the dock. You don't get picked every day . . . Just need enough to catch up."

The shame was almost too much to bear.

"Went to the relief office. Gave me twelve eighty. I need thirteen sixty more. To pay the bill. Get them back." Girding himself, he slowly looked up. "It pains me to ask . . . so much . . . but I sure would be grateful . . ."

Jim took off his hat and stretched it out, like the panhandlers on the street below.

The room was speechless now, the men uncomfortable with this specter of defeat among them. Finally, Mr. Allen dug into his pocket. "Sure, Jim, sure," he said and spilled several coins into Jim's hat.

"Thank you," Jim replied, then moved through the room, offering his hat. Every man gave, including the big one, Jimmy Johnston, the very promoter who'd suspended his boxing license and shut down his career.

Braddock completely circled the club. He stopped in front of Joe Gould only when there was no one else left. "I'm sorry, Joe," Braddock told him sincerely.

"What the hell do you have to be sorry about? Jesus, Jim," said Gould. "How short are you?"

Jim, who'd been counting as he went, replied in a hoarse whisper. "A buck fifty, I think . . ."

Gould winced, then reached into his rumpled suit and drew out his wallet, placing the exact amount into Jim's battered hat.

"Joe . . ."

But Joe Gould looked away, swallowed his drink. "Don't . . . don't mention it, Jimmy," he murmured.

With a final nod, Jim departed, his shoulders squared, his spine straight. He descended the long stairs, exited the side door, and passed the vagrants huddling around the trash-can fire.

Night had fallen and streetlights had already flickered on, illuminating the icy sidewalks. A few steps down the avenue, Jim walked by a store that had gone out of business. In the mirrored surface of the darkened glass, he caught a glimpse of his reflection and his steps slowed.

He'd seen that expression before, he realized. Years ago. On men his father's age, who'd lowered themselves to work those errand-boy jobs he'd held through his teens. It was the look of the man standing tall in his dusty suit to sell apples on Eighth Avenue, the face of the banker, in all his patched finery, waiting on line for hours at the Newark relief office, his hand out for pitiable public charity.

Jim had never before understood what it would take to make a man with such obvious pride willingly lower himself to such shattering depths. Tonight, with the money in his pocket to get his children back, Jim knew. Tonight, he finally understood.

The next night, Mae opened the door to their basement apartment and flicked on a light switch that actually worked. A golden glow finally dispelled the dismal shadows of the tiny space.

The door opened wider and Jay and Howard ran inside, followed by Jim, who was carrying the sleeping Rosy, draped over the cast on his arm. Mae took Rosy from him and put the girl to bed while the boys chased each other around the small space, happy and grateful to be home again.

Jim, dark rings circling his tired eyes, drank in the

sight like a thirsty beggar—joyful, relieved, and terrified at the same time. He was happy to see his family united, but now far too aware of how fragile their lives had become, how easily their world could be torn apart.

He couldn't sleep that night. He burned to change things, but he didn't know how. He only knew he would, at first opportunity.

The night before the Tuffy Griffiths fight, he'd felt like this too, keyed up and on edge. Jim had nothing real to battle tomorrow, no one he could actually haul off and punch, but he ached sorely for an opponent to face, someone to stand toe to toe with and fight.

Lying quiet and still, Jim listened to his wife's steady breathing, waited for the endless night to wane. At last, as the first rays of dawn peeked around the basement curtains, Jim rose and dressed silently. Before he left for the day to go to the loading dock, the coal company, the rail yards, or whoever would pay him a day's wage, he stood at the door and gazed at his family, unable to shake the fear that they would be gone—vanished, like his career and his fortune—by the time he returned home again.

A boxer entered the ring alone. If knocked down, he alone could pick himself up and keep the fight going. As Jim walked out the door and toward the winter sunrise, he grasped in a whole new way why those were the rules of his game.

ROUND SEVEN

I don't care who you are and how great you are, you're going to get hit . . . you have to be able to disregard pain.

—Tommy Loughran,
Light heavyweight champion of the world,
1927–1929

Newark, New Jersey
June 13, 1934

Paper streamers fluttered on warm gusts, brightening a Newark churchyard. The worst winter in years had faded finally, thawing the icy streets and transforming the freezing winds off Newark Bay into mild breezes.

The Braddocks had joined a dozen other families for the once-a-month birthday party mounted by their Catholic parish for children whose parents could not afford private celebrations. Jim stood beside Mae, while his children joined a dozen others around a weather-beaten picnic table, where two sheet cakes blazed with candles. As Father Rorick led the families in a rousing rendition of "Happy Birthday," Jim circled his wife's thin waist with his right arm, his hand finally free of its cast.

"Happy birthday to you . . . Happy birthday to you . . ." sang the crowd. When it was time to insert the child's name, the members of each family leaned in and sang a Babel-like jumble—

"Mitchell . . . Junior . . . Philip . . . Lisa . . . Bill . . ."

Mae leaned over her oldest boy and sang "Jay . . ."

"Happy birthday to you . . ." The children blew out the candles to a burst of applause. Howard tugged his father's arm. "I liked it more when we had our own cake."

Father Rorick overheard the remark and quickly spoke up. "Your dad every tell you I used to spar with him?"

Howard blinked in surprise, then shot a horrified look at his dad. "You hit the Father?"

Jim Braddock grinned. "As often as possible." He shared his smile with the priest as Howard took off with the other kids to eat cake and bat around the colorful balloons.

Father Rorick faced Braddock. "We miss you in service, Jim," he said.

Braddock frowned, glanced away. "I get an extra shift."

Rorick nodded but didn't walk away. He stood quietly and waited for Jim to do the talking. The wait was a long one, but eventually Jim asked, "You ever ask yourself, what's the reason?"

"He has his reasons. We are his children, Jim."

"I'm sure he does, Tom," Braddock replied, his eyes

following the gang of scrawny children in their tattered clothes. "But how would you feel about me if I treated my kids like this?"

Father Rorick was about to reply when Mae arrived, her expression troubled. "James . . ." she said.

Jim followed his wife's anxious gaze toward angry cries across the yard. Mike, his partner at the docks was sitting at the end of a long table, obviously drunk. His wife Sara, infant daughter in her arms, was shouting at him while the little girl squirmed and cried.

"Every day, fix the world," Sara charged. "How about fixing your family? What kind of father are you? Too proud to cross the lawn because she can't have her own birthday cake . . . And now you're drunk at church, for Christ's sake."

Mike leaned into his wife's face. "That a joke, Sara? Are you making a joke?"

Sara pushed him away. "I'm just saying it's enough."

All eyes were on them. Even the children halted their antics to gape. Mike smirked, knees wobbly, and opened his mouth to speak. Jim walked over and stepped between them, separating the angry couple.

"Hey, where's the ref?" he asked lightly.

Mike reeked of rot-gut booze and bad temper. He frowned at Braddock. "This is between husband and wife, Jim."

"How do you even call yourself that?" Sara cried, her baby hanging from her arm.

Mike lurched toward her, Jim stopped him with a firm hand to the middle of his chest. "Easy there, Mike. Maybe you've had a couple. No harm in that. Day of rest, after all . . ."

Jim had tried to keep his tone light, but Mike wasn't taking anything lightly. He glared, jaw moving, face flushed. "That the way it is? Man'll take your beer long as you're paying . . ." Mike shoved Braddock, who shook off the push without budging.

"There's no need for you to do this." Jim's voice was soft but firm.

Mike sneered. "Jim Braddock, big fighter . . ."

Jim easily slapped away Mike's punch, then grabbed the man's arm to steady him. Mike yanked himself away, stumbled.

"Mike, I got no beef with you."

"Couldn't make it in the ring . . . Why not take it out on his pal—"

Mike lunged for Jim again. Jim shoved the man aside and he tumbled to the concrete, smacking his head against the pavement. Blood gushed. Sara screamed, "Jim, no!"

As Mike stumbled to his feet, a scarlet torrent flowed from his scalp. Sara raced to his side, still clutching her baby. Mike pushed her away, glared at Jim, then his wife.

"Go to hell," he said. "Both of you."

Then Mike turned and fled the churchyard, ran down the street. When he was gone, Sara faced Jim, tears drowning her cheeks, her baby wailing in her arms.

"Jesus, Jim. He wasn't going to hit me . . . Jesus."

Finally, Sara hurried away, chasing after her husband. Jim looked up to find Mae standing a few feet away, tears in her own eyes. "Why was it so hard just to come over for the cake?" she asked.

Adrenaline pumping, Jim flared. "Maybe he just

needed a little time, all right? It's not so damned easy . . . Maybe he just needed a little time!"

Mae came right back at him. "Not at me, James Braddock," she cried, finger shaking. "Do you hear? I know it's hard. But not . . . at . . . *me*."

Hours later, afternoon light spilled onto the worn, cracked paving stones in front of the Braddocks' tenement. As Jim walked down his street, he noticed neighborhood kids of varying ages—Jay and Howard among them—playing stickball. On a stoop in front of their apartment house, Rosy sat watching her brothers. Jim joined her. As Jay chased a stray ball, he called, "No second shift at the yards, Dad?"

Jim stepped off the stoop, jostling his son playfully. "Yeah, but they only want kids. Go grab a shovel."

Jay grinned, snapped up the ball, and tossed it to his playmates. As he ran off, Jim tried to hide the worry in his eyes.

He turned to find Rosy watching him, eyes puzzled. Standing on the stoop, she was nearly the same height as her father. "Were you and that man fighting?"

"We were almost fighting."

Rosy put up her tiny hands, which were balled into little fists. "Teach me how."

Jim shook his head. "I can't, honey."

"Why not?"

Jim's eyes drifted to the door. "Because the cops might come back."

Rosy lowered her arms. "You mean Mommy?"

Jim nodded. Rosy put her hands on her hips. "You can too. Teach me, Daddy."

He tried to stare down his daughter, but Rosy was too much like her mother. When she threw him the knockout punch of all looks, he relented.

"Look," he began. "It's about the balance. Put your right here, twist your hips and throw that one—" As he gave instructions, he positioned the girl until she was posed like a tiny Gene Tunney. She squinted in concentration, then threw. Jim caught her fist in his big mitt.

"Wow, look at that!" he cried. "You got a better jab than I did."

As he and Rosy laughed, a familiar car rolled up to the curb, and the window rolled down.

"You are a brave man," called Joe Gould.

Jim smiled at his ex-manager. "Not really. Mae's at the store."

Rosy, still concentrating on her boxing lesson, let fly with another jab. Standing on the high stoop, she was high enough to clock her father square in the jaw. He blinked, impressed at her pint-size power.

"Okay, darling. Good shot. Now shadowbox while I talk to Uncle Joe."

Rosy pummeled the air as Jim walked up to Joe's roadster. Joe climbed out and Jim brushed the man's lapels. Gould's suit looked brand new.

"Still looking dapper, I see."

Gould shrugged. "Gotta keep up appearances." Then he smiled and punched Braddock's arm. "Good to see you, Jimmy." Gould looked around, checking out the street. Jim leaned against his car, waiting. "Nice day," said Joe.

Braddock leaned close to his ex-manager. "You drive all the way out here to talk about the weather?"

Gould shrugged again. "Maybe I was in the neighborhood."

"Joe, this is Jersey."

Only then did Gould laugh. "A point." He waited a moment, then spoke again. "I got you a fight."

"Go to hell."

"You want it, don't you?"

Braddock seemed doubtful. "What about the commission?"

"They'll sanction it. This one time and one time only." Gould frowned. "This isn't a comeback. This is *one* fight."

Braddock thought about it for a moment. "Why?"

"Because of who you're—"

Braddock brushed that question aside for a more important one. "How much?"

Gould shook his head, grinning. "Just once, ask me who you're fighting."

Braddock faced him. "How *much*?"

"Two hundred and fifty," Gould replied. "You're on the big show at the Garden . . ." Joe paused before delivering the bombshell ". . . tomorrow night."

Braddock turned and walked away. Jim had been partners with Gould for years. He couldn't believe the man would amuse himself this way, ribbing an old friend with a joke like this one.

Gould chased after him, coattails flying. "You fight Corn Griffin, Jimmy . . . number-two heavyweight contender in the world. Prelim before the championship bout . . ."

Jim faced him, eyes dangerous. "Joe, this isn't funny."

"It ain't no favor. Griffin's opponent got cut and can't fight. They needed somebody they could throw in on a day's notice. Nobody legit will take a fight against Griffin without training, so . . ."

Joe Gould looked away, then gave Jim a sidelong glance. When he spoke, his tone was apologetic. "I . . . I told them they could use the angle Griffin was gonna knock out a guy'd never been knocked out before . . . You're meat, Jimmy . . ."

To Gould's surprise, Jim didn't take offense. "You on the level?"

"Always."

Jim studied Gould for what seemed like a long time. On the stoop, Rosy had taken an interest in the conversation. During the long silence, she squinted, her little mind working.

Finally, Braddock grinned and clapped his rough hands on Gould's shoulders. Then he looked his manager in the eye. "Joe. For two hundred and fifty bucks I'd fight your wife."

Jim hadn't spoken to Mae since the scene between Mike and Sara earlier in the day. When Mae returned from the grocery store, he told her the good news Joe Gould had brought. Mae listened and then nodded silently. Jim knew his wife was not happy with the situation, so he kept on talking—about how long he would have to work at the docks or the yards to earn so much ready cash, and the fact that it was only one fight, not a comeback.

In the end, Mae told Jim to take the bout. It was, she told herself, only one more fight. No more than an exhibition, really—or so Jim told her. But that night, as her husband slept soundly for the first time in many months, Mae could not rest. Instead, she sat in the darkness on their lumpy old sofa. Wrapped in a tattered robe, she watched her husband sleep through eyes red from crying.

The next morning, when Jay and Howard went outside to play, they took Rosy with them. But instead of starting up a game of pink ball or stick ball, they headed across the street and down the block to the local butcher shop.

The door was locked and the blind was pulled down. Jay and Howard exchanged uncertain glances, but Rosy boldly reached out and tapped the glass with her tiny hand.

Sam, in a blood-stained shirt and apron, opened the door a crack. He peered down at the motley crew at his door and shook his head. "We're closed today," he grumbled.

Sam glared at Jay and Howard. Rosy stepped in front of her brothers. "Let me do the talking," she whispered, then pushed the door open and stepped through, followed by Howard and Jay.

Sam stepped back, beefy hands on hips. "Where's your folks?"

Rosy ignored the question. Head held high, she strutted right past the butcher and up to the counter.

"Well, look who's here," said the butcher, eyeing Jay, the salami thief. "Should I lock up everything?"

Jay flushed red but bravely stood by his sister, who was tapping her fingers impatiently on the countertop.

Sam stepped up to her, crossed his arms.

"I need a piece of meat, sir," said Rosy. "Peter's house, please."

"You mean *porterhouse*?" asked the butcher.

Rosy nodded.

"You got any money?"

The little girl shook her head. Sam sighed and his expression softened. "I can't just give it away, not even to a stray little lady and her bodyguards."

"How about something you dropped on the floor?"

But Sam shook his bald head. "I don't drop it. And if I do I clean it off. It's too precious."

"It's not for me . . ."

Sam scratched his unshaven chin. "Who's it for?"

"My dad," Rosy replied. "He needs it so he can win a boxing fight."

 **ROUND EIGHT**

I was always more or less the underdog. It didn't make no difference to me.

—James J. Braddock,
as quoted by Peter Heller in *In This Corner*

Long Island City, New York
June 14, 1934

PRIMO CARNERA VS. MAX BAER
HEAVYWEIGHT CHAMPIONSHIP FIGHT!
AND FOUR OTHER FIGHTS

The Madison Square Garden Bowl was where the Garden promoters took their fight cards in the heat of the New York summer. The outdoor arena was located just across the East River in the borough of Queens, and its bleacher capacity was more than twice the number of the indoor facility's nineteen thousand seats.

Tonight Jim Braddock's name wasn't on the marquee. He was no longer a headliner—and he couldn't have cared less. Two hundred fifty dollars and the chance to punch something real, to give as good as he got, were the only things on his mind as he entered the dressing room.

Outside, the fifty-six thousand capacity crowd hadn't crossed the East River to see Jim Braddock, and he knew it. They were here for the main event. The Italian-born heavyweight champ, "Satchel Foot" Primo Carnera, was set to defend his title against a promising up-and-comer named Max Baer, a powerful California-born fighter who'd forged the body of Apollo swinging a sledgehammer in his father's slaughterhouse. Baer's right hook was so deadly he had already killed a man in the ring.

Still, a few local sports reporters and fistic connoisseurs with long memories were intrigued to hear James J. Braddock was on the dock for the opening bout, wondering if it was the same boxer who'd ended his career in such humiliation, losing a title match to Tommy Loughran then shattering his right on Abe Feldman's skull.

Joe Gould had mixed emotions about what he'd set up. He'd been angling to get Braddock a fight ever since that freezing winter afternoon when Jim had arrived, hat in hand, in the middle of the Garden's dark-paneled, cigar-smoke-filled boxing club. Gould had pestered Johnston to no end after that, barging into his office unannounced and angering the Garden's powerful promoter in a half dozen separate incidents.

As fate would have it, Joe Gould had been waiting in Johnston's outer office for yet another chance to see the big man when Johnston got the bad news about Corn

Griffin's opponent. The boxer had backed out of the match due to a facial cut, just two days prior to the big fight.

Griffin, a private in the United States Army, was a rising star from down South who came to the big city looking for red meat. Johnston decided that, in order to attract the attention of the New York press, Corn would have to beat a has-been who used to be someone. Now it appeared that James Braddock would fit the bill, especially since Braddock's manager happened to be waiting in the outer office, and the guy had been badgering Johnston for months to put Braddock back in the ring.

Johnston had figured Gould for a pushover, but after he ushered the manager into his plush inner sanctum and made the offer, he discovered to his dismay that Braddock's manager was still angling for a better deal.

"How about giving us Dynamite Jackson?" Gould had asked.

It was a wily suggestion, to say the least, and Johnston was savvy enough to know it. Within boxing circles, the rumor was ripe that Jackson was outboxing Max Baer in sparring rounds at Baer's Asbury Park training camp. But the real reason Gould wanted Braddock to battle Dynamite was because Jim had beaten Jackson in 1932, and Gould figured his fighter could repeat that victory.

But Johnston didn't care what Gould wanted or what would make Braddock look good. He was in a bind with the Corn Griffin bout, and he wasn't in the mood for any of Gould's conniving.

"You're always on my neck to get a bout for that

washed-up heavyweight of yours," Johnston had bellowed. "But when I give you one, you turn around and want an offer to fight somebody else. Well, you tell Braddock that he fights Griffin, or he don't fight at all."

So Gould accepted the offer, and though Jim Braddock seemed completely sanguine about the coming bout, Joe Gould was secretly fighting panic. He was well aware that Jim had not boxed in over a year, hadn't trained at all, and had only one workout prior to the match—and Jim had complained the whole time that he was losing a day's wages at the docks to squeeze the warm-up into his schedule. Then, of course, there was the cherry on top, of which Jim had reminded Gould after arriving at the gate.

"I mean, Christsakes," Gould ranted, "a hundred and something fights, you never been knocked out—for God's sake, who goes and sells his gear?"

Gould brought shoes, gloves, and a robe to the dressing room. He dumped them on the bench. Braddock, seated calmly in his trunks while his hands were being taped, looked up as Gould shook his head and muttered. "Borrowed gear, borrowed robe . . ."

Jim lifted a boxing shoe. It was bright red, like a clown's. "Maybe I oughta get an aooga horn, chase him around the ring," he said with a wry lightness that Joe hadn't heard from Jim in a long time.

"You been drinking?"

Braddock pretended to frown. "Now why go and hurt my feelings?"

Gould slapped his boxer's naked back. Braddock hardly winced. "Well, you're too loose, you're spooking me," said Gould. "Sharpen up."

As Gould squatted to lace Jim's shoes, Braddock smiled. "Come on, Joe, we both know what this is, right?" He shrugged. "I get to put a little more distance between my kids and the street. And say goodbye at the Garden with a full house night of a big fight."

Gould shifted his attention to the other shoe while Jim fingered the worn gloves. "What's Griffin gonna show me that I ain't already seen?"

Suddenly, a loud rumble erupted from Jim's gut. "What the hell was that?" cried Gould.

Jim shrugged again. "They ran out of soup on the line this morning."

Gould jumped to his feet, leaned into Braddock's face. "How the hell you gonna fight on an empty stomach?" He ran from the room.

A few minutes later, the voice of radio announcer Ford Bond echoed through the locker rooms. "Good evening, and welcome to tonight's broadcast of the Primo Carnera, Max Baer fight for the heavyweight championship of the world."

Jim rose and shook out his arms, waiting to be announced. Gould burst into the room, a chipped bowl in hand. "Hash is all they had," he said, "eat fast."

"Where's the spoon?" asked Braddock.

Gould rubbed his neck. "It isn't there?" He glanced at the clock on the wall. "You gotta go anyway."

Braddock sniffed the bowl. "One bite," he pleaded.

Jim started to dip his fingers into the bowl, but Gould pulled him back. "Hey, I don't have time to re-tape you! Sit tight, I'll find one."

Gould rushed out again. Jim lifted the hash to his

nose, sniffed the greasy, hot meat again. The temptation was too much. He shoved his face into the bowl and began gobbling up the contents. He never noticed the dressing-room door opening.

"Good God. Am I seeing a ghost? An apparition?"

Jim looked up, hash dripping from his chin. A young man stood in the doorway in a rumpled suit, press pass pinned to his lapel. He smirked at Braddock, who'd been wolfing down hash like a starving mutt.

"Isn't that James J. Braddock, the Bulldog of Bergen?" He stepped into the room and pulled out his narrow reporter's notebook. "Saw your name on the card. Thought it *had* to be a different guy."

Jim set the bowl down and stood, wiped his mouth, cheeks, and chin with a towel and tossed it into a corner. The reporter stepped forward, threw a few shadow punches at Braddock.

"Come on, Jimmy. How's that right? No hello for your old pal?"

Braddock's eyes narrowed. "*New York Herald*, July 18, 1929," he said. "Byline, Sporty Lewis . . ."

When he heard his name, Lewis grinned.

"Proving Jim Braddock was too young, too green, and rushed to the top, Loughran wiped the ring with the Bulldog's career," Braddock quoted. "A sad and somber funeral with the body still breathing."

Lewis saw the look in Braddock's eyes and his grin vanished. "Look, Braddock, I don't fight the fights. I just write about them."

Braddock stepped up to Sporty, until they stood toe to toe. "Save that crap for the customers." Jim's glare was lethal. "You got me?"

The deadlock was broken by a Garden official who

appeared in the doorway. He pointed at Braddock. "You're on, pal."

Braddock moved aside, eyes still locked with Sporty's. Then he reached for the robe and stepped around the official. Sporty stared after him, pale and slightly shaken. When Braddock was gone, Lewis turned to the official.

"That guy," he said, wiping beads of sweat from his forehead. "What a washout."

A few minutes later, at his ringside seat, Sporty felt a cub reporter tapping his shoulder. He held up the program. "Who's Jim Braddock?" the kid cried over the roar of the mob.

Sporty looked over his shoulder. Braddock and Joe Gould were moving slowly down the aisle, toward the ring. He shook his head. "Get your pencil out, kid. I got your lead line for you: 'The walk from the locker room to the ring was the only time tonight that old Jim Braddock was seen on his feet.'"

When Jim reached the ring, he climbed over the ropes and warmed up on the springy canvas with a little dancing, ducking, and air boxing. He turned away from the reporters, and they noticed the name emblazoned on the back of his borrowed robe. The cub reporter, even more confused, scratched his head.

"Who's Fred Carston?"

Back in New Jersey, Quincy's bar was packed with a capacity crowd of mostly water drinkers. The bartender couldn't have been less thrilled. Quincy scowled as he dried a glass on his apron, then turned away from the nonpaying patrons to switch on the radio. The voice of Ford Bond filled the smoky tavern.

"Well, it seems Jim Braddock has come out of retirement just for tonight . . ." the announcer said.

The conversation died as the men looked at one another, doubting their hearing. One of the men from the docks shook his head in disbelief. "Nah. Can't be . . ."

All eyes turned to Mike, who sat back in his chair and shook his head, as surprised as everyone else.

"In this corner, Corn Griffin!"

The ref moved aside as the two-hundred-and-ten-pound Griffin leaped to the center of the ring and clapped his gloves together, then raised his veined, muscular arms above his head. The six-foot-two, freckle-faced kid wore black trunks and sported a crew cut and a confident grin. Though a virtual unknown in the Northeast, the Southern-born GI provoked a smattering of applause.

"And in this corner . . . from New Jersey . . . Jim Braddock!"

There was no reaction from the crowd.

Braddock nodded to the referee, whom he knew by name, then crossed to the center ring for the final instructions, but he didn't hear a word of the ref's spiel. Under the brilliant lights of the outdoor arena, he was taking the measure of his opponent. Corn was young, powerful, assured. A golden-boy heavyweight with a long reach and a massive right arm. After a moment, the ref banished the fighters to their respective corners.

Jim waited, eyeing Corn, who was playing to the crowd and ringside press—until the bell rang. Then Griffin came out punching, hard and fast, his smooth legwork like silk lightning. Jim ducked, danced, and weaved, doing all he could to avoid Corn's powerhouse blows, but the throws seemed to come from everywhere.

It took only thirty seconds for Jim to decide that taking this fight was a bad idea—his opponent was in top form, his jabs and body shots perfectly timed and hard to digest. Braddock's only goal now was survival. He had to walk away from this fight on his own two feet if he was going to put in a day's work at the docks tomorrow.

Jim absorbed a flurry of blows, then moved in close for the clinch. As the ref broke them, Corn straightened Jim with a stiff uppercut and Braddock blinked away motes of light exploding in his head.

In Braddock's corner, Joe Gould was shouting and waving his arms as usual, reflecting the shadow play of events in the ring. "Step inside those hooks, Jim . . . Keep your head down . . ."

It was just like the old days for the little manager, if not for the man in the ring. Suddenly, Jim spied a right hook out of the corner of his eye, and deftly knocked it aside with his left, surprised by his own move. Corn tossed a vicious haymaker. It caught the side of Braddock's head, and he went down hard.

As his back slammed the canvas, Jim's vision blurred and all clocks seemed to stop ticking. Vaguely, through a haze, he saw reporters on their feet at ringside, among them the sneering face of Sporty Lewis.

"Oh, and Braddock is down!" cried Ford Bond into the microphone he gripped in his fist. "A thunderous left hook from Griffin sends Braddock to the mat!"

The crowd in the Garden, more animated now, began to boo and shout catcalls. Back in Jersey, Mike waved at the other patrons in Quincy's bar, beckoning them silent as he hung on the announcer's words.

". . . And it's the count," said Bond.

"One . . . Two . . . Three . . ."

Jim struggled to rise.

"Four . . . Five . . . Six . . ."

He made it to one knee but was still clutching the ropes. The count would not stop.

"Hey, what's the rush?" Gould called to his fighter, balling his fists and air punching. "Two lefts, Jimmy. Pop, pop."

Finally Braddock stood, as shaky as a newborn colt, blood streaming down his sweaty, heaving chest from a cut inside his mouth. The ref stepped up to him and checked his pupils, held up two fingers, checked the cut.

"It's over, Braddock," the referee told him over the roar of the crowd.

James Braddock blinked. He peered over the head of the referee, surveyed Corn Griffin, who was waiting for the decision on the opposite side of the ring. With a crimson grin, Jim glanced at the ref. "He don't look that bad, Bill."

The ref shook his head, and began to raise his hand to stop the fight. Jim clutched his arm with two gloved hands. "Billy. Please. Let me go."

The ref hesitated, and their eyes locked. Jim nodded once, a silent plea. Finally, the ref stepped aside.

Corn Griffin was waiting. Like a bull he charged across the ring, leading with his right. Jim easily dodged the blow aimed at his head, but Griffin served up a nasty left jab that stole his breath. Jim responded with Gould's proscribed left jabs. Though ineffectual, Jim was surprised he could deliver a left at all.

The hammer struck the bell, and the fighters retired

to their corners. Braddock arrived, slumped onto the stool, took great gulps of the night air.

As a bucket boy poured water over his head, Gould was in his fighter's ear. "You're doing great, Jimmy," he cried, surprised at his own sincerity. "Run him all over the ring. He's big, he's going to get tired real fast."

Jim washed out his mouth and grinned, the expression a little less grisly than before. Gould grabbed his left glove and shook it. "You know the two jabs work. You gotta get your right in faster. You got to stop some of those left hands."

"You don't see any of them getting by me, do you?"

The bell clanged, and Jim was up. Though he moved a little better now, Jim was still on the defensive, still trying to avoid the pursuing Griffin, who was working for nothing less than a knockout. Braddock managed a few left jabs, and heard Griffin grunt at the end of one. But when Jim tried to toss Corn a right, he was clipped by an electric left that sent him reeling. Only a quick duck and dance spared him from being cornered on the ropes.

Braddock had circled to the center of the ring and was ready to fight when the strident clang ended the second round. Jim, face swollen with scarlet knots, slumped onto his stool. Joe Gould jumped the ropes and stepped in front of him, pouring water into his fighter's gaping mouth. Jim turned, spit the pink-stained water into the bucket, and hung his head. Chest heaving, heart pounding, Braddock only vaguely heard his manager's words, though they were screamed into his face.

"He's a half step behind you," Gould yelled. "You're

opening him up like a tomato can. If you don't believe me, sway. Sway, see what happens. Two jabs and the big apple." Gould's short arms beat the smoky air to a pulp. "Pop. Pop. Bang."

The bell clanged.

Jim moved out of his corner slowly, cautiously. Corn came out jabbing, aggressive. But each time Jim faded off him, and after two jabs, Jim swayed. True to Gould's words, Corn missed the move. Jim deftly stepped into Corn as the Southerner threw the next punch.

Jim blocked, but Corn's uppercut threw him into the corner. On the apron, Gould clutched his head with his hands. But to the manager's surprise, Jim swept underneath the charging Griffin, delivered two sharp left jabs that set the kid grunting—then Braddock delivered a mighty right that sent Griffin to the mat.

The ref jumped between the fighters and started counting. Over the man's shoulder, Jim looked down at his opponent.

"That's it!" screamed Gould from his corner. "Pop. Pop. Bang!" The little manager started to dance and throw windmills. A right, then a left. He stopped and stared at his left a moment, more stunned than Griffin. "Where in the hell did you get that left, Jimmy?" Gould whispered. Then he looked up in disbelief as the count continued.

"Three . . ."

Gould locked eyes with Jim, and howled. "Glory, hallelujah, where the hell you been, Jimmy Braddock?"

But Griffin got to his feet again. As the ref checked him out, Jim moved like a hungry animal, waiting to strike. There was a dangerous look in Braddock's eye that Joe Gould hadn't seen before, and it was Jim who was moving with confidence now, Corn Griffin who seemed shaken, dazed.

When the ref stepped aside, it was Braddock who charged forward. Two steps, followed by a series of punches impossible to count.

Gould was apoplectic. "No daylight! Close the shutters! Bring down the curtains. Throw him in the slammer! Send him back to the Ozarks or wherever the hell . . ."

Braddock was doing just that. The punches kept coming—like the unending rain on the soup lines, the incessant snow on the frozen docks—each blow more precise. Finally Jim delivered a hard right, and stepped away.

The crowd shared a gasp as Griffin just stared at Braddock, as if in shock. Then Corn pitched forward toward the canvas, his head suddenly too heavy to hold up. He landed with a slam and stayed there.

In the absolute stunned silence that followed, Jim spied Sporty Lewis on the sidelines. The reporter was frog-eyed. The next second, the mob exploded. Pandemonium swept the outdoor Garden Bowl, sending screams, hoots, and hollers into the June night, down Northern Boulevard and all the way over the Fifty-ninth Street Bridge. Joe Gould was certain they'd shaken the entire East Side of Manhattan by the time they were through. But nobody was more surprised than the patrons of Quincy's bar over in Jersey. The tattered, defeated men were laughing and cheering for the first time in memory as Ford Bond's voice echoed above the din.

"This is unbelievable! Corn Griffin, the number-two contender in the world, has been knocked out by Jim Braddock in the third round . . ."

In the center of the utter mayhem, Mike, a tear in his eye, just shook his head and smiled. As the others yelled and clapped, he simply whispered, "That a boy, Jimmy. That a boy."

In the locker room, Jim gobbled up the rest of the cold, congealing hash with a spoon while a cutman tended his face. A door slammed and a whirlwind entered—a whirlwind named Joe Gould.

"Jesus, mother and Joseph, Mary and all the saints and martyrs and Jesus—did I say *Jesus*?—where in the hell did that left come from?"

Jim swallowed, licked his swollen lips, then set the empty bowl on the bench. "Yeah, you did . . . say Jesus."

Gould rolled his eyes as Jim held up the spoon. "Good they invented these."

"The *left*, Jimmy," Gould shot back, hands on hips. "I'm talking about that *left* of yours."

Jim looked down at his left hand, turned it to examine the bruised knuckles. "When my hand was broke. On the docks. I had to use my left to work." He opened and closed the fist. "Got lucky, I guess."

Gould clapped his hands together. "That's something you ain't been in a long time."

Jim offered his manager a half smile. "Everybody's due."

"Due or not, I'll take it."

Braddock shrugged. "That was on hash. Imagine what I could have done on a couple of steaks."

Gould tossed him a towel. "Wipe your mouth. You still

remember how to satisfy the baying hounds?" He turned and walked to the door. But as he touched the doorknob, he turned. When he spoke again, his words were soft, for Jim only. "That was one hell of a good-bye."

The two shared a smile, then Gould yanked the door open. Outside was a mass of shouting reporters.

"Here, boys!"

The reporters swept in like an ocean wave, almost knocking the stout manager to the dirty concrete floor.

"Braddock! Hey Braddock!"

A dozen frenzied voices called as they swarmed the battered boxer.

Braddock met Gould's eyes. *Yeah*, he thought, *one hell of a good-bye.*

Later, as Gould and Braddock departed the Garden Bowl, the two paused at ringside to watch the closing round of the main event.

Max Baer, the young Apollo of the boxing world, was swinging at the skull of Primo Carnera with all the ruthless gusto he'd once used to swing his sledgehammer at slaughterhouse steers. In a pounding hailstorm of nonstop blows, he smashed Carnera to the mat with his fists.

"Imagine that hitting you," Gould said, awe in his voice.

Braddock grinned. "How about that guy we bought the cab company from?"

"That's an idea."

Baer was six three, two hundred and ten pounds to Carnera's six foot seven, two hundred and seventy. Carnera had the longer reach, but Baer was faster. All night he'd ducked and swayed, easily evading the Italian giant's frantic swings and returning them in spades.

In the ring, Carnera was bloody and beaten as he staggered to his feet, glove clutching the rope. Max Baer taunted the defending champ arrogantly. Carnera threw a few ineffectual punches, which Baer easily knocked aside.

Over the cheers, the voice of Ford Bond filled the arena.

"Primo Carnera has been knocked down for what has to be a record eleven times! And Max Baer struts around the ring in utter contempt of the heavyweight champion of the world!"

Carnera's massive bulk was heaving with fatigue and shock. With a barely audible growl, he thrust the referee aside and staggered toward Baer. The challenger waited patiently, a smirk on his handsome, unmarked face, until Carnera made it to the center of the ring. Then Baer stepped out of his corner and blasted the champ again and again. It was a massacre so terrible that even Joe Gould averted his eyes.

Jim touched his manager's shoulder, and they headed toward the exit without another glance back at the ring. Among the throng of reporters, Sporty Lewis watched them go.

 **ROUND NINE**

You gain strength, courage and confidence by every experience in which you really stop to look fear in the face ... You must do the thing you think you cannot do.

—Eleanor Roosevelt

The car door opened, and Jim stepped onto the cracked pavement in front of his apartment house.

"Sure you won't come in and say hello?" Jim asked.

Gould poked his head out the door. "You still married to the same girl?"

Jim nodded at the familiar routine. "Last time I looked."

Gould grinned. "Good night, Jimmy-boy."

Braddock watched the roadster roll to the next intersection and, then make a U-turn to head back to Manhattan.

Jim stood facing the front door to his basement apartment. The Braddocks no longer owned a radio— they'd hocked it along with everything else—so Mae and the kids didn't know, couldn't know, the outcome of tonight's fight.

Before he could touch the doorknob, the door swung open. Jay, Howard, and Rosy looked up expectantly. Mae stood silently, staring at her husband, her own face pale in the lamplight.

Jim presented a picture of defeat—battered head, shoulders slumped, a big frown on his swollen lips. But before the children's faces fell, before Mae could register joy or disappointment, Jim offered his family a triumphant grin.

"I won."

The kids shrieked and lunged, squeezing his waist, strangling his leg. Mae just stood there, speechless.

Jim felt a tug on his arm. "Daddy, Daddy," cried Rosy, "you have to see what I got you!"

"What's that, honey?" asked Jim.

Rosy tugged harder, drawing her father into the apartment. She ran to the icebox, pulled out an amazing sight, and brought it to him.

"Put it on your eyes," Rosy said, thrusting the thick red slab of meat into her father's hands.

Jim gaped at the raw beef. "Where did you get this?"

"They snuck off," said Mae, throwing her oldest boy a stern look. "Which we had a long talk about." Then she raised an eyebrow at her stubborn daughter. "I tried to take it back, but the butcher says he *gave* it to her."

"It's a porter's house," explained Rosy. "For your face." Then she attempted to tilt her head like her mama. "It's fix you right up."

Jim dangled the steak from his fingers, admiring the thickness, the marbling of succulent fat. He could almost hear the sizzle, smell the hot, juicy drippings. He licked his lips and hunkered down to speak to his daughter—fighter to fighter. "Darling, we have to eat this."

His two sons whooped. "Hoo-ray!"

But Rosy wouldn't hear it. "No!" Tiny hands went to little hips. "You have to put it on your face."

Jim offered the boys a helpless shrug, then tilted his head back and lay the cool slab across his swollen eyes. He sighed in mock relief, waited a moment, then lifted the edge of the meat to peek out.

"Okay, Rosy, how long do I leave it on?"

The little girl shrugged and shook her head.

"Did he fall hard, Dad?" Jay asked.

Jim grinned. "You should have seen the way he dropped."

"Timmm-berrr!" cried Howard. He raced around. "Timber! Timber! Timber!"

Jay turned excitedly to his mother. "Do the 'nouncer, Ma. Like when we was little kids."

Mae shook her head, surprised he remembered, but pleased too. "Well, what a memory," she told him. "Aren't you my little elephant."

Jay beamed, his gaze expectant.

Mae glanced at her husband, surprised to see the same little-boy expression on his face. He sat down at the table, continued to gaze expectantly.

"Yeah, Mae . . . Come on," Jim teased. "Do the 'nouncer."

"It's *announcer*, Jay," said Mae. Her eyes held her husband's. She moved to the table, touched Jim's shoulders, ran her fingers down his arm.

"Loud, Ma!" cried Jay, clapping.

Mae climbed onto her husband's thick legs, eyes

locked with his. "Introducing two-time state Golden Gloves titleholder . . ." her voice rose ". . . in both the light heavyweight and heavyweight division . . ." As she spoke, something awakened in her. The old passion. "The Bulldog of Bergen, the pride of New Jersey . . . And the hope of the Irish as the future champion of the world . . . James J. Braddock!"

Her final words were spoken loud enough to echo from the walls of the dingy tenement room. The kids went wild, hopping and cheering and laughing. But Jim and Mae didn't notice.

He touched her cheek, as if in thanks for her blessing, and she secretly wondered if she'd made a terrible mistake. Then Jim lifted his wife by her slim waist and set her on the floor. He rose and removed the steak from his forehead.

"Wow," he told his daughter, "this really worked great. I feel fantastic. Let's eat!"

He crossed to the stove, dropped the steak onto a cast iron frying pan and turned up the fire. The sizzling sound and the delicious smell soon filled the tiny apartment. The children jumped and danced joyously. In the middle of the commotion, Mae slipped into her husband's arms, leaned into his broad chest.

"Jim? Is it like you said before, just the one fight?" she whispered. "Or are they letting you back in?"

Jim shook his head, buried his nose and lips in her hair. "No, babe. It was just the one fight."

Mae sighed with relief, gave him a squeeze, then stepped away to tend the steak, thanking God she'd never have to endure her husband stepping into the ring again.

* * *

Dawn came early in June. By the time Jim rose, dressed, and started his walk to the Newark docks, straw-blond rays were already drenching the world with warmth. He walked east, toward the rising star, taking the same course he always took, through the city's poorest residential districts, across the landfill and industrial section. Yet something was different today. His limbs were sore, his face one giant bruise, but his steps were quicker than they'd been in months, his mood light.

With new eyes, he looked at the old dumping ground by the freight tracks of the Pennsylvania Railroad, the plot that needy families had taken over with junk-pile huts. He noticed for the first time how neat the garden patches were, how lovingly they were tended. He admired the flowers, the colorful flags, the patched-together latticework.

As he moved toward Port Newark's complex of warehouses and docks, striding across the gravel lot and toward the familiar locked gate, he became aware of the warmth on his face, appreciated how good it felt, noticed how the light transformed the murky blue chop of Newark Bay into a shimmering dance that dazzled the eye.

When he arrived at the fence, he joined the cluster of men for the long wait, his eyes glazed over, his mind replaying the Griffin fight, the knockout punch, the exploding roar of the capacity crowd. An hour flew like a minute.

Finally Jake, the middle-aged dock foreman, appeared, as he did every morning, and immediately began pointing out men. Jim straightened his boxer's shoulders.

"Six, seven, eight . . ."

The foreman's gaze moved over the crowd too quickly. By the looks of things, Jim figured he wasn't getting picked today. His mind had already begun working out alternate strategies. Leave here and hitch up to Union City, then walk to Weehawken, West New York, North Bergen.

The foreman's eyes skimmed over Jim, but darted back again. Jim took a half step closer, and Jake's finger moved that magical half inch. He said Jim's name and everyone turned to look.

"Nine."

Jim closed his eyes in relief. As fifty other men dispersed, Jim joined the chosen eight. Together they walked through the gate and moved toward the waterfront. Some of the men pointed at Jim and nodded. They reached the work area. A docked steamer's massive loading net held hundreds of bags of rice. Empty shipping pallets were lined up along the dirty, damp length of the wharf, waiting to be filled.

Jim noticed Jake approach him. "Listened in last night."

"Hey, Braddock," called one of the other men, "that really you?"

"Way to go," called another.

Jake took his folded newspaper from under his arm, held it open, and met Jim's gaze. "Didn't think I'd be seeing you back here again."

Jim blinked at the headline—

AMAZING!

BRADDOCK

KO'S GRIFFIN IN 3

He shook his head in disbelief. A few men crowded around to hear what he had to say.

"One night only," Jim explained with a shrug. "Purse was two fifty. My take's half. We owed a hundred twenty. Left me five bucks."

Jake laughed. "Makes you a rich man." Then his expression turned serious. "Good fight."

The men around Jim nodded in agreement.

"Sure was."

"You bet."

"And how."

Jim could see he'd stirred something in these men, standing there in their tattered clothes and patched-up shoes. He could see it in their weary, weathered faces. The yearning to come against what you can see—it was what they all wished for. Something real to stand toe to toe with and fight. The chance to see it coming for once and beat it back with your own fists.

Jim moved forward through a round of backslapping, and then took his place beside his partner. Mike Wilson nodded, a wordless greeting. The two grabbed their bale hooks and began their unloading work.

Hook, haul, drop . . . hook haul drop.

The cast on Jim's right hand had been off for months now, but he'd spent so much time and effort training his left hand to do this job, he now used it as often as his right, if not more. When the right got tired, he went to the left. When the left got tired, he went with the right. Alternating made the work easier.

Hook, haul, drop . . . hook, haul, drop.

Jim considered his silent partner. The two hadn't spoken since the churchyard celebration, that loud scene with Sara. Mike's handsome, young face appeared aged today. He was usually clean shaven, but this morning his cheeks and chin were covered with rough stubble, his bright eyes were downcast, cradled in dark half circles. His tall, lanky form was stooped, his narrow shoulders weighted.

Jim wanted to say something, but he didn't know what.

Finally, Mike spoke up, although his bloodshot eyes remained on the ground. "I wouldn't have hit her."

Jim nodded. "I know, Mike."

"I couldn't have lived with myself if I'd hit her."

Jim didn't know what to say.

"You get so angry with all of it," Mike went on. "You got to push somewhere. I'm getting things under control."

Hook, haul, drop . . . hook, haul, drop.

"So thanks for that," Mike added.

Jim glanced up to see Mike was looking at him now, his nod apologetic and grateful at the same time. Then he said, "You were going to win again, you could have told me."

"I knew? I could have bet on me too."

Mike smiled, but it was different. Strained. That old infectious grin had disappeared. Jim was sorry to see it go.

Hook, haul, drop . . .

"C'mon, Jimmy," Mike said at last, "how about you talk me through that last round?"

A tiny flame ignited in Jim's eyes. He cleared his throat. "Griffin comes out of his corner like a freight train, I swear . . ." Jim kept working. He'd been using his right till now. Without thinking, he switched to his left with smoothness, power, and flexible ease.

* * *

A week later, Mae was strolling down the street. In her hands was a thick package wrapped in white butcher's paper. She glanced down at her daughter.

"No more," Mae firmly scolded. "Now, say it, Rosy."

Rosy pouted.

"Say it," Mae repeated.

Rosy stalled by gazing down at the cracks in the sidewalk, where a variety of tall, green weeds were tickling her small legs as she walked along.

"Rosy!"

The little girl sighed. "Don't trade Daddy's auto-graph for free meat."

Mae bit her cheek to keep from laughing. "Why can't you ever listen to me?"

Rosy thought hard about this question, then an-swered with great seriousness. "I don't know."

This time, Mae couldn't stop the smile. Then she glanced up. A shiny roadster was pulling away from their dingy apartment house. Mae recognized the vehi-cle. It was Joe Gould's. Her smile vanished.

"Go play with the boys," Mae told her daughter.

Rosy ran off to join her brothers, who were playing pink ball in the shade of the tenement alley. With quick, worried steps, Mae headed inside.

The afternoon was beautiful. Sunny and warm but not hot, and the humidity that usually plagues this erst-while swamp was lower than usual. Mae wasn't sur-prised to find their stuffy apartment empty. After throwing the fresh cuts of meat into the icebox, she headed outside in search of her husband.

She found him behind the tenement building in what

passed for a backyard. More weeds than grass, a few damaged chairs scattered about. A pile of rusted pipes heaped at the yard's edge.

Jim stood strong and tanned in the middle of the scraggly outdoor space. Mae's breath caught a moment, seeing him so happy, so handsome in the sun. His broad shoulders tapered down to a lean waist, the thick muscles of his thighs evident through his slacks. His square chin was tipped up, his bright eyes peering confidently at the cloudless blue sky. He looked like a majestic bronze statue, still standing steady and unbroken, among the ruins of some devastated civilization.

Mae crossed the yard. "You daughter is now a celebrity in Sam's butcher shop."

Jim turned and Mae felt her heart stop. She saw it in his eyes—the old excitement. The reason he was so happy.

"Joe came by. He thinks the commission might be willing to reverse their ruling. He thinks he can get me another fight."

Mae said nothing.

"I'm going to stop working, get back into shape." Jim dug into his pocket, pulled out a wad of green. "Joe fronted us one hundred and seventy-five. So I can train."

Mae swallowed, had trouble finding her voice. "You said it was just the one fight."

"It's our second chance, is what it is. It's a chance to make you and the kids proud."

Mae's fingers clenched, her nails digging groves into her palms. She tried to keep her voice steady, her fear and anger under control. "Jim, we got off easy when you broke that hand. It's not that I'm not proud or grateful. I am. But what if something worse happened? And you can't work?"

Mae couldn't bring herself to paint the sign any clearer. She expected her husband could read it in her eyes. *What if you become a cripple, Jim Braddock? You've seen it happen to other men. What if you go and get yourself killed!?*

"What happens to us?" challenged Mae. "To the kids again? We're barely managing now."

Jim shook his head, disappointed at his wife's reaction. He gestured to their pitiful, rundown surroundings. Couldn't she see? Didn't she know? He was already killing himself—and for what?

"Yeah, Mae," he replied. "If I can't do better than I'm doing, we're not going to make it. Kill myself every day for a couple coins, and every week we slip behind a little."

Mae stepped closer. "We got out of it. We're back to even now." Her tone turned desperate. "Please, baby. I'm begging you. We don't have anything left to risk."

Jim wanted to reach out, take her in his arms, but he stopped himself. He couldn't give her what she wanted. There was so much at stake for their kids, their future, he didn't dare give in to her fears.

He touched her cheek with gentleness, but when he spoke again, his tone was unbendable iron. "I can still take a few punches, Mae. And I'd rather take them in the ring. At least you know who's hitting you."

He turned from her then, and Mae's hopeful expression crumbled. She stood there, feeling helpless as she watched him stride away from her, across the yard and into the dark doorway. But Mae Theresa Fox Braddock was far from helpless, and she knew it.

This isn't done, James Braddock, she promised. *No, it is not. Not by a long shot.*

The next morning, Jim rose at dawn and left the apartment house, not for the docks but for the gym. Mae left the apartment house too. She took a bus to her sister's, dropped off the kids, and rode a ferry across the mighty Hudson, toward the silver spires of Manhattan island, determined to storm one of its castles.

Mae's destination was a section of New York City known as the Upper East Side, a relatively small piece of property that displayed the grandest, most majestic apartment buildings and houses ever constructed in the United States. Elegant bluebloods, tycoons, and solid citizens resided together in these blocks amid exclusive clubs, luxurious penthouses, grand hotels, and stately museums. Millionaires Row was here, a Gilded Age playground along the east side of Central Park, where Carnegie, Astor, and Vanderbilt spent fortunes mixing periods and tastes in a line of sumptuous Fifth Avenue mansions resembling English castles, Italian villas, and French chateaux.

Two avenues over, on Park, the ostentation was less pronounced—"filthy rich" descending to merely "terribly moneyed." But it was still one of the broadest thoroughfares and most beautiful streets in New York. Two lanes of traffic were divided by a wide swath of well-tended grass, flower beds, and shrubbery. Trucks were banned from this gracious artery, but buses, cars, and drays constantly rolled up and down its lanes.

At one time, seven- and nine-story elevator buildings had lined Park Avenue, but after the World War, skyscraper apartments were constructed in their place. Mae had read somewhere that they'd been built on stilts to keep them free from the vibration of the New York Central railroad yards hidden below.

Walking north, Mae gaped at Villard House, a group of brown sandstone mansions surrounding a court and first owned by Henry Villard, a German-American railroad magnate. The ornate cornices, windows, and details had been fashioned to resemble an Italian Renaissance palace. Next came the opulent athletic facilities of the Racquet and Tennis Club, one of the most fashionable sports associations in the city. Mae remembered reading in one of the gossip columns that the two tennis courts inside with slate foundations had cost more than $250,000 to construct.

A pair of gentlemen in tennis whites, speaking earnestly about financing and real estate, burst out of a hired car and nearly ran her over in their haste to cross the sidewalk and enter the building.

Mae leaped back. "Goodness."

She continued her walk, aware no other street in the world came close to the amount of wealth concentrated among these buildings. Her sister had told her that apartment rentals here averaged as much as $1,500 per room annually—an obscene sum. She also knew farther uptown was the Frick Collection, a museum that housed important old paintings. And two avenues away was the Metropolitan Museum of Art, one of the greatest and most important museums in the world.

She vowed to take Jay, Howard, and Rosy to those museums for a visit someday—but not today. Today, she had business on Park, and she continued her trek between the double row of tall apartment buildings with all the intense determination that her husband displayed in the ring.

On the scrubbed sidewalk, she passed dignified men in white smocks—house servants—exercising pedigreed dogs or carrying armloads of parcels. Under each canvas-awning-framed entryway, she passed uniformed men, some simply standing guard, others hurrying to aid impeccably tailored gentlemen and ladies in their journeys from foyer to car, car to foyer.

On the small, dog-eared map of the city that she'd borrowed from her sister, Park was shown to stretch all the way to the uncovered railroad tracks at Ninetysixth, where it transformed itself into a slum tenement street in an area known as Spanish Harlem. But Mae wasn't going nearly that far.

When she arrived at the limestone building she sought, she tilted her head back, holding her little straw hat to keep it from tumbling. She tried to guess how many floors high the skyscraper went, but she couldn't even see the top.

Girding herself for what came next, Mae approached the door. Beneath the awning, the uniformed doorman, his brass buttons shining, tipped his visored cap and with a white gloved hand pulled open the beveled glass. Mae walked through, into an elegant lobby of rare marbles and dark wood. Framed oils hung on the walls and bronzed sculptures and potted plants sprung up from the waxed and gleaming floor.

Aware her shoes were broken down, her dress threadbare, her straw hat a sorry beaten-up thing, she nevertheless lifted her chin and walked toward the elevator door. The operator was dressed like the doorman.

She told him the floor she wanted as she moved inside and ogled the large, walnut-paneled car, deciding it was only slightly smaller than the entire basement apartment where all five Braddocks now made their home.

"Good day, Mrs. Reynolds."

"Good day, Johnny."

A matron stepped into the elevator behind her wearing a smartly tailored green summer suit, highly polished T-strap shoes, and an ostrich-feathered toque over perfectly styled curls. She seemed startled to see someone like Mae in her building, and, as the operator closed the door and the car ascended, the woman looked her up and down.

Mae felt her cheeks growing warm. Self-consciously she straightened her tattered clothes and nodded nervously. The matron nodded back with politeness, but Mae didn't miss the horrified expression in her gaze. It was the sort of look usually reserved for car accidents. Bad ones.

A few minutes later, Mae was standing on the fifteenth floor, digging inside her purse for a scrap of paper. She moved down the line of apartment doors until the number on the door matched the one she'd scribbled down.

Straightening her threadbare dress one more time, she raised her hand and knocked. Hard. She heard movement inside, saw motion at the keyhole. Then nothing. Just stillness beyond the portal.

Mae frowned and knocked again.

Still nothing.

"Open the door, Joe," she called politely. She waited ten more seconds, and when no one answered, she cocked back and let go—

"Joe, open the damn door! You're not going to hide in your fancy apartment and make my husband your punching bag all over again. We're starving and you're taking him from his work like some short little blood-sucking leech and I won't let you get him hurt like that again, do you hear me? I will not let you!"

The door opened a few inches. Joe Gould stood staring at her. "I guess you better come in."

Mae pushed past him and entered, as she moved inside, however, her steps slowed and the righteous anger drained out of her. She'd expected a space like the lobby or even the elevator—tasteful wallpaper, old English furniture, marble statues, framed oils, potted plants. But there was none of that. There was none of *anything*.

The apartment was completely empty. Just a wide expanse of polished wood floor and high bright windows. In the middle of the empty apartment stood Joe's wife, Lucille.

"Hello, Mae . . . We . . . we weren't expecting you."

"How is it?" asked Joe.

Lucille, an attractive woman with a genuine smile, nodded at her husband and took another sip from her bone-china cup. "Too sweet per usual."

Joe smiled back at his wife. The two of them and Mae were sitting on folding chairs in the middle of the empty living room, sipping hot tea that Joe had prepared. He glanced at Mae. "Yours?"

Mae nodded without speaking, still feeling off balance. She'd come here expecting a knock-down-drag-out, but Joe and his wife had been warm and civil. And their circumstances had left her in a mild state of shock.

"Sorry," said Joe, gesturing to the door. Clearly, he felt badly about not answering the door right away. "But you just don't want folks to see you down is all."

"I didn't know," said Mae, her voice not quite there. "I thought . . ."

"Yeah," said Joe fingering the lapel of his dapper, fawn-colored suit. "That's the idea. Always keep your hands up."

Mae's eyebrows arched. She realized that had been Joe Gould's philosophy all along. Keep up appearances. And never let the opponent get to you.

Joe shrugged. "Sold the last of it two days ago. So Jimmy could train."

Mae took a moment to absorb this. She'd always figured Joe Gould for a cagey opportunist. Not a man who'd risk his last few possessions on her husband's second chance.

"Why?" she asked.

"Sometimes you see something in a fighter. You don't even know if it's real, you're looking for it so bad." Joe glanced beyond the tall glass of the high window. "You can't have no hope at all. I guess Jimmy's what I hope for."

Mae's eyes widened. It stunned her to hear Gould express exactly what she felt for her own husband.

"He's really something, Mae."

She shook her head. "This is crazy. You don't even know if you can get him a fight, do you?"

"I'll get him a fight," Joe promised. "Last thing I do, I'll get him a fight."

Lucille reached over, lightly touched her husband's arm. "Honey, get us some more tea, would you?"

Joe rose, smiled at Mae. "I know who wears the pants." Then he winked and headed into the kitchen.

For a moment, the two women sat in silence. Finally, Lucille sighed, gestured to the empty room and said, "It's not the way I imagined it either."

Mae nodded, frowned at the floor. She knew Lucille was in as deep as Joe now, but she felt compelled to explain why she'd made the trip here.

"It's just that . . . I hated it. Every day he walked out that door for a fight. I even hated eating the food it bought,'cause it was like it came right out of him."

Lucille said nothing, just listened.

"We lost something when he stopped fighting," Mae admitted. "But I guess we got something too."

Lucille smiled but her eyes were sad. "Can you ever stop yours?" she asked. "When he sets his mind to do a thing."

"No. I wish I could. No."

"I never know who it's harder on, them or us. We have to wait for them to fix everything. They have to do it. And every day it seems like they're failing us. But really it's just the world that's failed, you know?"

"It's . . ." Mae's voice trailed off as she realized they could say more to each other, and probably would, but there really was nothing more to say. Outside, a passing cloud dappled the sunlight across the gleaming floorboards. Mae smiled. "This is a lovely apartment."

"Thank you," Lucille replied.

Then they continued sipping their tea.

ROUND TEN

American fighters train in establishments you are not likely to confuse with a Knightsbridge health club.

—Hugh McIlvanney, *The Hardest Game*

On Braddock's first day back in training, Joe Jeannette met him at the top of the creaky wooden steps of his Union City gym. The smell was the same—a combination of motor oil and gasoline from the garage below, mustiness from the gallons of sweat dumped daily into the air, and the distressed leather of punching bags and boxing gloves. The sound, however, was different. Absent was the usual noise of gloves smacking against bags, the slap of ropes on hardwood, and the grunting of fighters warily circling each other. At this early hour, the gym was empty, save for Joe and a corner man hanging a bag on a stout hook.

Braddock felt his adrenaline begin to pump the moment he set his foot on that first creaky step. When he saw Joe Jeannette's grin and the heavy leather bag just waiting to be smacked, his muscles actually twitched beneath his skin.

"Suit up and let me see how much you've forgotten," Jeannette told him. When Jim returned from the locker room, wearing boxing shoes, black trunks and six-ounce bag gloves, Joe Jeannette whistled. "You been training, Jimmy. Don't know where, but you haven't been training here."

"I've been working, Joe. Not training."

"Work? You mean to tell me you built that left from working? Show me."

"Huh?" Braddock grunted.

"Show me what you did when you were working."

Braddock shrugged. "Well, after I busted my right hand, I took a job at the docks. Heavy lifting, mostly. Moving freight around with a tie-hook." As he talked, Jim demonstrated his technique to the seasoned trainer—a swift punching motion with his left arm that sank the hook into a bale, which enabled him to lift and carry his end of the heavy freight. "After the cast came off, I started switching hands. But went to my left a lot anyway . . . out of habit."

Jeannette nodded. "That's because your right is your weaker arm now—but don't worry about that. You were always a hitter and we can fix your right in a couple of weeks."

"And my left?"

"That move you showed me with the hook, it's the perfect punching exercise. Your forearms—" Jeannette held them up. "You can see that the left is bigger, thicker than your right. You've been developing a lethal left and you didn't even know it. You were always right-hand crazy. That was your weakness. But you had a power punch so it didn't matter. But now—"

Jim lowered his arms, ducked into a fighting stance and threw a few air punches.

"Still got your old form, your old stance," Jeannette noted. "Guess we'll have to work on that, too."

Braddock straightened. "What's wrong with my stance?"

"Nothing," Joe replied. "For a boxer who's right-hand crazy. But you've got the potential to become an all-around fighter now, so you better start to train like one."

Jim moved around in a tight circle, throwing more jabs.

"You went hungry, too," Jeannette said softly. "I can tell." Jim flushed crimson. "No shame in that," he added. "Not these days. Good news is that all that hard work and no food has made you slim and chiseled and tough as nails. You're lean and lethal now, Braddock, no question about that. But I'm gonna make you even better."

Jeannette slapped Jim on his naked back. "Now lay into the bag. We'll see what we have to do next."

In the ensuing weeks, under the coaching of Joe Jeannette, Jim Braddock built up his right, increased his stamina, and put on a few pounds of solid, rock-hard muscle. After all those months of toiling for a living—at the docks, the rail yard, the coal shuttle—training with Jeannette seemed like a vacation. But nothing Jeannette taught him came easily. The man pushed Jim hard, and every week there came a new exercise, a new brace of skills and techniques to practice and absorb.

One afternoon, as they were working on Jim's timing in the center ring, a visitor crept up the rickety stairs and lurked in the shadows of the doorway. Joe Gould quietly watched as Jim Braddock pounded a punching bag to the rhythm of Joe Jeannette's banging tambourine.

"Faster, Jim. Pick it up! Come on . . ."

Jeannette cracked the instrument even faster, making it clang right behind Braddock's ears. Jim redoubled his efforts, delivering a fast flurry of powerful, alternating blows that dented the heavy leather bag and set it swinging on its hook despite the best efforts of the corner man to keep it steady.

Gould grinned and stepped up to the ropes, moving among a collection of lean, tough-looking youths in boxing gear who were also watching the action.

Jim spied Gould and paused. Jeannette smacked him on the back of the head with his tambourine. "Okay, okay, you got your left back. Big deal. Don't lock the knee. And you gotta be quicker."

Jim Braddock placed both gloves on the bag and pummeled it. As he threw, he tossed a glance at his manager. "You get me that fight yet?"

Gould smirked. "I tell *you* how to do *your* job?"

"Yeah."

Gould nodded. "A point."

Jim slapped the bag around a few more times, then caught it. The fighters outside the ring were moving closer to the ropes. Jim looked at them, then at Jeannette.

"Now what I got here is five pure fools thinking it would be an honor to get their heads beat in by you," said the gym owner.

Braddock sized them up. They were all big, strong heavyweights and light heavyweights with lean, hard muscles—some outweighed him and some had a longer reach. All were younger than Braddock by at least five years, and none of them looked like they ever skipped a meal, let alone stood in a long soup line to get one. Jim nodded. "Good."

He climbed out of the ring and shook his glove at Jeannette. "But I want a welterweight too. One with some spit and polish."

"That would be George," said Jeannette, directing Jim's attention to a compact fighter sparring on a mat in the corner. His fists were a blur, striking with a speed the wind would envy. George paused and saw Jim Braddock staring. Braddock lifted his glove, pointed with it. "Him."

George locked eyes with Jim Braddock, then looked past him to Jeannette. "He's still gonna have to pay me," George warned. "Even after I whup his ass."

Braddock smiled, knowing Jeannette had chosen the perfect sparring partner.

When Joe Gould left Jeannette's gym and climbed into his roadster, he was grinning too. He was still smiling an hour later when he waltzed into Jimmy Johnston's office at Madison Square Garden and planted himself in an easy chair across the desk from the busy promoter.

"You're going to sanction a bout between Jim Braddock and John Henry Lewis," Gould said.

Johnston looked up from the papers he was signing. The big man sighed and dropped the pen, leaned back in his chair. "Now what am I going to go and do that for?"

"You saw the papers. *News* had to run extra copies day after Braddock's fight." Gould flashed a confident smile. "People are sentimental."

"Yeah," Johnston replied. "So, tell me why I care."

Gould offered a bit of sympathy. "I get it. You're still sore over the way Braddock took down Griffin. Fine. I can understand that. It was a heartbreak. But look . . ."

Gould reached into his jacket and produced two fresh, expensive Cuban cigars. He carefully slid one across the desk toward Johnston, unwrapped his own.

Gould began his pitch. "You got guys fighting an elimination series over who gets a shot at Max Baer for the championship next June . . ."

It wasn't a question, and Johnston didn't deny or confirm the rumor that had been racing through fight circles all over the country.

"John Henry Lewis is your number two in line after Primo Carnera," said Gould. "And Lewis already beat Braddock once in San Francisco."

Gould leaned across Johnston's desk, offered him the flame from a sputtering Zippo. "Now, say you put Braddock back in the game against Lewis. Lewis wins, you get your revenge on Braddock, and your boy's had a top-flight tune-up with full publicity before Lasky, so what happens?"

Johnston puffed silently, staring into the corner. Gould slapped his desk. "I'll tell you what happens. *You* make some money."

Jimmy Johnston sat back, blowing smoke rings and considering the fading circles.

"Now, say by some minute, infinitesimal chance, Braddock beats Lewis," Gould continued. "You got a sentimental favorite to go up and lose against Lasky, and what happens? You make *more* money. Either way, you're richer with Braddock back in the ring than if

he's not. And we both know the name of this game . . ."
Gould rubbed finger to thumb—sign language for what
every promoter in this game loved. "And it sure as hell
isn't boxing."

This time it was Gould who sat back in his chair
and silently puffed on his Cuban, savoring the
smoke.

Johnston shook his head in awed dismay. "They
should put your mouth in a circus, Gould."

"Yeah. So what do you say?"

Mike Wilson was sitting in the bleachers watching Jim
Braddock spar with the welterweight named George
when Joe Gould returned to the gym. Gould strolled up
to the ropes as the fighters traded punches, distracting
Jim long enough for George to land a blow to his chin.
Braddock stepped backward and shot his manager a
curious look.

"I got you a fight," Gould announced.

Jim lifted his gloves to stop the bout. He walked to
the ropes and stared down at his manager.

"You're gonna fight John Henry Lewis again," said
Gould.

Braddock climbed between the ropes and landed on
the hardwood. "I could kiss you."

Gould backed away. "Say I was to beg you not to?"

Jim frowned. "Isn't Lewis one of Johnston's boys?
And isn't John Henry managed by some racketeer
named Greenlee these days?"

"You let me worry about that," Gould replied.

Braddock grinned knowingly. "No wonder you
won't pucker up. Bet you're all kissed out already."

Mike hopped down from the bleachers, approached the pair. "Lewis? He killed us in 'Frisco."

Gould raised an eyebrow. "*Us*? Who's this? Who's *us*?"

"Hey, Mike," said Jim, raising a glove. "No shifts today?"

"Lewis hasn't been beaten in ten fights," said Mike, ignoring the question.

"Joe Gould, Mike Wilson," said Jim by way of introduction. Gould looked at Mike, opened his mouth to speak—then shook his head. He reached around Braddock's broad shoulders and steered him to a corner.

"I ain't gonna bullshit you. Right now you're fodder, Jimmy. Fodder," Gould told him, eliciting a wince from Braddock. "But you win one and I can get you another. Win again and things maybe start getting serious."

Jim nodded, appreciating his manager's candor, if not his tact. Without a second glance, Braddock moved toward the heavy bag.

"Jimmy," Gould called.

Braddock turned back, saw the old fire in his manager's eyes.

"Win," said Gould.

The two men exchanged looks, and Gould departed. Braddock watched him go, then called over his shoulder. "Hey Mike, come hold the bag for me."

Jim placed his boxing shoes and his trunks into a paper bag on the bed. Golden light from the autumn sunset spilled into the room from the low windows. The paper crackled, and Jim stood in thought for a moment, already beginning to prepare mentally for the fight ahead.

Braddock turned to face his wife. Mae's face was pale as she folded the children's clothes, trying to hide her anxiety.

"I know this isn't what you wanted," Jim said softly.

Mae looked up from the laundry. Jim shifted on his feet, glanced at the floor, then into her eyes. "But I can't win if you're not behind me."

Mae set the clothes aside. Then she stepped up to her husband and leaned against him, her lips brushing his. "I'm always behind you," she whispered, holding him close.

As they embraced, Rosy signaled her brothers that the coast was clear. Jay and Howard escaped the apartment and raced quietly into the hall. Moments later, Rosy joined them, and they followed her out to the street. On the sidewalk, the children wormed their way through a crowd that had gathered in front of their building.

The trio burst into the butcher shop a moment later. Sam was weighing up some ham when the tinkling bell over the door interrupted him. He peered over the counter, to find Rosy—flanked by her stoic bodyguards—looking up at him.

"Rose Marie. Jay. Howard," said Sam suspiciously. "What can I do for you today?"

Rosy, her pale face pinched with concern, spoke. "My daddy's fighting a man who beat the living bee-Jesus out of him last time. What kind of steaks you got?"

Down the block, Jim emerged into the perfect fall evening to enthusiastic yells and a smattering of applause from the tenement neighbors gathered around his front stoop. As he stepped onto the sidewalk, the ragtag group clustered around him, slapping his back, pumping his hand.

"We're rooting for you, Jim," said an old man with stooped shoulders, eyes glistening.

"Take him down, champ!" cried another, from the back of the mob.

Then a familiar figure stepped in front of the rest. "How you doing, lefty?" said Mike Wilson. They clasped hands.

"How's Sara and the baby?"

Mike sidestepped the question. "It sure gives the guys a lift," he said. "You getting back into it, I mean."

Jim, unsure how to deal with praise, shrugged it off.

"I put two bucks on you, Jimmy," Mike continued. "Don't let me down, now."

Jim's expression darkened. "Mike, Lewis is favored five to one."

But Mike just smiled, demonstrating more confidence than Jim felt. "How else am I gonna get rich?" he asked, spreading his arms. "You know, maybe I could come along. Do you need some help in your corner?"

Jim shook his head, trying hard not to chuckle at the outlandish request. "I've already got my regular seconds," he replied, face somber. "You know how it is, huh Mike?"

Mike's shoulders slumped, but he laughed off his obvious disappointment. "Yeah, sure, Jim. I understand. Go get 'em, champ."

With a final wave to his neighbors, and a glance at the basement window where his wife stood watching, Braddock climbed into Joe Gould's car waiting at the curb. As they drove down the street, Mae Braddock at her window and Mike Wilson out on the sidewalk, both watched him go.

* * *

A punishing left jab snapped Braddock's head back. The arena had undergone some sort of earthquake, Jim decided, as he staggered, struggling to regain his balance. Braddock found himself against the ropes, looking up but seeing stars instead of the Garden's klieg lights. That powerful wallop was followed by another and another. Jim managed to recover, darting around his opponent to get clear of the ropes.

But John Henry Lewis wasn't about to let this big fish escape. The fast, lethal black boxer displayed a style well ahead of his time, and Lewis ripped into the Irishman with a series of perfectly timed combinations, once again pinning Braddock to the ropes with a flurry of blows.

At ringside, Ford Bond delivered blow-by-blow commentary to radio listeners. "Lewis, the uncrowned heavyweight champ, having beaten Rosenbloom twice in non-title fights, is here to repeat his 'Frisco performance and defeat Jim Braddock . . ."

Over the roaring crowd, Braddock couldn't hear Bond's words. Instead, the voice of Joe Gould boomed like cannon shot in his ears. "You're just fodder, Jimmy . . . *Fodder*."

As the black phantom closed to finish him, Jim ducked and weaved and slipped away from his opponent, dancing from the ropes to the center of the ring. Like a tidal wave Lewis surged after him, throwing and jabbing with arms as long as a soup line. His speed was dazzling, his force impossible to resist, yet Jim Braddock was demonstrating surprisingly quick footwork of his own, and once he escaped the ropes he mounted a remarkable defense.

Suddenly, Braddock spied an opening in the whirlwind and took it. He smashed a hard left into Lewis's head, followed by a pair of punches too fast for the other man to deflect. This time it was Lewis who danced away from his furious opponent, a look of shock on a face swollen with knots and gleaming with sweat.

But Lewis quickly shook off the blows along with his surprise. He locked eyes with Jim Braddock—who actually threw him, of all things, a smile. With an irritated grunt, Lewis closed on his opponent and they clashed in the center ring, the level of ferocity increasing with each jab, each swing, each punch.

For three rounds, the crowd had remained unimpressed while the two fighters danced and sparred and took the measure of each other, each trying to outbox or outfox the other man in what seemed was turning out to be a fairly timid display. But suddenly, in this ferocious fourth round—Jim Braddock's confident smirks no doubt goading Lewis on—the rule had finally been set, both fighters determined to yield no ground.

The furious exchange ended in an exhausted clinch that the bell broke before the referee had the opportunity. The fighters moved to their corners without a backward glance. Jim slumped onto his stool and Joe Gould hopped over the ropes. He checked Jim's face, then rubbed some life into his heavy, tired arms. While he worked the muscles, Gould glanced into the opposite corner, where he saw stunned confusion in John Henry Lewis's expression, and consternation on the face of his coach.

"Come on," the man screamed. "What are you doing? You beat this guy easy last time."

But Lewis just shook his head. Above the noise of the near capacity crowd, Gould could just make out the boxer's muttered reply. "He . . . he ain't the same guy . . ."

Behind them, Gould spotted Lewis's manager, gambler and racketeer Gus Greenlee, a big shot in the Negro Baseball League and owner of the Pittsburgh team. Under his fedora, the man chewed nervously on his big Cuban cigar, puffing like a chimney. Joe Gould cracked a smile and offered it to the opposing corner. Greenlee sneered back.

"Faster than I remember, even," moaned Jim Braddock. Gould looked up to find that Lewis wasn't the only fighter taken by surprise this round. Jim's chest was heaving, and sweat was pouring off him in a stinging, salty torrent.

Joe nodded, still working Braddock's arms. "Yeah, he's fast. But only in one direction . . ."

Jim traded a look with his manager, who stood and leaned into his ear. "He's always moving to the right," rasped Gould. "Cut down the ring. You gotta unload. You hit him, he's not going to like it. The more you hit him, the slower he's going to get."

Jim nodded, eyes flinty. Going into this bout, Braddock had known Lewis wasn't going to be a pushover. The son of an athletic coach for the University of Arizona, John Henry Lewis had been boxing since childhood, where he'd knocked down older kids during "midget" boxing competitions in his father's gym. Lewis turned pro at fourteen by defeating Buster Grant in a four-round decision. In his fifteenth professional match, Lewis defeated Sam Terrain in a fourth-round knockout beating that proved fatal when

Terrain died days later from injuries sustained during the fight.

Lewis had beaten Jim Braddock too, with a decision in San Francisco back in 1932. But despite his success and his well-connected manager, Lewis had not had much luck outside the ring since 1929. Though he was being groomed for a shot at the title, Lewis was just as financially strapped and fighting from hunger as Braddock himself. Both men's futures were riding on the outcome of this one match.

The bell clanged the start of round five. The sound had hardly faded when the boxers charged like mad bulls to the center of the ring, leather flying.

"The fighters are still toe to toe. No one is giving an inch," Ford Bond barked at his audience. "I have never seen a fight this ferocious go on for this long."

The sustained savage exchange finally broke. And it was Lewis who danced away, Jim who pursued him to the ropes, aggressively carrying the fight back to his opponent.

Lewis countered with a venomous combination—left, right, left. The power of those punches drove Jim back, but he quickly pivoted and tossed a surprise uppercut that heaved Lewis up, backward, and down again, leaving him wavering on one knee.

Jim stepped back, left poised to strike again as the ref jumped between the fighters and began the count—barely audible above the roar of the crowd.

Lewis stumbled to his feet, and the referee reluctantly waved Jim forward. Braddock didn't hesitate—

Years before, just two months after he'd KO'd Tuffy Griffiths, Jim had climbed into this very ring to fight

Leo Lomski. Jim had nearly KO'd Lomski too . . . *Nearly.* Instead of finishing him off, Jim had shuffled around and hesitated, squandering his opportunities long enough to give Lomski time to recover and win. Braddock wasn't about to let that happen again—

Rushing to the center ring, he delivered a trio of jabs. Lewis, still dazed from the knockdown, could not keep his guard up. Even Lewis's legwork slowed, until he could not mount an effective defense, leaving himself open for a tremendous right cross that sent him reeling into the ropes.

James Braddock threw up his arms and the crowd exploded. Their cheers blew off the roof, echoing loud enough to reach beyond the Garden's walls to the busy Manhattan streets outside. Loud enough to rock the richly paneled executive offices of the Garden's influential power broker, Jimmy Johnston.

Jim Braddock's upset victory over John Henry Lewis turned out to be a close win—a split decision rendered by the judges. A similar split opened among fight fans and members of New York City's sporting press. Impartial witnesses deemed John Henry Lewis the winner of the first four rounds since he'd clearly dominated his opponent with quicksilver moves, amazing flurries, fancy footwork, and perfect timing.

But after the fateful fifth round—when Jim Braddock had sent Lewis to his knees—the black fighter never recovered. His confidence shaken, Lewis's poor performance tossed the next several rounds to the boxer from New Jersey. John Henry Lewis's reputation was further tarnished by a low blow he threw at Braddock, unsportsmanlike behavior that caused Lewis to forfeit a round.

That low blow—hurled by accident in the heat of battle—knocked the wind out of Braddock, though he refused to show it. Fortunately, the stunning smash came near the end of the fight, and Jim thanked his lucky stars for the money Joe Gould had fronted him because he'd used the cash to increase his strength and stamina under the tutelage of Joe Jeannette, the king of endurance fighters in his day. Jim realized that if he'd showed the faintest trace of weakness during the closing rounds, the decision would have surely gone to Lewis and ended Braddock's fistic resurgence for good.

Most sportswriters gave Braddock his due, and a few even declared his performance against Lewis the pinnacle of his boxing career. But not everyone sided with the Bulldog of Bergen. Writers who favored John Henry Lewis were especially unimpressed with the "Jersey stooge." In their view, Jim had merely connected with a few lucky punches.

But the split in the press over Braddock vs. Lewis was inconsequential compared to the spotlight on the bout that followed, in which New York favorite Bob Olin overthrew Maxie Rosenbloom to become the world's light heavyweight champion. That titanic battle drew headlines away from the spectacular exhibition by Jim Braddock—media neglect that ensured Jim would enter his next fight with his underdog status as firmly fixed as ever. But it also made getting that next fight much tougher, an unpleasant truth that Gould never shared with his fighter.

As Gould handed Braddock his share of the seven-hundred-dollar purse, he offered some advice to go with it. "Always keep your hands up, Jimmy. Take care of yourself and keep in shape. Our luck has changed at last. I can feel it in my bones."

Jim trained fairly steadily after that, but he also went back to the docks to work part time to feed his family. Meanwhile, Joe Gould visited Jimmy Johnston's offices daily, pestering the promoter for another bout. He sometimes brought Jim Braddock along with him, as if to show him off. While Gould pressured Johnston for another Garden match, Braddock planted himself in the outer office where he charmed Johnston's seasoned, tough-as-nails secretary and guardian of the gate, Francis Albertanti.

Braddock became quite a fixture in subsequent weeks, and every time Johnston passed the fighter on his way in or out of his office, he muttered a curse under his breath. One day, Johnston protested out loud. "You've spoiled two guys for me, Braddock. Two fighters I was grooming for a shot at the championship."

"So," Jim replied with a guileless shrug, "when are you gonna throw me another?"

It would take a considerable amount of wheeling and dealing by Joe Gould to get Jim another bout, but circumstances helped his cause.

In December, 1934, a month after the Braddock vs. Lewis fight, Jimmy Johnston publicly announced what Joe Gould and many others had long suspected—that the Garden would soon host a series of elimination bouts to determine which fighter would be a suitable challenger for Max Baer's championship title. A rematch with the man Baer snatched that title away from was a given, which placed Primo Carnera at the top of the list.

Other contenders included Art Lasky, an up-and-coming, left-handed bruiser from Minnesota; Max Schmeling, who'd just returned to his native Germany to be celebrated by its newly elected chancellor, Adolf Hitler; Steve Hamas, a former four-letter man from the University of Pennsylvania; and "Big Ray" Impelletiere, whom Tommy Loughran had recently beaten in a decision despite a cut over Tommy's eye that almost stopped the fight.

Of course, Joe Gould wanted Braddock to have a shot at the title, but he ran into a hitch named Johnston. After his victory against John Henry Lewis, Johnston had concluded Braddock was more than lucky—he was *good*—and because he didn't want another of his rising young prospects to get smashed by the wild card from New Jersey, Johnston resisted Braddock's entry into the competition. But in his efforts to exclude Braddock, Johnston encountered a hitch of his own—Joe Gould, who badgered him day after day, week after week for another bout.

"How about a fight with Al Gainer?" said Johnston after Joe Gould burst into his office one chilly December afternoon.

Joe Gould waved that suggestion aside along with a cloud of cigar smoke. "How about Lasky?" he replied.

Johnston knew that Art Lasky—a fighter who'd chalked up a string of victories in the West—was a good deal slower on his feet than John Henry Lewis, the man Braddock had just defeated. So he refused to sanction the match, and said so.

"How about a series of bouts in the spring?" Johnston countered. "I can line up maybe five fighters for your boy, take him through next Christmas."

"How about Art Lasky?"

"Okay. But how about another fight *before* Lasky?" Johnston offered, hoping the other boxer would knock Braddock down and out of the running.

"I want Lasky," came Joe's reply.

Johnston threw Gould out of his office that day, but Joe came back the next, and the next. Gould stuck to his guns, and eventually Johnston—after listening to the confident Lasky crowd—began to believe that he'd been underestimating Art Lasky's fistic abilities and overestimating the boogie man named James Braddock.

In the end it was Jimmy Johnston who called Joe Gould into his office after Christmas 1934 to offer Braddock the Lasky match, with a contract that stipulated the bout would take place in the Garden on February 1, 1935. Gould fronted Jim some money and he went off to train. But on the eve of that fight, Lasky was stricken with pleurisy and the tussle was postponed—a sharp disappointment to Gould and Braddock, who were both sparring with hungry wolves at their debt-ridden doors as they waited for the long-delayed purse.

On February 1, the day the fight was originally scheduled to take place, Braddock paid a visit to Art Lasky in the hospital, posed for pictures and wished his future opponent a speedy recovery. The next morning, Jim rose early, kissed Mae good-bye, and headed back to the docks to scrounge for work. The fight was rescheduled for March 15, then postponed again by Lasky's trainers and the boxing commission, to March 22.

Gould exploded when he heard the news. "Another

postponement? They're afraid of Braddock, that's what they are. They're giving us the runaround, the dirty snakes." He complained loudly and long, but in the face of such rank favoritism toward Lasky, he could do nothing but agree to the change. Jim Braddock was again left waiting at the altar.

Two days later, Johnston called Gould into his office to inform him that the fight had been rescheduled yet again—to the original postponement date of March 15!

"Is that so?" Gould cried. "Well, they can go to hell. What do they think this is, anyway? What do they think I've got here, a four-round fighter or something? Well, we *won't* fight on the fifteenth, no matter what the commission recommends. I got a contract and we'll fight on March twenty-second—and that's that."

Before anyone could stop him, Gould stormed out of Johnston's office, went directly to Joe Jeannette's gym in Union City and instructed Jim Braddock to train for a fight on the 22nd. Then Joe Gould vanished. For the next two weeks, Johnston's men searched all over the city for him, but Braddock's manager could not be found. Only after it was too late to do anything else, and the New York press confirmed the fight's official date of March 22, did Joe Gould resurface at his familiar haunts.

By the time the date of the Lasky vs. Braddock fight arrived, Hamas and Carnera had been eliminated from competition, and Max Schmeling refused to return to the United States to fight Baer. With no one left to promote, Johnston understandably hoped for a quick and definitive Lasky victory, one that would push Braddock out of the competition altogether.

* * *

From the opening bell, it looked as if Johnston's hopes would be dashed. Braddock easily dominated the first round, beginning with a hard right that threw Lasky against the ropes. In the second and third rounds The Leftie from Minnesota seemed unable to penetrate Braddock's defense. Nose bloody, chin bruised, Lasky absorbed lots of punishment, though he managed to land a sinker to Braddock's chin in the fourth round before eating a left, right, left to the head that forced Lasky to retreat.

But the tide seemed to shift in the fifth round. Lasky flew out of his corner with a furious body attack that knocked the wind out of Braddock. Moving close, Lasky landed a right cross and left jab on Braddock's mug, followed by a body blow with his right. Braddock's response was tepid and misdirected—he was warned by the referee that he was hitting low—and he swallowed another body blow as the round ended.

Things got worse for Braddock in the sixth round, with Lasky planting a hard right to his chin and a left to the gut. As he backed away, Braddock managed to connect with Lasky's jaw, and tossed four shots to his head. But the damage had already been done to Braddock—Lasky came away from the sixth a winner.

Art Lasky's momentum continued in the seventh round, with Braddock continually backing away, Lasky always on the offensive. The eighth round ended with a near technical knockout when Braddock laid open a gouge under Lasky's eye, but the man's fury remained undiminished, and at the start of the ninth, Lasky came out fighting, landing successive hits to the

torso climaxed by a wallop to Braddock's stomach that
elicited a loud grunt. Meanwhile, Braddock's punches
seemed mistimed and ineffectual.

Announcer Ford Bond was beside himself. "After
his dazzling victory against John Henry Lewis, the
comeback of Jim Braddock has just hit a wall named
Art Lasky in the ninth round . . ."

Lasky had Braddock trapped in a corner and was
pounding him with bone-jarring shots to Jim's ribs.
Braddock just managed to escape—and rock Lasky
with a right to the chin—when the bell rang.

As Lasky crossed to his corner, he raised his fists in
triumph.

A corner man worked on Jim's bruises, and Joe
Gould leaned into his face. "He's a bull rusher," Gould
said. "He's going to keep doing this all night."

Jim looked up. For a moment the lights seemed to
descend from the ceiling and explode in his brain.
Gould shook him. "Where are you, Jim?" The lights
receded. Jim squeezed his eyes, shook the sweat and
water out of his hair. When he looked up again, the
lights were right back where they belonged.

"Jim!" yelled Gould. "This is Lasky's house. You
got to stop him breathing, you get me, Jim?"

Their eyes met, and a shared darkness passed between them.

"You hit him in the nose," said Gould, eyes blazing.
"You keep hitting him there, you get me? Make him
bleed—"

The warning buzzer sounded.

"—Fill his face with blood."

But Jim just couldn't pull it off. Instead, he tried to
hold Lasky back with his left, but the ploy didn't work.

In the eleventh round, Braddock found himself pinned into a corner once more. Arms down, elbows in tight to protect his ribs, Braddock's head was totally exposed. Lasky took advantage of the opening with a flurry of punches and jabs.

"Art Lasky is putting an end to a story that's been getting a lot of attention . . ." Bond cried into his microphone. His rapid-fire commentary was suddenly interrupted when Lasky dished up a right hook to Jim's temple potent enough to dislodge Braddock's mouthpiece and send it sailing across the canvas. It was the most powerful punch Lasky possessed in his arsenal, and the crowd seemed to grow still as they waited for the result.

Jim Braddock just stood there, holding Lasky's eyes, his ferocity undiminished. Without the referee's intervention, Braddock turned, walked calmly across the ring and retrieved his mouthpiece.

"I . . . I can't believe my eyes," cried Bond. "Braddock just took Lasky's best punch and it didn't even faze him. He's showing inhuman determination . . ."

Braddock popped the mouthpiece into place with a gloved hand. Then he grinned to the howling audience and closed on Lasky. Feeling fear for the first time, the man from Minnesota tried to end the round in a clinch, but a savage uppercut from Braddock's right snapped Lasky's head back and put an end to that failed strategy.

His confidence restored, Braddock came out swinging in the twelfth, landing blow after blow on Lasky's temple, his eyes, his chin. Lasky's cut reopened and blood seeped from the wound. Still Braddock pressed, continuing the assault on Art Lasky's cranium in the thirteenth and fourteenth rounds. Now Jim fought from

a distance, employing Gould's advice, repeatedly jabbing Lasky's nose, turning it into a red balloon.

By the start of the fifteenth and final round, both
fighters were displaying fatigue. Lasky managed to
make a show of charging, but was halted by Braddock's walloping left. With Lasky flailing, Jim landed
thudding rights, varying his attack with a feint to the
body, and finally a right cross that landed on his opponent's face. Lasky's nose exploded, blood drenched
the ring.

"This is incredible," said Ford Bond. "Braddock will
not be denied."

As Lasky staggered around the center of the canvas,
Jim was on him with a series of lethal punches that sent
his opponent to the ropes—the only thing keeping
Lasky upright as the final bell sounded, ending the fight.

The crowd was on its feet while the fighters were
still in the middle of the ring. Through the glare and
the tobacco smoke, Jim found Gould looking at him,
offering his fighter a respectful bow. Jim winked in reply, then threw his bloody gloves above his head and
punched at the Garden's ringing roof.

"And the winner is . . . James J. Braddock!"

The cheers were loud enough to reach across America's heartland, to Branson, Missouri, where their
echoes drowned out the sound of manager Ancil Hoffman's labored breaths, the click of heels across hardwood floor. He raced down a hotel corridor, to come to
a stumbling halt at the bridal suite.

He tapped the door, then pounded on it. A muffled
sound, then the door flew open.

"What?" roared a naked giant. Eyes simmering,

Max Baer gripped the doorknob with a powerful fist, chest heaving, muscles rippling like a pagan warrior god. Traces of crimson lipstick streaked his face, neck, and pectorals like tribal war paint. Behind the heavyweight champ, Ancil saw two young women sprawled across a queen-size bed, one stripped to her lingerie, the other stark naked except for silk stockings. Both were giggling, drunk.

Ancil met his fighter's angry glare. "Max . . . Jim Braddock just beat Lasky. He just got to be the number-one contender for *your* title."

Max Baer smirked. The women laughed wildly.

"I'm going to paste that guy," growled Baer. "He's nothing but a chump. Why not tell his manager to stand him on Fifth Avenue in front of the crosstown bus. If he can take *that*, maybe he can get in the ring with me."

Max was about to close the door when he paused. "Tell Johnston to get somebody who can fight back."

"You gonna bust your contract?" Ancil cried. "Too late. It's a done deal, Max."

Baer slammed the door in Ancil Hoffman's face. Peals of feminine laughter rolled after the fretting manager as he retreated down the hall.

ROUND ELEVEN

*Who are the better judges, the public or the
experts? I say the public.*

—Damon Runyon

"Ready to face the jackals, Jim?"

Joe Gould stood at the locker-room door. His hand
clutched the knob, shoulder pressed against the wood
as if he were holding back an angry mob armed with a
battering ram.

Braddock, slumped on a wooden bench, could hear
the reporters jostling for position in the corridor outside. He was still clad in his trunks from the Lasky
fight, robe tossed in the corner, towel draped around
his neck. Before he replied, Jim gazed at his bruised
hands, immersed in icy water to reduce the swelling.
He opened and closed his fingers inside the galvanized
steel bucket. Chunks of ice the size of bread loaves
bobbed in the clear water.

"Can't hold 'em back forever," Gould warned in the
usual rasping half voice that came from his constant
yelling in Jim's corner.

Braddock lifted his arms, shook his hands dry, used the towel to finish the job. "Ready," he said. A corner man whisked the bucket out of sight. Jim rose and faced the door.

Gould turned the knob and let go the flood. Flashbulbs popping, pens, pencils, and pads waving, the men of the fistic first estate burst into the locker room, filling it quickly, hurling questions—too fast and too many to answer, or even understand. Jim faced the group with a bemused smirk.

Whenever Jim faced the press, he always thought of Dempsey vs. Firpo in 1923. In round one Dempsey had knocked down the Argentine heavyweight seven times, but before the bell clanged, the "Wild Bull of Pampas" fired off an enraged combination that drove Dempsey outside the ring, where his kisser connected with a writer's typewriting machine.

Dempsey got up at the count of nine and finally knocked Firpo out in the second round to retain the title. Nevertheless, after all the bad press Jim had gotten over the years, he figured he knew exactly what Dempsey's head must have felt like smacking against that typewriter.

"Was it an easy fight, Jim?" cried one reporter, loud enough to be heard above the clamor.

Jim raised a bruised eyebrow. "Didn't feel like one."

"Who do you think will be next, Jimmy?" cried another.

Jim looked to Joe Gould, who gave a little shake of his head. Gould had confided the deal was as good as done, but it wasn't Jim's place to say it, so he shrugged. "Ask Jimmy Johnston."

"The smart money says Max Baer."

Jim crossed his arms. "You don't say?"

"Jim, Jim Braddock," called Sporty Lewis, who'd pushed his way to the front of the pack. "Will you fight Max Schmeling in 'thirty-five?"

"I would. But I hear Adolph Hitler wants Max to do his boxing in the Fatherland," Jim replied. "Won't even box Max Baer unless he crosses the pond."

"Yeah, like *that'll* happen," someone yelled.

"Even Madcap Maxie isn't that mad," yelled another, producing a ripple of knowing laughter. Since Hitler came to power in Germany, East Coast promoters had been forcing Schmeling out of most venues, though Jimmy Johnston still yearned to pair Schmeling with a number of American fighters.

"To what do you credit your victory over Lasky?" The man from the *News* waited for Jim's reply, pen poised over paper.

Jim thought for a moment. "I guess it's having a great family. A great manager, a great trainer—"

"And a great *left*!" Joe Gould croaked, punching air.

"Yeah, that too," said Jim.

After that, most of the questions concerned Braddock's future, questions he and Joe Gould both fended off, not wanting to tempt fate. After Jim offered the sportswriter for the *Hudson Dispatch*—the Union City paper—his own version of the Lasky fight, Joe yanked off his fawn fedora and waved the reporters out of the locker room.

"Come on, let Braddock alone now, ya bums," Gould insisted, pushing them out the door. "Jimmy's got a wife and kids to go home to. Ain't any of you guys family men?"

A string of guffaws was the reply.

"Nah," muttered Gould, "didn't think so . . ."

"Good job, Jim. I knew you could do it. Won me a quarter. Twenty-five cents!"

A rumpled suit hung from the little man's frame. He had dirty gray hair and missing front teeth. But his expression was Christmas morning.

Most of the fight fans had long since departed. The streets around the Garden were dark and desolate, but the moment Jim Braddock and Joe Gould had stepped out the door, a gang of fifty men closed around them.

The scene was markedly different from the group who'd greeted him after his Tuffy Griffiths KO back in 1928. Gone were the flamboyantly dressed high rollers with diamond tiepins and new fedoras, the flappers with mink-trimmed coats, fringed dresses, and silk stockings. In their place stood a rough bunch of men in tattered work clothes and scuffed shoes. Worn and lean with hunger, their bodies had been stooped by disappointment, toil, and want—yet when they saw Braddock emerge, they straightened. Defeated faces were resurrected, weariness turned to hope.

Jim was stunned by the sight. At his shoulder, Joe Gould grinned and croaked, "You sign a few, leave them wanting."

Braddock shook his head. "Nah, Joe . . . You sign them *all*."

Callused hands with broken fingernails waved press books, newspaper clippings, even betting sheets at the fighter. Jim moved among them, shaking hands and scribbling his name on whatever scrap was thrust upon him. He signed and talked and joked and shook hands until the crowd dispersed, over an hour later.

"Did I leave them wanting?" he asked, wandering over to Joe Gould. The manager had long ago sat down on some nearby steps to wait for his fighter.

"You sure did," Gould replied, dusting off his fawn coat. "So we gonna hit the spots."

"Home, Joe."

Jim was quiet for most of the drive, so Joe did most of the talking. He recounted the fight in his own colorful way twice when his roadster rolled up to the curb in front of Braddock's tenement building. The motor was still running when Jim opened the door. "Good night, Joe."

"Hey, aren't you forgetting something? Your cut of the purse." Gould reached into his coat, produced a thick wad of bills. The manager began to count out the cash and explain the breakdown of expenditures. Jim lifted his bruised hand to silence him.

"I trust you, Joe. You know that. And so does Mae."

Gould smiled and thrust the cash into Braddock's hand. Jim glanced down at the small fortune, then thrust it into his coat. "I'd invite you in, but it's late," said Jim. "The kids are asleep."

Gould opened his mouth to speak, then realized no words were necessary. He waved good-bye, threw the roadster into gear and peeled off down the street, kicking up soot and discarded newspapers like the March winds.

Before Jim entered his tiny apartment, he paused under a naked bulb in the hallway and counted the cash. His aim was to divide the money into two neat piles. When he entered the apartment, he placed one bundle in the mason jar Mae still used for a bank. The other he tucked into a wrinkled envelope he'd been holding on to for what seemed like an eternity.

Mae and the children were asleep, and he was careful not to wake them. He'd tell them all about his victory over Art Lasky tomorrow. Jim undressed, folding his clothes and draping them over a chair, then slipping between the clean white sheets. Beside him, Mae shifted on the mattress. He gazed at her until he nodded off, but he didn't sleep long. When the first rays of the chilly March dawn streamed through the window, he rose and hurriedly dressed, managing to slip out before Mae and the children stirred.

The windswept sidewalks were empty. He strode toward the center of town along sidewalks damp from an overnight shower. As Jim crossed the square and approached the Newark courthouse, pedestrian traffic increased. Inside the relief office, it was warm. Braddock joined the men and women already standing on line. As he waited patiently for service, several people seemed to recognize him. One man showed a local paper to the fellow at his shoulder. Inside, a three-column article, complete with grainy photograph snapped in Braddock's locker room right after the bout, outlined Jim's surprising victory at the Garden.

Waiting patiently, hands folded in front of him as he wended his way slowly to the front of the line, Jim ignored the curious, sidelong glances. When it was finally his turn, he stepped up to the counter and greeted the now familiar woman with a nod. He drew the official white envelope, which bore the seal of the State of New Jersey, out of his pocket, slid it across the counter. The woman picked it up, peeked inside.

"Let me get this straight," she said, displaying the cash. "You want to give the money *back*?"

Jim purchased a dozen long-stem roses from a florist on his way home—a wildly extravagant gesture, but his way of apologizing to Mae for not waking her the night before, or this morning, to tell her about the fight. He knew his wife would be upset about that, but Jim hadn't wanted to celebrate his victory over Lasky—or even acknowledge it—until he returned all the money the relief office had given his family over the last few months. Now that the weight of that shame had been lifted, Jim felt a hundred pounds lighter. The aches and pains from the fight were forgotten and his steps were buoyant as he opened the door to his family's apartment.

His smile dissolved when he found Sara Wilson there, sitting on their old sofa, her eyes red-rimmed from crying, the baby girl in her arms racked with a hacking cough. Mae looked up when he entered, pale face somber. "Mike's gone missing," she told him softly.

Jim crossed the room. He dropped the flowers onto the table, spying Jay, Howard, and Rosy huddled in a corner where Mae had banished them, straining hard to hear what was going on.

He crouched down in front of Sara, placed his hands on her shoulders. "How long?"

"Three days," Sara cried. "I've been staying at my brother's since Jake cut him—"

"Jake cut him?" Braddock gulped. That was bad news. The docks provided the only reasonably steady work around, but not if Jake the foreman didn't pick you out of the pack of hopefuls. "When?"

Sara wiped her eyes with a dirty cloth. "Maybe a week after you left the docks for good. You know how Mike gets. All his talk. So much trouble."

The baby coughed. Sara caressed the girl's face as if she saw Mike there. "He's been sleeping nights down in the Hooverville. My brother didn't have room for both him and us."

She looked up at Jim. "He said he was doing some strategy work for you. He had a little cash coming in, down at the gym all the time. It made sense, you being friends and all . . ." Her voice trailed off. More tears dewed her eyes and Jim could tell Mae had already dashed this fantasy. "Last night, he was supposed to meet me down at Quincy's," Sara continued. "He never showed . . ." She clawed Jim's sleeve with clutching fingers. "Something's wrong, Jim. I know it. He'd never miss one of your fights. He just wouldn't."

Jim looked down at her, surprised by this revelation. Then he faced his wife. Silently, she gestured toward the mason jar that contained his fight winnings—the family's rainy-day money. Jim nodded. "Look," he told Sara, gently pulling her hand from his arm, "you and Mae go down to Rexall, get something to fix her cough. I'll go—"

But Sara wasn't listening, lost in a nightmare of her own. "I give up," she said softly, staring into nothingness. "That's what Mike said before he left last time. I should have known something was wrong. 'I give up,' he said."

Mae and Jim were startled by her words.

"I'm sure he's fine, Sara," said Jim, trying to hide the lie. Mae touched the woman's shoulder, a silent re-

inforcement. But Sara didn't believe it, and she broke
down. Her baby cried too, its tiny face flushing redder
than a cutman's rag.

Two strides took Jim to the front door. "I'll . . . I'll
just go round him up . . ."

Braddock thrust a bill into the driver's hand, stepped
out of the cab. Sinking below the Manhattan skyline,
the sun was a milky ball, casting its feeble rays through
passing clouds over a barren expanse of trampled grass
and tall, barely budding trees. But Braddock knew that
the vast, mock wilderness of Central Park was not so
empty as it seemed, that something beyond the chilly
March wind stirred there.

Since the crash of 1929, more than a hundred thousand New Yorkers had been evicted from their homes.
Tens of thousands of them—many who once considered themselves middle class—were now living in
their cars, in empty lots, subway tunnels, or on the
street. By autumn 1930, the first shantytowns had
sprung up along the banks of the East and Hudson
Rivers. This Central Park "Hooverville"—named after
the ineffectual chief executive who presided over the
crash and its devastating aftermath—was the largest
and most famous of these makeshift settlements.

Among the ruins of the half-demolished Croton
Reservoir in the middle of the park, men lived in water
mains, storm drains, even in ditches they dug into the
earth with their bare hands. The more skilled and in-
dustrious among them constructed rough huts or tents
assembled from scraps of lumber, bits of canvas, plywood, cardboard—any material they could find.

The denizens of this desperate shantytown lived on a

subsistence level. They ate what they could buy, scrounge, beg, catch or steal. In time, no creature that inhabited the park with the starving masses was spared: Pigeons, squirrels, songbirds, and even rats were trapped and devoured daily.

Jim had heard that most of the flocks of sheep who placidly grazed in the area of the park known as Sheep Meadow had been moved upstate by now, but, as he moved farther into the park, he realized a surreal evacuation was in progress. It appeared the last remaining few dozen or so sheep, who'd evaded the previous move, were now being herded out by groundskeepers into immense corral wagons lined up along a wide cobbled trail. Flanks twitching, steam billowing from their nostrils, the baying flock nearly trampled Braddock in their feral panic. One of the many cops on horseback, overseeing this process, whistled a warning and waved Braddock away with his nightstick.

Jim moved away from the barnyard chaos, jogged down a gentle slope, descending at last into the jumble called Hooverville. As Braddock wended his way among ramshackle huts of cardboard, he heard moans and coughs from within, mingling with the constant howl of the March wind.

Among the structures, shadows lengthened with the setting sun, the wavering glow of trash-can fires becoming the only source of light in the darkening park. Jim moved through legions of men, dressed in all manner of clothing from rags and tatters to soiled evening wear. They sprawled on old easy chairs that spit stuffing, ate at broken card tables, drank from vegetable cans or bottles.

Jim warily approached an old man hunched over a

roaring fire in an empty barrel—he was cooking something, though Braddock was not sure exactly what.

"Excuse me."

The man turned, grinned wide enough to display missing teeth. Others emerged from the shadows of a leaning shanty. They eyed him, tipped their hats.

"Evening sir," said the taller. "Offer you a bite to eat? It's fresh."

The cook used a stick in his hand to prod the food, carbonized fur hide cracked to reveal pink flesh. Juice sputtered into the fire. Another man reached forward, waving a bottle under Braddock's nose. He smiled and waved the offer aside.

"I'm looking for a friend of mine." Jim glanced around. A sea of faces watched him, eyes shining in the half-light. "Is there someone in charge?"

The man with the bottle chuckled, a deep, throaty sound. "Ain't that the question of the day?"

Jim heard the clop of hooves. Two policemen rode by, flanking a groundskeeper herding a small group of sheep. The men's hungry eyes followed the woolly animals.

Jim moved deeper into the park. The shanties seemed to go on forever, their rude construction a mirror in reverse of the tall, stately skyscrapers of glass and granite that ran up Fifth Avenue. Coming upon a tent, Braddock peered inside to discover a makeshift hospital. The air stank of disease, and wet, tubercular coughs filled the dusk.

"Mike! Mike Wilson?" he called.

Sick, bleary eyes met his cry, but no reply, and Jim moved on. A man lay sprawled on the ground, his legs flung wide. Jim stepped over him and into the path of a

pair of running policemen, who yelled for him to
move. He turned to see where they were heading and
saw a knot of mounted cops in the distance, a swarm of
men around the horses' legs. He smelled smoke, saw
flames wafting up from a distant commotion. Shouts,
howls, angry whinnies, and bleating sheep echoed
across the lawn.

Another cop charged by Jim on horseback, nearly
trampling him. Pistol drawn, arm raised, the officer
looked as if he were leading the charge up San Juan
Hill. Jim followed the cop toward the chaos, but before
he could get to its center, he slammed into a mob, a
solid wall of bodies.

"Mike Wilson!"

The tide ebbed and flowed. Braddock was swallowed up by the press of men. Smoke from the burning
shanty in the distance blew over the mob in a dim,
choking cloud. Finally, he broke free.

"Mike . . . Mike!"

"Jim . . . Over here."

Braddock turned expectantly, but the man who'd
called his name wasn't Mike—just another inhabitant
of Hooverville, a once prosperous man now trapped in
financial limbo. "Braddock, right? Seen you fight."

Jim looked beyond the man, searching the milling
throng, forced to blink against the poisonous fog.

"Frank Gibson. City National," the man said. "Hope
you don't want a loan."

Braddock pushed past him, across sere grass. He
dodged a wild-eyed unfortunate with blood streaming
from his head, and finally arrived at the center of what
had been a riot: the Sheep Meadow.

Horses and men had clashed together here just min-

utes earlier. Police, on foot and horseback, had re-
gained control and were now herding the men like
sheep, away from the overturned wagons. Someone
had set a shanty on fire and the yellow flames were
throwing flickering light on moaning men who'd been
struck down by nightsticks and were now dotting the
ravaged lawn.

Two police on twitching horses pulled up near Jim.
"We was just trying to clear the sheep, Sarge," said the
young one. "But these guys got more guts than a
slaughterhouse. One started getting all political, shouting, angry—then they charged us."

Jim closed his eyes, knew it was Mike. All his talk.
All his angry talk.

"Jeez, that ain't no royal flush," said the sergeant.

Jim began looking for Mike among the fallen on the
grass, then near the overturned corral wagons. As the
police freed the work horses from their harnesses,
forced to shoot two with broken legs, vagrants and
blue-uniformed men lifted the wagons to expose shattered bodies beneath.

"Some crazy nut tried to release the sheep," one cop
told another. "Horses got spooked, wagons went over.
Starkers just didn't get out of the way in time."

From beneath the wheels of one wagon, a man with
a crushed leg howled. The men heaved together, lifting
the heavy cart to free the trapped man—only to reveal
a second in a pool of blood.

"Jesus," said a cop, choking, seeing the corpse.

Sirens blared in the distance. Jim's eyes continued
searching.

"Hey, Jim." The voice was soft and filled with agony.

Jim turned and winced. Stepping over another mangled corpse, Jim knelt on the cold, gore-splashed ground. With his fight-scarred hand, Jim smoothed the hair from Mike Wilson's face, wiped blood from his cheeks with the sleeve of his coat.

The sun had set by now and there wasn't much light, but Jim was able to see that his old partner's body was badly out of alignment, his face was ghostly white. Still, when he saw Jim, a smile creased the corners of his blood-flecked lips.

"You win?" he rasped. Mike waited for the answer, his eyes glazed with pain but expectant too.

Jim nodded, leaned closer. "You're gonna be fine, Mike. You're gonna be okay.

Mike managed a weak nod, squinted up at Jim's face. "Yeah . . . I know it . . ."

Then the chill wind shifted, and the smoke from the burning shanty drifted over the two men, blotting out any remaining light.

Mike Wilson's funeral was a somber, frugal affair. Even with Jim and Mae's help, Sara could not afford a headstone to mark her husband's grave, not even a decent coffin. A cold, desolate potter's field near the Newark rail yards was his burial site. He was laid to rest in a shallow grave, in a cheap plywood casket, under a cloud-covered sky.

Mourners were sparse—it was a workday and Mike's few friends were pragmatic out of necessity for a day's wages. At any rate, death and tragedy were common coin these days and certainly no reason to break with grueling routine. So only Jim and Mae

Braddock, along with their children, stood with Sara and her baby girl as her husband's remains were lowered into the ground.

After Father Rorick's softly intoned benediction, Jim spoke haltingly of his friendship with Mike, of Mike's love for his wife, his family. Not said were the words that had blistered his thoughts the night Mike had died. *Stupid, pointless waste.* Jim knew what it was to feel crushed, to want to strike out, strike back, but like Ben, who'd pulled that gun on Jake at the docks last fall, Mike's righteous anger, his useless riot, had done little to help his wife, his child, and least of all himself.

Standing next to the man's grave, Jim didn't want to think about those things, so instead he thought of how sorry he was, how he wished he'd have known how bad things had gotten for his friend, how he wished Mike would've laid aside his pride just long enough to ask for help. And yet, Jim could not forget Mike's selflessness, either—how he risked his own spot at the docks to help Braddock hide his injured right hand, how Mike did double the work while Jim healed. Or the way Mike helped two strangers who were about to be evicted, just because he could.

Mae Braddock stood beside her husband, only half listening to his hesitant words. Her attention was too focused on Sara. The woman appeared to garner small comfort from the muttered sentiments, the prayers, the promises of a better life beyond this one. Instead, Sara silently gazed at the horizon, as if mulling over the lonely, husbandless days that stretched out ahead of her.

A tear dampened Mae's frozen cheek. Shed for Mike and his stricken mate—but also for herself. Some part of her feared she was peering into a reflection of her own future. Maybe not today, or tomorrow—but one day, Jim could suffer the same fate. Trembling, Mae realized how completely lost she would be if she found herself in this same cemetery, watching her own husband being laid to rest for all eternity.

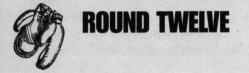

ROUND TWELVE

I would like to say to the boxing fans and to the public at large that I will be in the best shape any athlete can possibly get into for the fight. . . . I know what this fight means to me. . . . And it will be some fight.

—James J. Braddock, 1935

I insist on having an ambulance at ringside. Jim is a nice fellow, and I wouldn't want to see him die on my hands. He won't last a round.

—Max Baer, 1935

Madison Square Garden
March 24, 1935

Photographers circled the long draped table in the center of the vast arena, vulturelike. Flashbulbs popped, muted lightning. A hundred reporters waited patiently while Jim Braddock and Joe Gould mugged for the cameras, good-naturedly sparring for the title of most photogenic grin. Jimmy Johnston sat next to Gould, ignoring the cameras.

Mae sat in the front row, ankles crossed, gloved hands folded demurely in her lap. She wore a new yellow dress and matching hat, her smile sincere though nervous.

The light show continued for a few moments, then one of Jimmy Johnston's boys waved the photographers back, and a man in the third row stood, pad and pencil in hand.

"Frank Essex, *Daily News*. You got a lot of reporters here—" Laughter and cheeky applause interrupted him. "You can see a lot of people are interested in this fight. You got anything to say to the fans, Jim?"

"I guess . . ." Braddock rubbed his chin. "I guess I'm grateful for the opportunity. Not everybody gets a second chance these days . . ." His eyes claimed Mae's. "I guess I got a lot to be grateful for."

A craggy man stood next, nodded, shoved back the brim of his fedora. "Bob Johnston, *Boston Globe*. Two days ago we ran a story about you giving your relief money back. Can you tell our readers why?"

Jim nodded, sure of his answer. "I believe we live in a country that's great enough to give a man financial help when he's in trouble. I've had some good fortune so I thought I'd return it. Let them give it to somebody else who could use it, because they were good enough to give it to me."

Reporters scribbled his words as fast as he spoke them. A few sneered at his cornball reply. Most nodded approvingly.

"Wilson Harper, *Associated Press*. What's the first

thing you're going to do if you make world champion, Jim?"

"Well, I guess I gotta go out and buy some pet turtles."

The reporters paused in the scribbling, looked up, not sure they heard him right.

"Did you say turtles?"

Jim nodded, kicking up his New Jersey lilt. "When I was leaving the house I told my kids I was going to bring home the *title*. They thought I said *turtle*, so naturally I can't let them down."

More laughter, and some reporters headed for the phone booths, certain they'd gotten the quote of the day.

"Get the turtle for his kids!" Joe Gould roared with laughter. "'Cause of his accent, see?"

"John Savage, *Blue Ribbon Sports*."

Jim faced the new reporter. He stood in the second row, directly behind Mae. Braddock didn't like the gleam in the man's eye.

"Max Baer says he's worried he's going to kill you in the ring. What do you say?"

Mae could not help but look down at her hands. Jim noticed the gesture, then met the reporter's gaze with his own.

"Max Baer is the champion," Braddock said in a loud, firm voice. "I'm looking forward to the fight."

Enthusiastic cheers and whistles greeted his reply. Mae felt eyes on her. She looked up to see Jimmy Johnston, sitting at the long table at the front of the room, watching her.

"Jack Greenblatt, *Chicago Trib*," a voice called from one of the last rows. "What changed, Jimmy? You couldn't win a fight for love or money. How do you explain your comeback?"

Jim found Mae's eyes. "Maybe I know what I'm fighting for this time around."

"Yeah, what's that?"

Jim shifted in his chair, adjusted his tie. "I just got tired of the empty milk bottles, is all."

Then the man seated right next to Mae Braddock stood. Instead of directing his question to the men at the table, he faced her.

"Sporty Lewis, *New York Herald*," he began, touching the brim of his hat. "Mrs. Braddock, my question is for you. My readers want to know, how do you feel about the fact that Max Baer has killed two men in the ring?"

Mae stared at the man, speechless. Lewis pressed his advantage. "Mrs. Braddock, are you scared for your husband's life?"

A photographer slipped in front of Mae. Crouching, he snapped a picture. The flashbulb exploded in her face, and a fire erupted in Jim's eyes. He leaned forward in his chair, ready to lunge for Sporty's throat.

"She's scared for Max Baer, is who she's scared for."

Sporty turned toward the table, saw Jim glaring at him. Joe Gould rose, waved his arms like a referee. "Okay, boys, one more question and we'll ring the bell. Save some ink for the baseball scores."

Reporters shouted for attention. Mae hid her expression under her hat until Sporty Lewis drifted away to file his own story. When she felt him go, she released a held breath. Her tiny fists clenched as she fought for control.

Jim answered the last question, his eyes seeking her out. But Mae refused to look up. In the years they'd been together, she'd never doubted her husband before.

She didn't want him seeing any doubts in her now, but she couldn't erase the fear from her eyes, or the terrible image of Sara Wilson standing alone in that potter's field, pondering her lonely future.

Fine, old wood polished to a sheen lined the interior of the Garden's exclusive boxing club. Stout leather chairs, sculpted end tables topped by Tiffany lamps, and inlaid card tables had been arranged strategically by the domestic staff. A pool table dominated one corner, its felt dappled by afternoon light filtering through open blinds in the tall windows.

Dominating it all was Jimmy Johnston's desk. The powerful promoter was usually surrounded by members of the New York boxing commission, his army of assistants, and a smattering of privileged hangers-on— gamblers, mobsters, members of the fourth estate. Now the only thing in the room besides Johnston was a movie projector, a roll of film spooled and ready.

Braddock entered the club, Joe Gould at his side. Cutting a swath through thick clouds of cigar smoke, Jim mused that he had come a long way since the day he'd passed the hat around, accepting charity from the men in this room—and from the man seated at the desk. It took all of Braddock's willpower to walk with his head erect, chin jutted, as he met a man who'd seen him stooped so low.

Joe Gould stepped in front of his fighter as he approached Johnston. "Said downstairs you wanted to see us."

"Gould . . . Jim," said Johnston with a wave of his cigar, not bothering to rise.

"Mr. Johnston." Braddock's nod was respectful.

Johnston dug into the pile of newspapers at his arm, spread the early edition of the *Daily News* across his desk. He tapped the editorial page with a thick-fingered hand. "Right here, editorial says this fight is as good as murder. It goes on to say that everyone associated with it should be hauled into court and prosecuted afterwards."

Joe Gould moved his jaws, but did not open his mouth.

Johnston shifted in his stuffed leather chair, crumpled the edge of the newspaper in his big hand. "Says the paper's getting all sorts of letters from people . . . people saying that you're their inspiration. Like you saved their lives or something."

It was Jim's turn not to respond. Johnston appraised the fighter, then stood. He moved around the room, closing the blinds, blocking out the sunlight.

"You ask me, it's all crap," Johnson continued. "My balls and my brains are for business, and this is business—got me?" He approached Jim, his face stopping inches from the fighter's. "You *will* know exactly what you're up against, and my attorney, Mr. Mills, will witness I have done everything in my power to warn you."

A private door opened. A small man with a smaller moustache entered the club, followed by a young, wide-eyed stenographer, her scarlet lips parted in surprise at seeing Jim.

Braddock blinked, crossed his arms. "I saw the Carnera fight."

Johnston ignored Braddock. He walked to the projector, threw the switch. A lackey killed the lights as the clacking machine began to roll the film spooled inside it.

"Carnera's height saved him," said Johnston matter-of-factly as he watched the bright square of blank white light on the wall.

"He was knocked down twelve times," argued Gould.

Numbers danced in the light. *6, 5, 4 . . .*

"Exactly," Johnston replied. "It would have been worse if he was shorter. Baer had to punch *up* to hit him, which took a little power out of his swing."

3, 2, 1 . . .

Two blobs appeared. They flickered, danced—a blur. Johnston twisted the lens and the smudge became a picture.

"Baer versus Campbell," said Johnston. The film showed a quick close-up of grinning lips, jaws chewing a mouthpiece, curly hair, gloves clapping in anticipation. "That's Frankie Campbell. Stand-up fighter. Knows how to take a punch."

Quick jump to the ring. Campbell, head down, throwing haymakers at Baer.

Johnston faced Braddock. "His style familiar, Jim? Like looking in a mirror, huh?"

As Braddock watched, Joe Gould stepped forward. "He don't need to see this."

"He'll see it or I'm calling off the fight," Johnston warned.

The image jumped, Campbell stepped forward with as good a left jab as Braddock had ever seen, almost as good as his own. Baer easily blocked, then countered with his right. The punch—too fast to see—had a strange and awesome power. Absorbing it, Campbell spun, yet remained on his feet. Dazed, Campbell let down his guard, and Baer's hammerlike fist smashed against the side of his unprotected head.

Campbell pitched to the canvas, bounced. Arms limp, legs wide, he gazed sightless at the roof. The referee kneeled over the stricken fighter and Baer's trainer pulled him away. Campbell's corner men scrambled under the ropes, rushed to the center of the ring.

"See that combination?" Johnston said, breaking the ominous silence. "Campbell didn't go down on the first one. Tough guy. It was the second punch that killed him—on the spot."

Gould stepped up to Johnston, stared up at the big promoter's face. "Consider your ass fully covered. Now cut it off, will you—"

"No," said Jim, surprising Gould and Johnston both. "Run it again."

Johnston appraised Braddock, expression thoughtful. Then he switched the projector into reverse, and played the footage once more. As the death punch played again, lawyer Mills averted his eyes. His stenographer pouted her red lips and swallowed.

When the show was over, the film flapped in the projector until Johnston cut the power. The lackey restored the lights and then impassively opened the blinds.

Johnston returned to his desk and sat down. "The autopsy report said Campbell's brain was knocked loose from the supporting tissue." He puffed his cigar, but the stogie had lost its heat. He held it out of his mouth, looked toward Gould for the usual light, but the little manager just glowered and kept his Zippo in his pocket. Johnston tossed the dead stogie on his desk.

"Remember Ernie Schaff? Stand-up fighter, nice guy. You lost one to him in 'thirty-one."

"I remember him," said Jim.

"Ernie took one of those on the chin from Baer. He was dead and didn't know it. Next fight, first jab put him to sleep forever. Detached brain, they said."

Johnston shot a look at Gould. "Joe? No snappy comeback?"

Gould looked at his fighter. "Guess it ain't my skull the guy's going to try and stove in."

The Garden promoter grinned. "Want to think about it?" He leaned back in his chair, waited for their reply.

Braddock slapped his palms down on Johnston's desk. The cold cigar bounced, rolled to the floor. Jim leaned in close.

"You think you're telling me something?" Braddock asked. "Sitting here with all the cash you need to make the right choice? You think triple shifts or working nights on the scaffolds ain't as likely to get a guy killed?"

Johnston shrank back in his chair, Jim leaned even closer.

"How many guys got killed the other night, just living in cardboard shacks to save on the rent money? Some guy just trying to feed his family. Only nobody figured out a way to make a buck seeing how *he* was gonna die." Jim's lips curled, his smile fierce. "My profession." He thrust a thumb into his chest. "I'm more fortunate. So I guess I've thought about it all I'm going to." Braddock stood tall, his glare still pinning Johnston's back in his chair. The promoter looked away.

"All righty then." Johnston slid a card across the

desk. With his duty discharged, his smile turned con-
ciliatory, but Braddock thought he saw a cobra curled
up behind the man's eyes.

"You guys eat here tonight," Johnston said. "Take
your wives. On me. We'll snap some pictures on your
way out. You change your mind tomorrow, at least we
get some good press out of it."

Jim reached into his pocket, pulled out two bills and
some loose change. He laid the money on the desk.
Johnston looked down at it, the card waiting at the end
of his fingers.

"It ain't a bribe," said Braddock. Johnston looked up
at him, puzzled.

"Two bucks, ten," Jim explained. "I already paid
back everybody else."

Jim turned, headed toward the door.

"Jim," Johnston called. Braddock turned. "I got reels
of all Max Baer's fights. You can come up here, use the
projector any time you want."

Jim's jaw worked a moment, then he nodded, turned,
and left the club. Joe Gould snapped the card out of
Johnston's hand and followed his fighter. When they
were gone, Johnston reached down and lifted the cigar
from the thick carpet. Somehow his stogie had gotten
crushed. With a curse, he tossed it into the trash can.

The Continental Club was still the same, thought Jim,
as "Braddock, party of four" was shown their table.
Graceful, curved walls paneled with blond wood, tables separated by etched-glass panels. Exquisite Art
Deco fixtures, furnishings. A piano player stroking out
classy tunes in a muted corner.

The saucer-shaped, upholstered booths were jammed with well-heeled customers. White-coated waiters raced to and fro, shouldering silver trays brimming with china and crystal. There were no hard times here, not like the grimy world beyond these elegant walls. The world of tenements, wharves, rail yards—of Hooverville and potter's fields.

Jim, Mae, Joe, and Lucille ate, drank, and laughed the night away. Now, with the remains of a fine meal on their plates and the ladies visiting the powder room, Joe and Jim faced each other across the linen-draped table. For a long time, neither spoke. Braddock broke the silence. "Since when did you get quiet?"

Gould chuckled, then grew serious. "These last three fights," he said in a low voice. "We sure showed 'em, didn't we?"

Braddock glanced at his manager suspiciously.

"Look, I put you in some bad situations," said Gould. He glanced away then. His mouth moved, but no words came out.

"What are you getting at, Joe?"

Gould squirmed, adjusted his collar. "Jim. You're the toughest kid on the playground. But this Max Baer. It's a whole other thing. You got nothing to prove to me or anyone."

"You losing faith in me, Joe?"

Gould tapped his index finger on the smooth table top. "Never. Not for one goddamn minute."

Jim knew it was true, could see it in Gould's eyes. So what was the problem? Why was his manager talking about throwing in the towel before round one?

Mae and Lucille suddenly appeared, hair and makeup restored.

"Jimmy," Mae purred, running her finger up his arm. "Can we get silver faucets?"

"Yeah, I'll order a dozen." He curled his arm around her slim waist, pulled her close.

Gould raised his hand. "Now, as promised, the *piece de resistance*." He yanked a rolled-up newspaper out of his back pocket, slapped it down. "Little bird told me to check the evening edition. Let me see here . . ."

He flipped through the pages to the sports section, then began to read. " 'Boxer Jim Braddock has come back from the dead to change the face of courage in our nation—' "

Jim blinked. "Who wrote that?"

"Sporty Lewis."

Joe shook the paper under Jim's nose. He swatted it away. Gould continued where he left off. " 'In a land that's downtrodden, Braddock's comeback is giving hope to every American.' "

Mae curled her fingers around her husband's.

" 'People who were ready to throw in the towel are finding inspiration in their new hero, Jim Braddock.' " Gould paused to scan their faces. " 'As Damon Runyon has already written, he's the Cinderella Man.' "

"Cinderella Man?" Jim didn't look happy.

Mae squeezed his hand. "I like it," she laughed. "It's girly."

"Oh, this is going to be fun," groaned Braddock.

A server arrived to clear the table. Mae's eyes darted to her husband. "Jim."

He stopped the waiter. "Not quite done here, friend." The man nodded, slipped away. Mae drew crinkled waxed paper from her purse, carefully emptied each plate onto it, and folded it around the food scraps. Lucille looked away.

"I'll get the bill," said Joe, waving the card in his stubby finger. "Johnston's a big spender, and he's leaving a big tip." He winked. "A *peach*. Gotta love the guy."

Mae closed her purse, glanced up. Suddenly she tensed.

A broad-shouldered giant had just walked through the front door accompanied by two young women. Glittering playthings in gaudy finery, one hung on each of his brawny arms. But it was the man's shock of black hair, volcanic blue eyes, and savage, dynamic presence that drew everyone's attention. Conversations faded and died as the barbarian in bone-white evening clothes strode confidently to the polished oak bar. In the silence, a man sitting nearby whispered to his female companion. "It's Max Baer."

Mae touched her husband's arm. "Jimmy . . ."

Braddock's mood darkened. He turned to Gould. "You think Johnston set this up?"

"Sure. Few extra pics for the dailies," said Gould. With his manager's eyes, he appraised the fighter leaning against the bar across the room.

At over six feet and close to 200, the bronzed Baer had prime attributes for a ringman—slim waist, massive shoulders, long arms, and strong legs. Baer was also young, twenty-six to Jim's twenty-nine, and he had the deadliest right punch that Gould had ever seen, probably the most powerful in the history of boxing. His record included twenty-four KOs but he hadn't gone undefeated. Back in 1931, he'd lost to Tommy

Loughran, just like Braddock, but Gould knew that Dempsey had coached "Madcap Maxie" afterward, instructing him to shorten his punches to prevent the telegraphing that had cost him the match.

Baer was still a crude swinger, however, and he'd never bothered to develop a left, so Gould knew there were ways to beat him. And yet, he couldn't get that Long Island City Bowl massacre of Primo Carnera out of his head. The Italian giant had gone down eleven times at the business end of Baer's gloves.

Gould's gaze moved over the shapely females on each of Baer's arms, typical accessories for the on-the-town fighter, who'd been romantically linked to movie actresses, chorus girls, and Broadway starlets. There wasn't a more colorful character than Madcap Maxie in the boxing world, and the New York press loved him. Gould could see why. At a time when the country had hit the skids, Baer had made people feel better by having such a good time himself. Whether he made or lost money, Baer kept smiling, kept hitting the Broadway nightspots and picking up the tab. He'd made a movie with Myrna Loy, opened a song-and-dance revue at the Paramount, and had frequent roles in radio dramas.

"Boys, I've got the world by the tail on a downhill pull," he'd told the press not long ago, "Hollywood, the stage, radio—how that dough is going to roll in. You guys will be writing about how I light cigars with thousand-dollar bills."

The Roaring Twenties had never stopped for the champ, who'd famously pulled up to New York's Plaza Hotel five years earlier in a sixteen-cylinder Cadillac driven by a chauffeur. He had ten pairs of trunks and thirty suits of clothes, and an entourage that included a secretary, a manager, and a trainer. But Gould knew Baer had traveled more than just a continent from his beginnings in his father's California slaughterhouse, where he'd killed steers with a sledgehammer, skinned them, and hoisted their carcasses up to drain. With his copy of Emily Post, he'd managed to smooth the rough edges, learning how to order a meal in a fine restaurant, eat salad with the correct fork. Nevertheless, no matter what social circles the heavyweight now traveled in, Gould had no doubt the man was still capable of delivering killing blows.

Joe's attention moved away from Baer when he noticed a white-coated waiter approaching their booth, a silver tray with crystal champagne glasses in one hand, an ice bucket in the other. He set down the tray and pulled a champagne bottle out of the bucket, displaying its label to Braddock and Gould. "From the gentleman at the bar . . . Mr. Baer said to wish you *Bon voyage.*"

Jim looked at Mae. The blood had run out of her face. He stood. The alarmed waiter backed up.

"Jimmy—" said Gould.

"Get the coats, Joe."

Unable to grasp the situation, Mae didn't even try to restrain her husband as he crossed the dining room, excited whispers joining gawking expressions all around.

Leaning against the bar, Baer watched him approach, flashed a grin that displayed even, white teeth. His companions, a blond and a redhead, caressed Braddock with curious looks. Max set his martini on the bar, crossed his thick-muscled arms.

"If it ain't Cinderella Man," Baer bellowed loud enough for the spectators to hear.

They stood toe to toe. "Thanks for the champagne, Mr. Baer. You keep saying in the papers how you're gonna kill me in the ring."

"Yeah, so?"

"You know I have three little kids. You're upsetting my family."

Baer leaned into Jim. "Listen to me, Braddock. I'm asking you sincerely not to take this fight." His tone was unexpected. More of a trusted attorney than a deadly pugilist. Baer paused, scanned the room—wary of being overheard. "People admire you. You seem like a decent fellow. I really don't want to hurt you. It's no joke, pal. People die in fairy tales all the time."

Max waited for a response. Braddock's gaze was stony. The chandelier above them could have been the sword of Damocles.

Suddenly a flashbulb popped. Shouts. "Max! Jim! Maxie!" A half dozen photographers and reporters burst into the club, running roughshod over the head-waiter. Max whirled to face the camera, showing teeth.

"You know, I was thinking . . ." Baer's voice was loud, now, the usual hot air inflating his chest. "Smart thing would be to take a fall. Circus act's over, old man."

Jim's browns met Baer's blues. "I think I'll try going a few rounds with the dancing bear."

Joe Gould suddenly pushed through the photographers and reporters, appeared between Braddock and Baer.

"That's a good one," he laughed, too hard. His face darkened. "Okay. Let's keep it in the ring."

Mae and Lucille stood nearby, wrapped in their coats, watching the confrontation with stunned expressions. Baer noticed Mae, bent low so he could peer into her face.

"You should talk to him, lady. You are sure too pretty to be a widow."

The women on Baer's arm tittered. Jim balled his fist, leaned forward, ready to lunge. Gould held his fighter back. "Simmer down."

Baer's smirk was mocking as he consumed Braddock's wife with his admiring gaze. "On second thought, maybe *I* can comfort you after he's gone."

This time it was Gould who leaped, fists swinging, snarling like a rabid dog.

"Joe!" shouted Lucille.

Braddock seized his manager's coat, dragged him back.

While Jim struggled to keep Joe Gould in check, Mae stepped up to the bar. Baer watched her, his sky-blue eyes curious as she reached out, grabbed his martini, and dashed it in his face.

Flashbulbs popped. Baer chuckled—a deep, menacing rumble. He accepted the attention of one of his girls as she dabbed his white coat with a linen napkin.

"Get that boys?" Baer asked the photographers. "Braddock's got his wife fighting for him."

Jim thrust Gould aside, stepped up to Max Baer, went nose to nose with his mocking face. The moment lasted long enough for a photographer to capture it for all time.

Then Braddock lips curled, but it wasn't a smile. "Yeah," he said, "she sure is something, ain't she?"

Braddock turned, took his wife's hand, led her away.

Baer caught Mae's eyes before they left. Jim saw the exchange and a cloud passed over his face. Joe Gould, arm around Lucille, pushed the fighter toward the door.

Baer's laughter followed them into the street.

BAER TICKET SALE TO BEGIN

Tickets for the Max Baer-James Braddock heavyweight championship fight at the Madison Square Garden Bowl on June 13 will be placed on sale at the Garden box offices tomorrow morning at 10:30 o'clock, according to an announcement yesterday by James J. Johnston, Garden promoter. Prices will be $2, $5, and $10, plus tax, with ringside seats $20, including tax.

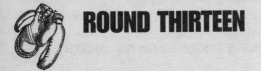

ROUND THIRTEEN

Baer was a guy that could hurt you . . . But I always said that Max should have been an actor instead of a fighter.

—James J. Braddock,
as quoted by Peter Heller in *In This Corner*

"Now, here's how you work a combination." Still dressed in his Continental Club clothes, Jim loosened his tie, draped his suit jacket on the back of a chair and knelt on the floor, ready to demonstrate the tricks of his fistic trade to Jay and Howard.

"You have to keep your head down, chin tucked. Like this." Jim struck a classic boxing pose.

Squinting in concentration, Howard lifted his fists and gamely tried to mimic his father. Jay, a little taller and longer limbed, had an easier time of it, his fighting stance a spitting image of Jim's.

At the basement apartment's cracked sink, Mae stood scouring a cast-iron skillet she'd used to warm the smuggled leftovers for the kids. As her husband talked, she felt her fingers tightening on the wire brush, her circular motions becoming more violent.

"Okay, now give me a left, right, left," said Jim.

Skinny arms windmilled, earnestly battling air. When Jay threw his right, he lifted his chin. Jim reached forward, gently bumping his son's jaw with a closed fist.

"Oops," said Jim with a wink. "See what just happened?"

"Yeah!" Howard cried. "Jay got *clocked*."

"You know why?"

The boys shook their heads.

"He was so busy punching, he wasn't paying attention." Jim threw slow-motion punches. "Never take your eyes off your opponent."

Mac spoke without turning. "That's enough, now."

Jim glanced at his wife, unable to suppress his pride. "There's more than one fighter in the Braddock family, tell you that."

Jay bounded around the cramped basement apartment, sparring against an imaginary foe. Howard looked up. "What about the *left*, Dad?"

Jim tucked his own chin, then feinted a straight jab at his son's nose. "Like that?"

Howard followed the jab until his eyes crossed, then nodded enthusiastically. Suddenly, Jay tossed off a right that threw him off balance. The boy slammed into the easy chair, rocking it.

Mae whirled, exploded. "I said that's enough, Jay Braddock!" The dripping skillet slipped from her hand and clattered to the hardwood floor.

The boys froze, doe-eyed. Jim stared too.

Mae clutched the edge of the sink with one hand. She'd tried to be stoic, but her head was pounding, the elegant dinner turned rancid in her stomach. "No boxing in the house. No boxing out of the house. No boxing, period."

Ignoring her husband, Mae pointed at her slack-jawed sons. "You are going to stay in school. Then college. You are going to have professions. You are not going to get your skulls smashed in, is that clear?"

Before the boys could reply or even retreat, Mae turned her back on her family, yanked open the basement apartment's door and ran out.

Jim hustled the boys off to bed, tucked them in. He comforted Rose Marie, who'd been startled awake by her mother's loud voice.

Mae hugged herself against the damp April chill, her back turned against the dingy apartment house, against her husband. Instead, she faced the dismal silhouettes littering the dark weeds of the tenement's junk-strewn backyard—broken chairs, discarded pipes, and rising above it all a smokestack in the distance spewing choking fumes. A siren wailed somewhere north, and she suddenly saw the smirk of Max Baer in those billowing clouds. The sneer of Sporty Lewis—

"Mrs. Braddock, my question is for you . . . My readers want to know, how do you feel about the fact that Max Baer has killed two men in the ring?"

Mae heard Jim's steps behind her. He was coming for her, would want to know what was wrong.

"Mae?"

She didn't turn to face him. She just couldn't, not until she told him how she felt. In the distance, the siren's wail faded. She swallowed her nerves, tried to summon her courage, then finally confessed to her husband the secret she'd kept for so many years.

"I used to pray for you to get hurt—"

Jim stepped back, the words hitting him physically.

"Just enough so you couldn't fight anymore," she added quickly.

He blinked, speechless.

"And when they took your license, even scared as I was, I went to the church and thanked God for it. I always knew a day might come where a fight could kill you. I just knew . . . and now it's here."

Braddock stepped forward, touched her shoulder, turned her to face him. "You're just getting the jitters."

Mae shook his hand away. "There's more to it." She closed her eyes and for a moment was back at ringside all those years ago, enduring the spectacle that had made her vow never to watch her husband fight again . . .

Blood. She'd seen blood before in a boxing match, but never so much, and never so much on Jim. He'd been brutally slammed to the canvas that night, his face bruised, streaked in crimson. And the men around her, the bookies, the reporters, the fight fans, they just kept talking about Jim as if he were some racehorse they'd laid a bet on. "Ain't showin' much stamina," or "He ain't got the legs," or "Nix to the odds with this guy . . ."

Mae opened her eyes in the tenement yard, found her husband's gaze in the shadows. "We've got enough now. Why can't you stop?" Her voice was pleading.

This time it was Jim who turned away.

Mae's fists balled. "He's killed two men, Jim. Why fight him? What's worth it?"

Jim frowned. Stared at the grimy brick wall. "This is what I know how to do."

Mae watched his broad shoulders. Waited for him to turn back to her, to take her in his arms, to tell her he'd change his mind.

But Jim didn't turn. A part of him wished he could—the part that wanted to be a good husband, to give Mae anything she asked for. But life hadn't made that possible for him. His wife just didn't understand how he felt, how Mike Wilson felt. They were capable, strong, hardworking men, but the world had told them they were helpless, worthless. They were proud husbands and fathers who'd found themselves unable to take care of their wives, their families. He wanted to tell Mae about the thousands of other men living on the streets, in the shantytown Hoovervilles, the ones who'd gathered around him outside the Garden when he'd won the Lasky fight—men who were in the same fix as he was, and who now looked up to the boxer they called the Cinderella Man with something like hope in their eyes.

Jim struggled to find the right words, then turned and slowly shared them. "I have to believe I have some say over our lives, see? That sometimes, I can change things. If I don't . . . It's like I'm dead already."

Mae bit her lip, seeing the stubbornness in her husband's face. "I need you to be safe . . . so much."

Jim lifted his chin. "Look around, Mae. Nothing's safe anymore."

Mae's anxiety shrank and her rage rose. Her husband appeared to be brushing off her fears as inconsequentially as snowflakes from his sleeve. In her mind, he was treating her the very same way he had last summer, when she'd stood in this very yard and pleaded with him not to return to the ring. But she wasn't backing down this time, she told herself. This time was different. This was his life.

"I stood by until now. For all of it." Mae's eyes, damp with tears of fright had turned to stone. "But not for this, Jim. I just can't."

"Mae—"

"So you train all you want. Make a show of it for yourself, for the newspapers. But you find a way out of this fight, Jim." Mae's voice went cold. "Break your hand again, if you have to. But if you set foot out of this door to fight Max Baer, I won't be behind you anymore."

On June 13, 1935, Joe Gould pulled his roadster up to the curb, cut the engine. He stepped onto the sunwashed sidewalk, blinking against the glare. It was early—too early for reporters to show, to ask endless questions and take endless photographs. Too early, even, for the milk man. But it was already uncomfortably hot on the streets of Union City, outside Joe Jeannette's gym and Gould knew it was bound to get hotter as the day progressed.

He paused at the gym's front door to savor what remained of his morning cigar. Though Gould hadn't crossed the river in three days, he had been working harder than ever. Full time, and then some. All for Jim Braddock.

While keeping the public happy and hungry, and the fistic press close and at bay at the same time, Gould was also trying to line up contracts to secure Braddock's future. Not fight contracts, either—these were deals for testimonials, endorsements, appearances, for advertisements and speeches. Lucrative contracts signed in advance and set to pay off in the event that Braddock won the championship title.

Boxing tradition allowed the heavyweight champ a two-year grace period before he was required to fight another challenger. That unwritten law allowed fighters who battled their way to the top spot an opportunity to make real money, provide for their retirement from the ring. With odds running ten to one against Braddock, Gould wasn't having an easy time securing the best deals. But he refused to accept anything less.

"When Jimmy wins the title, you'll be back," he'd told anyone with doubts. "And by then the price will have doubled—tripled, even."

Gould's goal was to make sure that at the end of the day, Braddock received one of the biggest paydays of all times. It was the least he could do for the man who would step into the ring with Max Baer that very evening, the man he had pushed to the limits of his physical and mental endurance each and every day for the past six months.

An example of this intensity had come early on, with the manager's choice of sparring partners. Though Gould retained Joe Jeannette's picks—including George Robbins, the quick and wiry welterweight—he also recruited a quartet of sturdy sluggers from across the country. The biggest of the bunch was Paul Pross, a two-hundred-ten-pound German boxer whose father died on the Western Front the day he was born. Not only did Pross outweigh Braddock, he also had a longer reach.

Norm Barnett was another heavyweight. A former University of Maryland fullback who came in at 205, he ducked and swayed better than most champs, and he punched like a mule kick.

For stamina, Gould found Jack McCarthy, a beefy Massachusetts Irishman who'd sparred with Jack Sharkey and was still quick on his feet after hours of grueling work. For quickness and hitting power, Gould hired Don Petrin, a speed artist who'd been kicked out of Max Schmeling's camp for showing up the German in front of the national press.

"Together they formed the best set of sparring partners to prepare a heavyweight since Dempsey's days," wrote Lud, sports reporter for Union City's *Hudson Dispatch*. Similarly, in his own column, Sporty Lewis compared the preparations for the Baer versus Braddock bout with the hoopla leading up to the Dempsey–Tunney title fight of 1924.

Gould thought it an apt observation. Back in 1924, after studying Jack Dempsey's technique on film, Gene Tunney easily evaded the champ's rushes to be crowned the new heavyweight champion. It helped that Dempsey was overconfident and out of shape as a result of his playboy lifestyle, and there was a parallel here too. Max Baer had not stopped making outrageous statements to the press about how easily he was going to defeat Jim Braddock. His latest demand—that an ambulance be posted at the Madison Square Garden Bowl to rush Braddock to a local hospital—was only the latest in a long string of contemptuous stunts. To Gould, Baer's hot air sounded an awful lot like over-confidence, which was something Braddock, like Gene Tunney, could exploit.

Also in the spirit of the Dempsey vs. Tunney bout, Braddock had made good use of Max Baer's fight footage provided by Jimmy Johnston. At the start of training, Braddock, Gould, and Joe Jeannette reviewed those films daily for hours at a time, often watching two or three fights in the same sitting.

"Watch him," said Jeannette when they viewed the Primo Carnera title fight. "After all this time, Baer's still a sharpshooter. Dempsey tried to fix him but it didn't stick. Madcap Maxie still telegraphs every move."

Jeannette, as intent as Braddock in going for Baer's jugular, ran the footage back and forth until the film broke. While Jeannette and Jim talked strategy, Gould—who'd watched Baer's power punches with mounting dread—secretly concluded that strategy could get Jim Braddock only so far. Probably not far enough.

After that, sparring became all-out war with both sides taking punishment. By early May, the workouts at Jeannette's gym had become furious punching bees with six, seven, even eight three-minute-round bouts mounted every afternoon around four o'clock. During these grueling marathons, Gould alternated sparring partners so that Jim faced a fresh fighter every single round.

The press was surprised to find there was real boxing going on at Joe Jeannette's gym, and flocked to see more. In the early going, Braddock's performance did not impress those who witnessed it. Heavyweights

Pross and McCarthy connected regularly with right handers—so many that one newspaper reported that Braddock had been "hit fifty times on the lug in eight rounds." Other sportswriters wondered whether the challenger and his manager had gone complete crazy. Things had become so brutal that Braddock's training camp became known as Murderers' Row.

But if Gould was crazy, there was a method in his madness. Every day Braddock was learning how to withstand right-hand punches, and how to block them too. In the long run, these harsh tactics paid off in spades. By the beginning of June, less than two weeks before the fight, Gould and Jeannette both agreed that Jim Braddock was in the finest shape of his boxing career. Though Jeannette voiced doubts about Jim's ribs, both agreed that Braddock could easily go a full fifteen rounds.

That same afternoon, Murray Robinson of the Newark *Star Eagle* had heard Gould, in a burst of exuberance, crow, "Look at Braddock, will you! He's going to be in wonderful shape, if he lives!"

Gould had laughed when he saw his words printed in the paper the next morning—until Lucille reminded her husband that Mae Braddock would be reading them as well.

The honk of a passing newspaper truck interrupted Gould's revelry. He sucked on his cold stogie, then tossed it into the street. At the top of the stairs, Gould found George Robbins in the ring, punching air while Braddock sat alone in the corner, face grim, a flak jacket wrapped tightly around his torso.

Gould frowned and approached Joe Jeannette. "What's wrong with him?"

"Came in. Warmed up. Hasn't said two words."

Gould studied his fighter, unhappy to see the flak jacket. "So, how's he doing?"

Jeannette shrugged. "He's in the best shape of his life. But he's old, he's arthritic, and his ribs aren't right since Lasky."

Gould knew about the ribs, fretted about them, too—just like Joe Jeannette. But he also sensed something else was bothering Braddock. Maybe it was money, which was bothering everybody. Or maybe it was personal. Braddock had a wife who wasn't particularly happy about his choice of profession, and a family he had to clothe and house and feed. Thankfully, Joe Gould could only imagine what that was like.

Well, whatever the issue, Braddock sure didn't have time to deal with it now. Not with the title fight just hours away.

Braddock stood just then, faced his manager. But before they could speak, a bucket boy hurried up to them, spoke into Gould's ear.

"The press is here," said Gould. "Peel that rig off or Baer'll see you got a rib problem."

Jim stripped off the flak jacket and the bucket boy hustled it out of sight. A crowd of jostling men rolled up the steps and burst into the gym. A few began barking questions as soon as they spied the challenger. Gould watched, frowning, as Braddock turned his back on the clamoring mob and climbed into the ring.

After the morning antics staged for the press had ended, Gould was summoned to Jimmy Johnston's office for a last-minute powwow concerning what the press called "the referee problem." The issue started when the New York Boxing Commission named Jack Dempsey as referee for the title fight. Braddock objected—not on personal grounds, as he was a great admirer of the former champ. Jim was upset with the choice because at one time, Dempsey had trained Max Baer, and had owned a piece of the fighter once too.

Jim and Joe Gould both doubted they would get a fair shake. Gould told the commission that any ref they named was fine with Braddock, so long as his last name wasn't Dempsey.

Meanwhile Baer's manager, Ancil Hoffman, objected strenuously to the commission's second choice, an experienced ref named Arthur Donovan. Donovan had refereed the Carnera versus Baer fight. Though Baer was declared the winner hands down, both Baer and Ancil thought Donovan shortchanged them with his final score. During the weeks that the dispute had raged in the press and in the commission, neither side had given in. Despite the hastily called meeting with the commission on the very day of the fight, it appeared that Baer and Braddock were going into the title bout without knowing who their referee would be.

After the press vanished to file their stories and Gould departed for the city, Jim told Jeannette he wanted to spar some more, but Joe refused. "Go home, Jim. Get some rest. You're gonna get plenty enough sparring tonight."

So Jim Braddock went home, unsure of the welcome he would receive. He came through the front door, leaned his rucksack against the wall. The house was empty except for Mae, who stood silently at the kitchen table, the daily newspaper spread flat on its surface.

Jim smiled a greeting but Mae looked away. Her face was tight, closed. A wall. Her back to him, Mae crossed to the sink, then walked away.

Alone at the kitchen table, Jim read the headline.

**WORLD CHAMPION FIGHT TONIGHT
BAER VERSUS BRADDOCK IN
LONG ISLAND CITY BOWL
MANY WORRY FOR BRADDOCK'S LIFE**

Jim walked stoically to the bed, began to undress. He lay sleepless and alone as the sun crossed the sky and morning became afternoon.

At four o'clock a cab arrived and waited on the street, engine idling. Local well-wishers began to gather in front of the tenement house. His kids were out there with them, romping and playing.

Mae stood at the basement window, her slim form tense, face pale. Something split open inside him as he watched the afternoon sun gleam golden through her brown hair, saw how her blue eyes reflected the sky. At that moment, he longed to touch her, pull her into his arms.

She followed him out the door, and he made his way to the street, shaking hands and accepting his neighbors' benedictions.

"Go get 'em, Jimmy!"

"Come home with that title, now!"

"Knock him out!"

"You show 'em!"

"We're behind ya all the way!"

Howard raced up to him. Jim snatched his son's belt, lifted the squirming boy, lowered his head and kissed his forehead. Still cradling his youngest son, Jim bent lower to kiss Jay too. The boy smiled up at him. His smile was proud, but his brow was crinkled with worry. Little Rosy was next. Jim caught her up in a bear hug, buried his face in her sweet dark hair.

The crowd grew even bigger, the shouts more zealous. Finally, Jim released his daughter and faced his wife. For a moment Mae didn't move. Then she stretched up and kissed him.

He bent close, his eyes asking, hoping. "I can't win if you're not behind me."

"Then don't go, Jimmy."

The moment hung into forever, each waiting for the other to relent. Finally, Mae turned and pulled the children close. Jim watched as she pushed her way back through the throng, taking the children with her as the crowd closed ranks, swallowing them up.

Jim climbed into the waiting car, slumped into the cushioned seat. An hour later, the cab was rolling through the canyons of Manhattan's skyscrapers. They crossed town along Forty-second Street, passed Times Square and idled at a long Sixth-Avenue red light. Jim sat up straighter in his seat, peered curiously at the sight ahead.

"What's that?" he asked the driver.

"What's what?"

Jim pointed.

"Bryant Park," the driver said in a "where *you* been anyways?" tone. Then he laughed. "Sorry, Mr. Braddock. Guess you ain't been getting' around much . . . with your trainin' and all."

The cabbie kept talking. Told Jim that New York City had a new mayor now. Jimmy Walker, that crooked official who'd previously held the office and done little to nothing to help the city's destitute and unemployed, had been convicted of corruption and run out of town by a crusading judge. Now a man by the name of La Guardia was mayor.

After the worst winter in recent memory, the new mayor had gone to see President Roosevelt, secured federal assistance, hired a city parks Commissioner by the name of Robert Moses and got six hundred unemployed architects and engineers working again. Then they'd hired field superintendents and unemployed men.

By the time summer's warmth sent the people of New York into their parks again, the citizens discovered that something had changed. Those newly employed crews had completed seven hundred different renovation projects. They'd repaved thirty-eight miles of cracked walks, repaired countless broken fences, repainted buildings and benches, reseeded lawns, resurfaced ruined tennis courts, and planted more than ten thousand trees.

In Central Park there was a new zoo, and one in Brooklyn's Prospect Park too. More playgrounds and swimming pools were being planned for the future including one in Astoria, Queens, that would accommodate 6,200 bathers. And there were big plans for the New York shorelines, from the Bronx to Brooklyn and Queens—talk of new beaches and parkways, new construction . . . all of which meant new jobs.

Jim gazed at Bryant Park, stunned. He remembered

only a seedy lot being there—an empty five-acre space of weeds and wandering vagrants with the crumbling remains of a plaster statue at the west end. All that was gone now. In the heart of midtown Manhattan sat a completely green space. A formal garden with two hundred London plane trees, flagstone walkways, and a large, elegant stone fountain. It was a beautiful space, remade by an army of unemployed—for all the public to enjoy.

The cabbie drove on. As they crossed the East River to the borough of Queens, Jim rode silently, preparing his mind for the fight, running the Baer fight films through his head again and again, hearing Jeannette's words, Gould's advice, trying for anything that would block out Mae's stony face, her cold words.

Finally, the car rolled down Northern Boulevard and pulled up to the Madison Square Garden Bowl, Jim gazed out the window at the mob standing outside the outdoor arena, waiting to get in. Men and women, young and old. Their clothes were worn and tattered, their faces creased with the hard struggles they went through every day of their lives. Yet they had a bright look in their eyes—expectation, possibility, hope. Jim caught a reflection in the car window, saw himself in the midst of all that.

He studied his face in the window, and recognized something about it. Gone forever was the self-assured man who'd KO'd Tuffy Griffiths with ease. Gone too was the hopeless wretch who passed his hat at the boxing club and accepted relief from the government to feed his family. In its place was every man who'd ever been savagely beaten down by hard times yet wouldn't stop fighting.

That's when Jim knew. No matter what happened tonight—whether he walked away with the title, or perished inside the ropes—Jim would not give in. He would die trying.

On the streets of Long Island City, Queens, the temperature soared above eighty degrees before noon and continued to rise. In Jim Braddock's expansive dressing room at the Madison Square Garden Bowl, a clattering fan provided a sultry breeze that did little to cut the torridity.

Jim sweated in his trunks, robe draped over a chair. He was waiting for the weigh-in ceremony to begin. Thirty minutes ago they had been told "any minute" by one of Jimmy Johnston's lackeys. Meanwhile the physician and judge had arrived and were ready to preside, the commissioners were on their second cigars, and the press was clamoring. The only thing missing was Max Baer.

"There's Jimmy Johnston, puffing like a chimney," said Joe Gould. He stood at the dressing door, open a crack. "Leave it to Madcap Maxie to be late for his own funeral." Gould crossed the room. "Are you hot? I'm hot."

"It's hot, Joe."

Three powerful knocks. The third swung the door open and it banged the wall. Max Baer filled the doorway, silk robe flowing over his hard-muscled frame like a blue waterfall. He made for Jim right away, a · half sneer, half smile plastered on his face. Gould, a pit bull in sea-green trousers and yellow polo shirt, leaped between the fighters.

"Get away from here, you bum," snarled Gould, poking his finger into Baer's hard-muscled chest.

Baer stopped, looked over Gould's head, to Braddock. "I got something to say—"

"If you got anything to say, say it tonight—in the ring," Gould cried.

Ancil Hoffman appeared, tie loose, harried. He pushed the champ out of the dressing room.

"Yeah, all right, I'll go," Baer said peevishly. In the hallway, Baer lashed out at another spectator, Mike Cantwell, his old trainer. The fight world knew they hadn't parted on good terms. Flashbulbs popped and angry words were exchanged.

Gould slammed the dressing room door, twisted the lock. "It's like a goddamn dime novel out there."

After that, Gould strutted like a bantam. "I sure fixed Baer's wagon," he crowed, chest puffed.

"You sure did," said Jim.

Another knock. "Five minutes," barked a voice.

Jim rose. Gould lifted the robe and held it. "Ready, champ," he said, slapping a broad shoulder.

"Ain't we jumping the gun, Joe? Last time I looked, I was the challenger."

"I says champ and champ I meant," Gould replied. "You better get used to it, Jimmy boy."

In the hallway, General Phelan, the New York Boxing Commission head, was admonishing Baer and the sputtering Mike Cantwell, an elderly gent in a straw hat.

"Here, here, cut that out." Phelan sniffed. "I'm running this thing and I want order."

Peace was restored. Joe and Jim squirmed through the throng packed into the weigh-in room. Among the swarm of officials, reporters, photographers, and handlers, the heat was so furious it seemed like hell had opened and the devil was breathing fire in every direction.

Jimmy Johnston looked on as Max Baer, in black trunks, stepped up to the officials. Johnston, angry over Baer's late arrival, couldn't hide his sneer. Flashbulbs popped as the heavyweight champion stripped off his robe, threw up his fists, and climbed onto the scale.

"Two hundred and ten pounds," the judge declared.

Already down to his navy blue trunks, which were emblazoned with a large green shamrock, Jim climbed onto the scale.

"One hundred and ninety-one pounds," said the judge.

Braddock stepped down—and into the path of Max Baer. The champ shook his head.

"How's the story go?" roared Madcap Maxie, mugging for the press. "The clock strikes midnight, the coach"—He shot a look at Joe Gould—"turns into a pumpkin, and the Cinderella Man loses her skirt."

Laughter rippled the crowd. Gould glowered. Braddock shrugged, unfazed. When Baer flashed a dangerous grin at Jim, Braddock grinned back.

Around them flashbulbs exploded like heat lightning.

"Watch it, now . . . Here it comes. Right there . . . Art Lasky wailed him good . . ."

Max leaned forward in his chair as he watched the movie screen—grainy black-and-white footage of

Lasky versus Braddock. As Baer watched, Lasky moved in, slammed Braddock's torso and the Irishman reeled.

"His ribs are mushy," said the trainer. "I got it on good authority. If you can connect with his right, tap Braddock on the ribs a few times—sharp jabs. He's weak, you can hurt 'em."

Baer sneered. "I won't need to smack his ribs. I can floor this mug any time I want to—put him on the canvas. What's important is that I give 'em a good show before I kill the guy."

The trainer frowned, turned off the projector. Maxie's redhead rose and switched on the lights. On a long couch in a corner, the blond yawned, stretched like a lazy cat.

Baer's dressing room was all show business—makeup lights circled the mirror, photos of Baer with various celebrities and movie stars hung on the walls, stood in silver frames on countertops. Mammoth bouquets of bright flowers were strewn about, sent long distance by the cream of the Hollywood establishment. Actors, producers, and directors all loved Maxie, adopted the heavyweight champion as a member of their exclusive "club"—mostly because his arrogant, self-aggrandizing manner mimicked their own.

A knock. The door opened and Ancil Hoffman burst into the room. Baer stood, faced him. "You get it there like I told you?"

"Yeah," said Ancil.

"You sure!" Baer roared.

"The ambulance is at the back gate, Max," Ancil cried. "Jeez, calm down. There's a doc there, too. I just checked it myself."

Max cursed, shook his head. He turned to peer into the mirror.

"That's all I can do for him, then," he said, his voice hoarse. "Now Braddock's on his own."

Mae Braddock spent the rest of the day at her sister Alice's house. Jay and Howard played in the yard, Rosy drew pictures on the sunny front porch. Alice and Mae drank coffee, shared lunch, and spoke of many things. Both women carefully shied away from any discussion about the real reason for Mae's visit.

But as the shadows lengthened, the conversation lagged. Mae's silence grew longer. She glanced more often at the Art Deco clock on the mantel, as the afternoon waned. When Alice offered her a glass of her favorite wine, Mae declined. Distractedly, she gazed out the window until Alice gave up trying to engage her.

Then, at five o'clock, Mae rose abruptly, pinned on her hat. Wordlessly, she crossed to the front door, where she paused.

"No radio, Alice."

Mae's sister frowned, nodded.

"I'll be back soon."

As Mae strode across the lawn, Howard and Jay watched her go, and Rosy looked up from her pencils.

She walked alone for a long time through the deserted streets of Newark. The shadows stretched until they darkened the streets. All was quiet until she came to Father Rorick's church.

Though no regular service was scheduled for this hour, people were streaming through the open doors. Inside, the lights were bright. Mae wondered as she crossed the courtyard if a funeral or even a wedding was in progress. Then Mae spied Father Rorick at the door and approached him.

"Father?" she asked, puzzled. Peering around him, Mae saw that the church was full to brimming, with people lining up in the aisles as well.

"Hello, Mae," said Father Rorick.

"I came to pray for Jim."

"You too?" said the priest. He stepped back, directing her gaze to the church's interior. "So have they."

Mae blinked, surveyed the full pews, the people in worn clothes praying on their knees in the aisle, and shook her head.

"I don't—" Her voice faded as realization dawned.

"Maybe sometimes people need to see someone do it so they can do it themselves," said Father Rorick. "They think Jim's fighting for them."

Mae looked over the crowd again. She saw men from the docks, vagrants from the street, women and children who'd been abandoned—all of them thrown aside by the world, challenged to summon enough fight inside themselves to keep going. They looked up to her husband, Mae realized, all of them. Jim Braddock had become their example . . . if he could fight and win, maybe they could too . . .

"Yes," Mae whispered. "I understand now."

Mae turned, hurried into the street. As her heels clicked down the sidewalk, she noticed knots of men and women gathering in doorways, outside of shops. Through open windows and doors radios blared. They were all tuned to the same station—the announcer excitedly teasing the title fight about to begin.

The same thing was happening at Quincy's bar, in Sam's butcher shop, at the docks, the rail yards, the

coal shuttles—even the Newark relief office. Any-
where there was a radio, a crowd of hungry, eager people crowded around to listen.

It wasn't only happening in Newark, either. The
fight of the century and the fate of the Cinderella Man
had become the fodder for national news. From coast
to coast, from the Mexican border to Canada—all
across the nation, from rusty factory towns to the hot,
barren farms of the Dust Bowl, idle fisheries to ramshackle shantytowns—men without jobs, women without hope, tuned in to hear the boxer Damon Runyon
dubbed the Cinderella Man fight. They listened and
hoped that Jim Braddock would beat the odds that had
all but crushed the rest of them.

They prayed that Jim Braddock would win. That he
would finally become the prince, the king, the
champion—and that this fight would not end their
beloved Cinderella Man.

The crowd roared, a palpable wall of noise that shook
the walls, wafted upward, into the warm night sky.

In his dressing room, Braddock felt the tension. He
sat patiently on a wooden bench while Joe Gould taped
up his hands. The echoes from the vast stadium rum-
bled in their chests like the growl of a hungry lion. Joe
ripped the tape, tossed the roll onto the bench, slapped
his fighter's broad back.

"Who beat John Henry Lewis?"

Jim smiled. Their old game. "That would be me."

"Who whupped Lasky?"

"As far as I can tell, that would have been me too."

Joe grinned. "Who—"

A knock interrupted him. Braddock's back was facing the door, but Gould looked up. When it opened, a small, frail, familiar shape swayed like a slender reed in the doorway. Gould's grin widened. Jim noticed his manager's look, swiveled his neck. Mae Braddock's eyes met her husband's.

"I tell you," Gould said. "That's a bet I shoulda taken."

"Joe . . ." Gould looked up. Jim put his finger to his lips. "Shhh."

Gould rose. " 'Scuse me a minute." He slipped past Mae, out the door, closed it behind him.

For a long minute, no words came. Finally, Mae spoke. "You can't win without me behind you."

Jim swallowed, spoke. "That's what I keep telling you."

"Thought it looked like rain, you know. Used what was in the jar." Mae handed Jim a brown paper bag, bulky and heavy. The paper crinkled as he opened it, stared at a brand new pair of boxing shoes inside.

"Maybe I understand some," Mae said, eyes shining. "About having to fight."

Jim rose, caught her up in his powerful arms. They kissed and kissed again. Mae's words flowed in a torrent. "I don't know what I was saying, I'm always behind you Jimmy, with you and inside you and in love with you. So you just . . . just you remember who you really are."

"Who's that?"

"You're the Bulldog of Bergen," she said, smiling through her tears. "The pride of New Jersey. You're everybody's hope and your kids' hero and you're the champion of my heart, James J. Braddock."

They kissed again. Then, with a devilish grin, Jim

leaned close to his wife's ear. "You better get home.
Boxers hang around places like this, and you don't
wanna get tangled up with that crowd . . . Nice girl like
you . . ."

Mae laughed. Her gaze was brave, stoic, despite the
fear that still threatened to engulf her.

"See you at home, okay?" she whispered, fighting
hard to bite back more tears. "Please, Jimmy . . . See
you at home."

Jim nodded. "See you at home."

ROUND FOURTEEN

. . . Letters came to Braddock from all over the world. . . . most of them were from those whom life had treated shabbily . . . from those who had been left alone in the world and who were plodding in a weary way, hopeless until this big guy had come swinging back from obscurity to show them how a losing fight could be won.

—John D. McCallum,
Encyclopedia of World Boxing Champions

Madison Square Garden Bowl
Long Island City, New York
June 13, 1935

Jim Braddock closed the dressing-room door, moved through a long, dimly lit corridor to the shadowy stair-well. Someone called his name, the voice reverberating off the slate gray blocks of the concrete walls. A stage-hand wished Jim luck, watched his back as Braddock climbed the steps.

Ushers and concession workers gaped at the sight of Jim. He nodded politely, then stepped out into the aisle of the open-air stadium. For a moment, he saw the bruised color of the blue-black night, then a blasting glare blinded him as a spotlight swung to illuminate his walk to the ring.

Around him, the typical buzzing noises of the packed stands instantly became muted, the crowd's hushed whispers a sibilant hiss. Jim couldn't see the throng, but he was bewildered by their strange silence.

Slowly, Jim's vision returned, allowing the shape and form of the Garden Bowl to come into focus. From where he stood, at the top of the dark stadium, the ring seemed miles away, an illuminated postage stamp. The small roped-off square shimmered under the klieg lights like a dazzling diamond set on black velvet in a jeweler's glass case.

Where Jim stood now was as far away from that sparkler as a man could get. These were the cheap seats, paupers' row, hayseed heaven—and they were packed. Beneath the night sky, bodies jammed every row, every seat. But these weren't the usual fight-going folk. They were *Jim's* people, his forlorn fans. They came from Newark, Hoboken, and Weehawken; Woodside, Red Hook, and Crown Heights, wearing their very best shabby finery, heads held high for the first time in recent memory. There were so many of them here, Jim realized, so many. They sat quietly, reverently, like hollow-eyed ghosts, silent, expectant.

"God Almighty."

Jim knew their expressions—from the streets and docks, the coal house and rail yards. Men hurting for jobs, seeing no chance of a future. Women robbed of once happy homes. Some looked as if they could stand a good meal, or a stiff drink. Others seemed to have drifted over the East River from Hooverville in rags and tatters. Yet they were here tonight, using precious money they'd begged or earned—cash they should have spent on food or the rent—to buy a little piece of the Cinderella Man's shimmering gem of a dream and take it home.

He'd never seen these people before, yet Jim knew them—from the streets, the basements, the junkyards, from Sam's butcher shop, Andolini's grocery, Quincy's tavern, or a million other places like it, in a thousand other towns. Places where the beaten down congregated in a mutual pact of shared disillusionment. But there was no disappointment tonight. Instead, Jim saw awe, joy, anticipation. Their eyes followed him with wide, hopeful expressions. For the first time in years, they were transfixed by a belief in something bigger than themselves, a conviction that a fight could be won. Jim Braddock was a fairy-tale comeback that would end tonight in this place, happily or not. And they'd come here to be a part of it.

As Jim moved down the aisle, he began one of the strangest walks any boxer had ever taken to the ring. As he passed each row, the people rose to their feet, as if the bleachers were church pews and they were at Mass, standing out of respect for the celebrants' procession. Jim caught the nods, the smiles, the waves. Some reached out to touch his robe, his arm, his hair. After what seemed like an eternity, the eerie silence was broken when someone shouted his name.

Jim Braddock had spent so many years being called a bum, being jeered at, booed, discounted and written off, he didn't know what to do, really, when at the sound of his name, the pent-up emotions were released in a stadium-quaking explosion of applause.

As he approached the ropes, the cheers persisted, rising into the starry sky. That sound continued its journey across America, carried over the airwaves to radios across the nation, so loud the clamor merged into a sustained barrage of white noise. The voice of the announcer vainly tried to cut through the cacophony, but was forced to pause and wait for the shouts and applause to fade.

Back in New Jersey, Alice had been fixing a light supper for her sister's children. The soup was hot, the table set, so she went to the porch to find Jay, Howard, and Rosy and bring them inside.

She noticed immediately that Rose Marie was gone. Her pencils were lined up in a neat row on the porch step; the drawing she'd worked on most of the day was now being blown around the yard like a fallen leaf. There was no sign of Howard or Jay either, yet they'd been playing pink ball in the now darkening streets when she had gone inside to cook.

Alice tamped down her worry and went back inside, searched every room of the house, but the Braddock brood were nowhere to be found. She raced down the stairs to check the basement, loudly calling their names.

"If you're playing hide-and-seek, I want you to know that the game's over now," she cried.

No answer. Heart racing, Alice ran up two flight of stairs to check the bedrooms. Then she checked under the beds. Still no sign of her niece and nephews.

Alice was about to go outside and scour the neighborhood when she heard a muted roar—cheers and applause. The sound was coming from the back hallway. Then she spied the electrical cord running from the socket to the closet, and the empty table where her Edison radio usually rested.

She pulled open the door. Jay and Howard were huddled around the radio, which they'd dragged into the closet. Rosy was there, too, her eyes defiant. Ford Bond's familiar voice boomed out of the wooden box. Alice, hands on hips, wore a disapproving face. The boys' eyes were desperate.

No words were exchanged. At the sound of a bell, Ford Bond's distinctive voice announced the entrance of Jim Braddock. Realizing then that her cause was lost, Alice surrendered. Making room on the floor, she sat outside the open closet door and listened to the play-by-play along with the children.

"This is Ford Bond, live from the flats of Astoria and Long Island City," he screamed into his microphone. "I don't know if you can hear me out there. I can't hear myself. Madison Square Garden is on its feet and the noise is deafening!"

Braddock, still stunned by the response, was suddenly flanked by dozens of photographers, vultures circling carrion. Bulbs flashed, incomprehensible questions were shouted, adding to the general chaos around him.

Ford Bond clutched his microphone like an umbrella handle in a hailstorm, shouting into it at the top of his lungs. "We saw people lining up to buy tickets tonight . . . People who looked as if they were spending their last dollar. But they're here now, and thirty-five thousand strong. Listen to them!"

The announcer held up the microphone to capture the noise of the caterwauling mob. Jim Braddock climbed over the ropes, scanned the audience. As soon as his feet touched the canvas, the noise intensified, buffeting him like a gale-force wind.

Behind the back row, Max Baer emerged from the same doorway that Braddock had passed through. Ignored, he listened to the approving crowd, jealousy darkening his handsome features. His eyes fixed on Braddock inside the ring, basking in the applause. Baer's manager, Ancil Hoffman, and two corner men appeared at Baer's side. The boxer tapped Ernie Goins, one of his two corner men, with his glove, and then moved down the aisle, flanked by his entourage.

As the audience became aware of Baer's presence, a wave of respectful silence rolled down the stadium bleachers in a muted waterfall that matched his feral strut. Max felt the public's dread and savored it like fine wine. By the time he climbed into the ring, his chiseled features were a smirking mask, his every move, every gesture an arrogant challenge.

With both fighters inside the ring, the managers and corner men behind the ropes, photographers and members of the sporting press hurried to their ringside table. Typewriters were already clacking as Sporty Lewis, in his wrinkled seersucker suit, squeezed between the bodies of his packed-in colleagues and sank into his chair. He tossed his sweat-stained hat onto the typewriter in front of him, nodded to the cub reporter assigned to the seat beside his.

"All ready, kid?" Lewis yelled over the noise.

"Yeah, but for what?" the young reporter replied.

Sporty winked. "You never been to a funeral?"

Max Baer trotted around the ring like a stallion, accepting the boos, insults, and catcalls tossed his way as if they were an ovation. Gould, who'd slipped unnoticed into Braddock's corner, called Jim over. Alone in the center of the ring, Baer soon grew tired of his own antics and the crowd's scorn and moved into his corner too.

A moment of tense drama followed as the men in both fighters' camps awaited the arrival of the all-important third man. The ongoing dispute over the referee continued right up to the wire. Nothing had been resolved at Jimmy Johnston's last-minute powwow that morning. Gould and Braddock still nixed Dempsey; and Hoffman and Baer rejected Arthur Donovan. Adding to the mess was General Phelan, chairman of the boxing commission, who insisted that the referee be licensed in New York State. At the moment, as the fight was about to begin, neither Baer nor Braddock knew who the referee would be.

A gray-haired man built like a fireplug appeared at the ropes and climbed into the ring.

"That's Johnny McAvoy, from Brooklyn," Gould informed Braddock, relief evident in his voice.

"Yeah, I recognize him," said Doc Robb, Braddock's cutman. Ray, Braddock's other corner man, agreed. "Me too."

Gould's cherubic face beamed. "Lucky break for us. We'll get a square deal from Johnny. He's on the up-and-up. A real straight shooter. I tell ya' Jimmy, with McAvoy as ref, and Kelly and Lynch for judges, it's a great night for the Irish."

Baer's corner seemed complacent with the choice. Ancil shrugged, Ernie Goins nodded his approval.

Baer didn't know McAvoy from Adam, but he wasn't Arthur Donovan, so Max was fine with the commission's selection.

The referee spoke with the boxing officials for a few moments. Then, leaning over the ropes, he addressed Charley Lynch and George Kelly, the title fight judges. Finally McAvoy adjusted his bow tie and moved to the center of the ring. Hands on hips, he summoned the boxers and their corner men.

"I want a clean fight," McAvoy said in a whiskey voice. "When I say break, I want you to step back, 'cause I won't say it twice. And remember"— McAvoy's eyes caught Braddock's—"protect yourself at all times."

McAvoy stepped away from the huddle. "Shake."

Braddock and Baer touched gloves. Max flashed white, straight, movie-star teeth. Braddock's expression stayed neutral. Before they broke and returned to their respective corners, Ernie dangled a gold watch in front of Jim's face.

"One minute to midnight, Cinderella!"

Gould lunged at the man, caught himself, then waved the punk back to his own corner. "You ain't worth it, ya little turd," he muttered, climbing out of the ring.

Braddock stripped off his robe to reveal a scrapper's body, lean and sculpted with a rock-hard chest and thighs clad in blue trunks with a green shamrock emblazoned on the right leg. On the other side, the Californian was down to his black trunks, his powerful, bronzed muscles rippling under the glare of the stadium's man-made daylight.

Ancil spoke intensely to Baer, who kept waving his manager off with a grimace of annoyed impatience that said he'd heard it all before and was sick of it already. Jim leaned into the ropes, closed his eyes. He seemed relaxed, calm, almost as if he were praying.

"Keep your hands up, Jimmy," said Gould.

Jim nodded.

At ringside, Ford Bond was nearly whispering into his microphone. "Jim Braddock's rise from the soup lines to number-one heavyweight contender has truly been miraculous. Now, never in all my years, have I seen the arena so quiet."

Then the clang of the bell crashed through the silence to mark the start of the fight.

ROUND 1

Braddock leaped out of his corner, lean and determined, a lunging predator. Before Baer even made it to the center of the ring, Jim was on him, a light tap with his left followed by a stiff right to Baer's body.

Braddock's tactic—to catch the champ completely by surprise with an aggressive, well-directed attack— was the same one Baer himself had used in his first round with the German Max Schmeling in the title fight back in 1933. Braddock knew this because he'd watched the film. Yet Baer seemed unprepared for the assault, and shaken by Braddock's unexpected intensity.

The Cinderella Man's no-fear ferocity lifted the audience out of their seats.

But Baer recovered quickly and came back at Braddock with a short uppercut that missed Jim's chin by less than an inch. Braddock stepped away, circled Baer until he spied an opening in the champ's defenses, then closed on him again.

This time Baer was ready, delivering a left hook that smashed Jim's ribs and set his teeth grinding against the mouthpiece. Jimmy swallowed the punch and spit it back in the form of a twisting hook—right into Baer's side.

Spun by the blow, Baer dropped his fists, leaving himself wide open for a combination. Braddock let him have a long, stinging right to the face. Baer grunted, sneered. Braddock let fly with another right, then a left, and a final terrific right that bounced off the champ's iron jaw.

Max grunted, clinched with Braddock in a sweaty embrace. Baer blinked then grinned through the mouth guard. "Now, now," he said, a parent chiding a naughty child. Before Braddock could reply, McAvoy barked, made them break. Braddock danced away, his foot-work dazzling, and then he charged again.

Jim's three early rights, all of them robust, had stunned Max Baer, as much by their authority and con-trol as their power. For the first time, Baer realized that Braddock had the kick of a mule in his arm. But the champion refused to show any discomfort to the audi-ence. He began to clown instead. As he easily blocked several jabs, using his powerful right to swat them aside, he laughed and pranced. But Jim relentlessly pressed his advance and they clinched again.

"Calm down, old man," Baer said. "I'll let the fight go a few rounds."

The ref pushed them apart. As he stepped back, Baer

hooked a sneaky left to Braddock's body. Though it was too weak and too low to hurt Jim's vulnerable ribs, the punch was followed by a right that sent Braddock's teeth rattling. Jim ignored the splinters of light, sent two soft lefts—return postcards—to Baer's cranium. Then Braddock walloped his opponent with a third left, this one with real muscle behind it.

Baer didn't appear to feel the punch, though he came up short with a counter tossed at Braddock's head. As Madcap Maxie danced away, the bell clanged to end the round.

The champ had clearly lost the round on points, yet he strolled casually to his corner with an air of smug superiority, still confident that he could end this fight at any time with one deadly punch.

Meanwhile, the crowd's raucous cheers rang heaven's doorbell. Even the members of the first estate, who figured to a man that the fight would be over by now, were stunned by Braddock's driving performance. Sporty Lewis outwardly speculated how many minutes into the second round Braddock would remain alive, but he removed his suit jacket and loosened his tie while he talked, secretly realizing, after a look at Braddock's focused control, that he was in for a long night in the summer heat.

At the ropes, Gould met Jim with a ready grin. "Did you see that look on Baer's face when ya clocked 'im?" the little manager cried.

Braddock spit out his mouthpiece, nodded. "Yeah. He was *grinning*."

"So use that magic left of yours to wipe that smirk off his goddamn face."

Jim glanced across the canvas expanse, to see Ancil giving it to Baer. Once again, Baer waved his manager away, spoke words broad enough to lip read: "I'll kill him when I'm ready."

Doc Robb checked Braddock's face. Like any good cutman, he was prepared to stem any blood flow before it limited Braddock's vision. Ray slipped Jim a towel, passed him some water. Finally, Gould leaned in.

Decades of experience had taught Joe the difference between a good corner man and a lousy one. The lousy one crammed the boxer's head full of stuff he'd never remember. The good one gave his fighter one usable tactic between each round—just one decent tip his guy could use to maybe turn the fight around.

"Your left, Jimmy," Gould barked into Braddock's cauliflower ear. "Remember your left."

The bell rang—

ROUND 2

The audience couldn't believe their eyes when Braddock came out swinging at the sound of the bell. Reporting from ringside, even Ford Bond seemed perplexed by this unforeseen turn of events.

"A fight that no one expected to go one round has gone two," cried Bond. "But only because Max Baer is toying with Braddock—there is no other word for it. He's hardly thrown a punch and is laughing at Braddock's every strike."

Jim delivered a long left to the champ's smirking face, but missed with his follow-up and Baer snickered. They traded lefts, then Baer ripped a hard right to

Braddock's body. Jimmy replied with three straight rights, bashing the sneer off Maxie's mug.

Eyes flashing with fury, Baer rushed Braddock—his first charge of the match—but Braddock stopped him abruptly with an uppercut at close quarters that snapped Baer's head back. He roared, coming back with a combination, but the assault was ill-timed and glanced off Braddock's head without doing damage. Jim doubled down, presenting Baer with two straight lefts to the head, two crushing rights to his jaw.

"Look at Braddock take those belts and come back!" Ford Bond cried. "Where did he get that left he's feeding Baer?"

Max stepped back, bought time by grooming himself. He wiped his gloves on the back of his trunks after landing a punch as if he didn't want Braddock's sweat or blood to soil the leather. While Baer preened, Jim stalked, then landed a stiff, whip-fast jab that put a moment's wobble in Baer's muscular legs.

Jim tried to press his advantage, but Baer rushed him, distracting his opponent with a wildly swinging left while smashing his lethal right into Jim's bum ribs. Braddock reeled, the power of Max's blow flattening his lungs.

Gasping for air, Braddock struggled to counter with a flurry of punches that ended when they fell into a clinch.

"The champ has clearly hurt the challenger," said Ford Bond. "Braddock is wobbling, appears ready to drop . . ."

The crowd roared their disapproval.

Inside the hug, Baer managed a bull's-eye to the ribs again. Braddock's mouth gaped like a beached fish.

"That the right spot, old man?"

Jim knew every boxer's hits were different. Some fired in hard, penetrating bullets that dug into your muscles, others threw haymakers that broke like boulders against your head. Max Baer's punch felt like a leather-covered sledgehammer, like the gore-covered mallet he'd used to bash the skulls of cattle in his father's slaughterhouse.

The bell sounded. McAvoy separated the fighters. Baer gave Braddock a patronizing pat on the back as they moved to their corners.

Braddock collapsed onto his stool. Gould pulled on the waistband of the blue trunks to help Jim breathe. Doc Robb treated his cuts. Ray poured water into his mouth, but Jim gagged and coughed it up.

"Air," he gasped.

Jim's crew hovered over him until the warning buzzer sounded. Gould examined his ribs. "They ain't busted. Not yet."

Across the ring, Baer was mugging for the reporters, acting like he was on crutches. His thumb jerked in Braddock's direction. Sporty Lewis and the other ringside sportswriters guffawed.

"What's with the clowning around?" Ray asked Joe.

"Ah, he just wants to put on a good show for the rubes," Gould replied. "All Hollywood, that Maxie."

Jim took in the dancing bear act, knew he himself had thought like that once, back when he only worried about giving the crowd a good thrill, handing them the big knockout they were salivating to see. He'd risk a victory on points just to get a dramatic finish—just to hear those cheers, win the approval of the promoters, get that next headliner's spot.

Watching Baer's antics, Braddock realized that pleasing the crowd didn't matter to him anymore. Jim wasn't boxing to thrill reporters, please promoters, or wow the crowd. He was boxing for his family's future. He wasn't even fighting Baer. He was fighting to beat back the thing that had beaten him.

Suddenly, the bell sounded. One minute was up. Three minutes to go.

ROUND 3

Despite his battered condition, Braddock burst out of his corner, leather flying, for the third time. He pummeled Baer's head while the champ battered Braddock's torso.

"That's the way, Jimmy, get him good." Gould was at the ropes, punching the air, yelling himself hoarse. It was all he could do to help his fighter now, so Joe kept up the raspy tirade.

Jim delivered two lefts to Baer's face, then a left and right combination to the skull. Baer drove his own left into Braddock's midsection, the glove sunk muscle deep. Gould winced, knowing that if Baer'd had a real left, Braddock might have tumbled. But Maxie was no all-around fighter—he was a heavy hitter with a bone-crunching right and a left that was weak as hospital coffee. As Gould expected, Braddock shrugged it off.

Dancing backward, Braddock flecked Baer's face with double long-lefts, but Jim's fatal right arrived too high to connect and Gould cursed.

"Lower the swing, Jim," cried Gould.

Meanwhile, Baer stepped around Braddock's defense and continued to pound his battered midsection with both hands. Soft leather slapped against hard muscle, and Gould winced when he saw it. Some of Baer's stomach smashes were too close to the danger zone, and Joe angrily called for Baer to keep his punches up.

Jim tried to counter with a combination, but Baer easily blocked. Then Braddock stung him with a right to the jaw, the sound reaching Gould's ears over the din of the crowd. Baer snarled like a beast, eyes wild, nostrils flaring.

"Protect yourself, Jimmy!" Gould warned—too late. Baer slammed Braddock's body with another stiff right. The punch was visibly low and the referee moved in, warning Baer to keep his fists up.

Gould panicked when he saw Braddock dropping his guard. Baer saw it too. Max had smelled Jim's blood and now he wanted to taste it. Before Gould could warn his fighter what was coming, it came.

Baer slammed Jim's temple with a vicious left. Braddock's knees wobbled and Gould froze in dread. Baer skipped across the canvas, making faces and aping Jim's obvious agony.

Joe considered throwing in the towel just then. He turned toward Ray, but the corner man yanked the cloth out of reach.

"Give 'em a chance, Joe," Ray said.

"Easy for you," Gould replied. "You don't have to face Mrs. Braddock."

A few seconds later, Jim was straightening without reaching for the ropes, and Gould breathed easier.

A bemused Baer rubbed his gloves on his trunks, flicked his nose and charged. This time it was Braddock who scored—a long right, then a left jab that made Max's backward-lurching head look like a punching bag.

"That's right, that's the way!" yelled Gould bouncing up and down as Ray snapped his towel in the air.

When the bell rang, the audience leaped to their feet.

ROUND 4

The opening bell's clang had barely faded before Baer and Braddock were both out of their corners, standing toe to toe, trading left jabs to the head. Baer's were an exercise in futility. He'd throw and throw and throw again, but Jim's half steps made Maxie miss by inches. Braddock's footwork was never better, and most of his own blows hit home.

In desperation Baer shifted his attack, going for the torso. After several heavy smashes, he was gratified to see a red bruise appear on Braddock's left ribs. As Jim sucked air, Baer was certain every breath produced lancing agony for his opponent.

To buy time, Braddock drove a volley of sharp left jabs to Baer's head, but the champ wasn't going to let that continue. He draped his heavy arms over Braddock in a clinch. This time Baer didn't wisecrack; he needed the wind just to remain standing.

After a beat, McAvoy called for a break, but instead of releasing him, Baer tried to wrestle Braddock.

"Dirty fighting!" bellowed Joe Gould from the ropes. "Baer's a stinking rat!"

McAvoy exploded at the breach of fistic etiquette. Shook his finger in Maxie's face. "I warned ya, Baer. I say break once and I don't say it twice!"

Max released Braddock amid boos and catcalls.

Legs braced, Baer pulled up his trunks, shook the sweat out of his shock of black hair. Turning his back on Braddock, he threw up his hands by way of apology. Out of the corner of his eye, Baer could see Braddock had let his guard down.

Without warning, Baer spun, delivering a thundering right to Braddock's sinewy torso. That crimson bruise was like a target, and Maxie aimed for it. His glove slammed flesh, dug deep to grind the ribs to the bone. But to everyone's surprise—especially Baer's—Braddock countered with a left-right combination before retreating.

Baer snarled his frustration, threw a right hook and cursed when it grazed Braddock's jaw, barely touching his opponent a split second before the round ended.

ROUND 5

Ancil Hoffman rubbed the back of his neck in dismay. He could see plain as day that Braddock's ribs were mashed, yet the man was controlling the round, repeatedly jabbing his fighter, throwing Max off guard and off balance.

Joe Gould's shouted instructions to "protect your goddamn ribs, Jimmy" had not gone unheeded, and Braddock had doubled his footwork to elude his opponent. Baer was going for the knockout now. Ancil could see it in his eyes, the way he telegraphed his punches, and Ancil knew Baer was timing his throws wrong, waiting for the chance to use the sledgehammer rather than wearing his opponent down, which was obviously Braddock's strategy.

But no matter how many times his man sent a punch

forward, Braddock wasn't accepting delivery. The challenger slipped and pivoted, dodging every blow the champ tossed at him.

Ancil winced when Max Baer's own lunge threw him off balance. Braddock, by contrast, was gliding so gracefully away from Maxie's swings he made the champ look like a stumblebum. The crowd booed. Even some of the reporters laughed. "Traitorous bastards," muttered Ancil.

Baer was equally infuriated. He charged Braddock, but his uppercut slapped nothing but air. Braddock's terse reply was a stream of long jabs that rained on Baer's face. Blinded by leather, Baer clinched. Before McAvoy could break the fighters apart, Baer rose up and smacked Jim with an illegal backhand.

Ancil cursed, hammered the ropes.

Gould was hopping mad. "What the hell, McAvoy?!" he bawled. "Wake up, you wet son of a bitch, wake up!"

McAvoy chuffed, shot Gould a peeved look. Then he tapped Baer's head, held a warning finger under his nose. The champ could hardly see it. Even locked in a clinch, Braddock was tagging Baer, finishing with a right to his jawbone.

"Come on, break it up," Ancil bellowed.

But the clinch only got tighter. As Baer grappled, Braddock butted his head against the champ's chin. Baer's teeth rattled under the mouth protector. Then the champ roared, enraged.

"No, Maxie, no!" Ancil cried, even as Baer lifted Braddock and tossed him against the ropes.

The crowd howled for Baer's blood. With loud boos, they pitched balled-up newspapers, cigar butts, food wrappers into the ring. Max turned and contemptuously saluted the grumbling mob. Then he shook his gloved fist at Jim Braddock's nose, who eyed him warily under sweat-soaked hair.

The bell closed out the round.

In the corner, Ernie worked Max's shoulder. Ancil Hoffman hopped over the ropes and screamed at his fighter. "What the hell are you doing?!"

Max sneered, eyes on Braddock. "Don't worry about it."

"Then quit screwing around!"

Ernie spoke up. "Boss, I think Maxie stopped screwing around a while ago—"

Ancil's thorny glare shut the corner man up.

"Relax," gargled Max, spitting water.

Ancil followed Max's gaze to the opposite corner. Gould was huddled tight with Braddock.

"Yeah, sure. I'll relax," said Ancil. "After we walk out of here with that title."

ROUND 6

A snarling Max Baer drew first blood. The champ came out swinging, driving three terrific uppercuts home within the opening seconds of the round.

Blood flowed from Braddock's nose, his mouth. Baer saw the crimson torrent and was back in the slaughterhouse, breathing the metallic tang of freshly spilled gore, feeling the life-and-death power of his smashing hammer, the cracking skulls shocking his arm, building his body into the Apollo of the boxing world—a godlike standing he had no intention of relinquishing, least of all to a broken-down bum three years his senior. Baer grunted with animal satisfaction.

Braddock came back with a weak left that creased Max's face. Baer fired back with a short right uppercut that threw Braddock back. He closed to finish the aging Irishman, when suddenly, Baer found himself on the receiving end of a wrecking ball.

From somewhere, Braddock summoned enough raw power to dispatch a devastating right to Baer's jaw. Max's knees sagged, the stadium lights faded, came back brighter than before. He fought for air, tasted leather as Braddock rattled his head with one, two, three left jabs.

Through a hazy fog, Baer wobbled on the canvas. He threw, determined to continue the slugfest, but Braddock's left was evcrywhere, delivering body blows like Baer's chorus girls delivered kisses—though Braddock's connections were a tad less gentle.

Baer repaid Braddock in kind, dishing up a flurry so fast and furious that Jim gasped for breath. Baer stepped in to press his advantage, but his eagerness turned his punches wild and wide, and he missed his target. Braddock didn't. His left dug into Baer's face. Surprise left Max with a lowered guard, and Braddock's glove hammered the champ's temple.

Thunder and lightning struck together, splitting Max's vision. He staggered. Through a red veil he saw Braddock's silhouette. He wanted to strike back, but his right eye throbbed, began to close.

For the first time in this title fight, Baer was relieved to hear the bell that ended the round. As he stumbled to his corner, Baer vowed to finish the challenger off in the next, even if he had to kill Jim Braddock right here and now, in front of tens of thousand of the Cinderella Man's pathetically devoted fans.

ROUND 7

Joe Gould watched Max Baer burst from his corner and knew by the gleam in the fighter's eyes that the champ was finished clowning. Crouched, fists raised, Max Baer was all business. The audience sensed the change as well, and were swept to their feet in quiet alarm

"Keep sliding, Jim," Gould bellowed, his voice hoarse. "Just keep sliding to the right. And don't rush him."

But Jim was unafraid, and met Baer in the center ring. After hurling a glancing body blow, Baer took a left-right combination to his outthrust jaw. Max fired back with a long right that barely missed Braddock's head—Joe Gould could hear the swish of leather cutting air, the collective intake of breath from the audience.

Baer missed with another wild right and Braddock popped him with a hard jab, then another. Baer threw his weight against his foe and they fell into a clinch.

"I'm getting bored, old man," hissed Baer, loud enough for the people at ringside to hear it.

McAvoy moved quickly to pull them apart, and Baer used his muscle and weight to toss Braddock around.

"Watch that!" the ref warned.

Max connected with a quick set of slams to Jim's sweet spot, the blotchy red bruise on his vulnerable ribs. The last jab hit below the belt, and Gould went crazy—

"Dirty stinking rat! Pay attention, McAvoy!"

Braddock grunted in agreement. "Keep 'em up, Max."

Max smiled—a deadly poisonous thing—delivered a stunning combination to Braddock's torso, his head.

"That *up* enough?" Baer roared.

Through the brutal surge of agony, Jim forced a half smile. "Yeah, Max. That's fine."

Gould could see his boy was hurting. That the tenderness in his ribs was going to bring him down. But Jim swallowed the pain, found a way to slap Max back with a jerking jab to his head before falling against Baer in another clinch.

McAvoy yanked the boxers apart as the bell clanged. But Baer, whether he hadn't heard the signal or simply ignored it, shoved the ref aside and landed a series of combinations on Jim, who came back, raging mad, with a powerful uppercut followed by a left hook. They were the most forceful blows Jim could muster. Max Baer just laughed.

As McAvoy jumped between the boxers, they glared at each other over the referee's bobbing head.

At ringside, Ford Bond's tinny voice spewed words faster than the challenger's fists—

"Baer, a crude swinger but heavy handed, had smashed former champion Max Schmeling into defeat on his way to the title and cruelly battered the huge Primo Carnera to become champion. He had been expected to blast Braddock out of the fight. But here it is, the end of the seventh and Baer and Braddock are dead even."

ROUND FIFTEEN

No contender for a title ever entered the ring conceded so little chance. Braddock was regarded by many of the ringsiders as a pathetic figure, as merely a pugilistic sacrifice to the glory of Baer.

—Damon Runyon, 1936

Mae came through the front door, unpinned her hat. The house seemed empty.

"Alice?"

She stepped into the parlor. A lamp was glowing, a newspaper spread open across the couch. A meal was set on the kitchen table, uneaten, and the dining room was dark and deserted. Then Mae heard a voice— muted, familiar. The sound was mingled with the noise of a crowd.

Mae found them in the hallway, gathered on the hardwood floor around the open closet door: her sister Alice, Jay and Howard at her side, Rosy resting on her elbows, staring intently at the radio, listening to the distinctive voice of announcer Ford Bond.

"In the seventh round, Max Baer staged a slashing outburst. He tore into Jimmy Braddock with a series of vicious uppercuts. The crowd was impressed with the champ's display and waited for big things from Max Baer in the eighth round. But they didn't count on Braddock's determination to finish the fight, and it was the champ who took it on the chin . . ."

Rosy saw her mother in the doorway. "It's the cops."

Jay and Howard looked up. Mae loomed over them. Howard's guilt was all consuming. Jay's was mingled with defiance.

". . . By the ninth round, it was an established fact that Braddock has fought better than anybody thought he could, though some would say that it is only because Baer allowed it. The proof of their assertion came in the tenth round, when Max Baer completely dominated the ring . . ."

Mae reached for the cord in the wall. Jay caught her eye. "Please, Ma."

She peered into their pleading faces—including her sister's. Against such odds Mae couldn't help but surrender. But she stubbornly refused to listen herself. Wordlessly, she walked away.

On the radio, the bell clanged, signaling the start of the eleventh round.

ROUND 11

Raging mad, Baer stormed out of his corner, his eyes a black abyss. Jim saw him coming, danced to the right. Max stayed with him and ripped away, pinning Braddock with a right-left combination.

Jim tasted the leather, blinked to clear his eyes. Then

it came. Baer's sledgehammer right—the punch that buried Frankie Campbell, that turned Ernie Schaff into a walking dead man. It seemed to Braddock that he'd been lifted off the canvas, that his legs had been cut off. He felt weightless and heavy at the same time. Mind floating, knees unable to support his weight

"Oh," screamed Ford Bond. "What a tremendous shot by Baer, flush on Braddock's chin . . ."

Jim stumbled backward, felt the ropes cut into his back. He heard the crowd's roar, the announcer screaming over the chaos.

". . . Braddock is reeling against the ropes while Baer stands like a wood chopper waiting for the tree to fall!"

Suddenly, ridiculously, the cry of his youngest son, Howard, popped into Braddock's frazzled mind. "Tim-mmm-berrrrr!" With it came the memory of his family, of what he was fighting for—and against. Like an approaching subway train, reality roared back, the howls of the audience battering his ears. Jim felt the ropes, let them carry his weight for a moment. He knew he'd been hit, but it was nothing new. Baer might have smashed him, but no harder than he had been smashed by the Crash of 1929. He'd forced himself to keep going after that knockdown. To get up again. And he got up now. Back on his feet.

Through eyes suddenly focused, Braddock saw Baer hovering near. Braddock grinned. Referee McAvoy stepped aside to allow the fight to resume, but Baer just stared at Jim, an expression of frustrated disbelief on the champ's broken face.

Braddock shifted his weight, bounced back on his feet. Baer shrugged, tucked his chin into his chest and moved in to finish the job. Braddock lashed out with a sharp right that took the champ off guard. He followed that jab with another—then another.

Baer staggered back, startled as blood burst from his lips. He touched the gloves to his face, they came away red. Baer wiped his gloves on the back of his trunks—the opening Braddock was waiting for. Braddock stepped in as fast as he'd moved in the first round and nailed Baer with an explosive right. Baer wheeled in a half turn, caught his balance.

He turned back to Braddock, insulted that the challenger would interrupt his preening ritual, and lunged with looping rights that failed to connect. With each miss, Jim stabbed at Max. A jab, a cross, another jab. Braddock felt the strength flow back into his limbs with each swing.

The tumultuous screams that filled the stadium drowned out the sound of the bell, and Johnny McAvoy had to pull the fighters apart. As he stumbled back to his corner, Max Baer spat blood.

"Doc, get over here!" Gould screamed. Braddock was hardly on the stool when the cutman started working under his eye, cleaning and closing the deep wound. The gash had been torn by Baer's sledgehammer, which Braddock had survived, to the champ's dismay.

Through streams of sweat and blood Braddock focused on Joe Gould. The man's face was flushed, he seemed close to tears. Jimmy tried to cheer him up with a wisecrack—"Do I look that bad?"—but his lips felt like wet putty.

"Jimmy," said Gould. "Win, lose, or draw . . ." His voice caught.

Jim smiled under the surgery. "Thanks, Joe. For all of it."

Gould's mouth moved, Braddock lifted a blood-stained glove. "Joe. Stop talking."

Mae gave up pretending. Pretending to relax in the living room. Pretending to read the newspaper article she'd been staring at. Pretending she could not hear the muted sounds from the radio in the next room. Pretending that her husband was safe and fine and not battling for his life.

Finally, Mae threw aside the paper, rose from the couch, and crossed the living room. She peeked around the corner, into the hallway. The closet door was still open, Alice, Jay, Howard and Rosy transfixed by the voice of the sports announcer.

Lurking just around the corner, where her children couldn't see her, Mae leaned against the wall and listened too.

ROUND 12

Baer and Braddock faced each other, swapped left hooks. The motion seemed futile until Braddock's lightning combination sent Baer scrambling backward in an effort to escape.

Braddock moved with him to press the attack. Then Baer lifted a gloved fist and stuck it in Braddock's face—not to strike him, but to blind the challenger to his real swing, a lethal right cross.

From the sidelines, Joe Gould recognized Baer's trademark move, opened his mouth to scream a warning.

Gould didn't have to. Joe Jeanette had spied the move while viewing Baer's fight films weeks before, clued Jimmy to the trick, made him train for endless hours to be ready for just such a maneuver. Braddock deftly slapped Baer's left aside and stung Max with a sharp jab. Then he circled to the right, out of Baer's reach.

"He's slow, Jimmy!" howled Gould. "Dance around him. You know what to do. Baer's a bum."

Baer, angry and off balance, threw a futile swing that cut the night air. Jim slipped behind his guard and walloped the champ with two of his own. Baer slapped his glove against Braddock's face to hold him back. Jim faked right, skipped left, hammering the champ with two more well-placed clouts. Helpless and outboxed, Baer slipped into a clinch. The champ slapped his glove against Braddock's ruined ribs, eliciting a grunt.

As the referee pulled the fighters apart, Baer cuffed Braddock on the chin with a desperate backhand. Braddock shook it off, found a gap in Baer's armor and pounded him some more.

The crowd was roaring, driven to a frenzy by conflicting emotions. Joy. Terror. Disbelief. Even the jaded members of the press seemed stunned.

"Am I seeing what I'm seeing?" cried Sporty Lewis.

"It's a funeral, all right," shouted the young reporter at his shoulder. "And Max Baer is the guest of honor."

But Lewis didn't hear the kid's words. He was already on his feet, screaming at the top of his lungs—just like everybody else.

Soon the chant rolled down the aisles toward the ring, a tidal wave of sound.

"Braddock! Braddock! Braddock!"

Sporty Lewis joined the chorus.

Through a haze of pain and confusion, Max Baer heard the chanting, the cheers. Gripped by a berserker rage, the champ charged Braddock, left swinging. His blows connected fast and hard—the last one below the belt. The leather glove sunk deep into Braddock's gut. He folded up around the fist as the air shot out of his lungs in a hiss. Jim stumbled backward as the bell clanged, ending the round.

Joe Gould was over the ropes, lunging at the champ before the sound of the bell had faded. "Why don't you just kick him in the balls, you asshole!"

Johnny McAvoy intercepted Gould and hauled him back to the ropes.

"Let me have a shot at him, you son of a bitch," Gould continued to rage.

Doc Robb grabbed Gould's belt, helped the referee hoist the little spitting-mad manager over the ropes, out of the ring. Meanwhile Braddock, puffing hard, sank onto his stool.

Baer was bleeding from a new cut and his right eye was swollen nearly shut. But he stood in the center of the ring, refusing to move into his corner, until Johnny McAvoy crossed the canvas to face him.

"That last low blow will cost you the round, Max," the referee said.

Baer snarled at the man, waved him away like royalty dismissing a serf, and moved to his corner. Ancil leaped the ropes, pushed his face into Baer's. "You're behind. Are you listening to me? You wanna lose the goddamn championship to this nobody?"

Max shoved his manager aside.

From her secret vantage point, Mae listened to the thirteenth and fourteenth round with mounting dread. With one final round to go, she moved out of the shadows and approached her children.

Howard and Jay looked up fearfully—afraid she was going to make them stop listening. Somehow, Rosy understood Mae's real intentions. The little girl smiled, slid sideways, patted a spot of floor right next to her.

"Sit here, Mommy," she said.

Mae paused for a moment, then sat on the floor to be with her family. On the radio, the bell clanged.

"It's the fifteenth and final round," reported Ford Bond. "The crowd is yelling for Braddock to stay away because Max Baer is going for the knockout . . ."

Mae went pale, turned slightly away to hide her fear. Jay and Howard didn't notice their mother's reaction, but Alice frowned. Rosy reached out and touched her mother's hand.

". . . But Braddock is not staying away," the announcer continued, "and Baer is delivering the biggest punches of the fight—maybe of his life!"

Howard was pale now, his lower lip trembling. Jay put on a brave face, but Mae could see her oldest boy felt the same as his brother. Both were worried their father would be hurt, would not come home that night—or ever.

". . . But Braddock is not only standing . . . He is moving forward . . . Boldly, bravely bringing the fight to his opponent . . ."

ROUND 15

The people in the cheap seats had surged forward, stamping and screaming, completely surrounding the fistic field of battle. The mob was a solid wall of flesh and bone that pinned Joe Gould, the reporters, the judges—everyone at ringside against the edge of the blood-stained canvas.

Inside that ring, Jim Braddock and Max Baer were knotted, bloodied, battered, and snuffing like winded horses. Sweat streamed down their swollen faces as they gasped for air. Eyes locked on his opponent, each fighter warily circled the other, stalking, waiting for an opening.

Suddenly they slammed together like charging rams. Max Baer was sailing punches, every last one with knockout power. But the shots were wild, anxious, and ineffective. Braddock was still standing, and more, he was coming on with his signature left jab coiled and ready.

"Take a walk, Jimmy!" yelled Joe Gould.

At ringside, Ford Bond, jostled by the maddened crowd, clutched his microphone like a lifeline. "This is not boxing, folks!" he cried. "This is a walloping ballet!"

To the men in the ring, the final seconds seemed to stretch into an eternity. There was no other place, no other time, no other world beyond this square of roped-off canvas. The howling mob vanished, managers and corner men disappeared, the referee and the judges ceased to exist. Only the other fighter was real.

Braddock moved forward aggressively, scoring with a string of well-placed jabs that rocked the exhausted Baer. But the champ took the raps, waiting for the opportunity to send his challenger to the mat.

Braddock danced sideways, but his movements were sluggish. He tossed a jab that glanced off Baer's bruised chin. But as he threw, Max saw an opening— and that was all the heavyweight champ needed.

With his mythic right arm, Baer clocked Braddock in the temple. The patented sledgehammer spun Jimmy, leaving him wide open for the second half of the deadly combination—an uppercut that seemed to start at the floor and climb upward to the sky over Queens, with only Jim Braddock's chin in the way.

"Baer is swinging with a tremendous blow," bellowed Ford Bond. "I don't know how Braddock is going to survive it!"

A tomblike silence fell over the arena as the crowd waited for the Cinderella Man to topple.

But Braddock decided to die another day. With a ducking pivot, he avoided the savage uppercut and countered with a brace of hard lefts. Max loomed so close he was practically standing on Braddock's toes. But Jim dodged a clinch to deliver his own smashing uppercut that lifted Max Baer off his feet. The fighters were still trading blows when the bell clanged.

"It's over! The fight is over, and the referee is pulling the fighters apart," cried Ford Bond.

It took all of Johnny McAvoy's considerable

strength to thrust the men away from each other. Gould leaped into the ring and dragged Jimmy to his corner. Slapping his back, the junkyard dog of a manager grinned like a satisfied cat.

Over the chaos, Sporty Lewis reached into the ring, tugged hard on Referee McAvoy's trouser leg. The ref tried to shake the reporter off, but Sporty hung on like a hyperactive terrier.

"What!" bellowed McAvoy.

"How'd you score it, Johnny?"

McAvoy counted out loud. "Nine . . . Five . . . One. I call it even."

"Even?" Sporty's eyes went wide in stunned disbelief. McAvoy hustled away to consult with the judges.

The chaos inside the Garden had not diminished with the end of the fight. The fans, pressing close to the canvas, waited to hear the officials declare a winner. Bond fired a steady dialogue into his microphone. "The crowd, which was on its feet for almost the entire fight, is still standing, yelling for who they clearly believe to be the winner of this fight . . ."

He didn't even have to hold up his microphone for his listening audience to hear who the crowd was pulling for.

"Braddock! Braddock! Braddock! Braddock!"

Minutes later, Braddock was still leaning on the ropes, head back. Doc Robb wiped the blood out of his eyes, worked on closing a deep cut. Gould yanked the laces out of Jim's gloves, watching the judges the whole time.

"I don't like it, Jimmy. Every time they take this long for a decision they're deciding to screw somebody."

A shadow fell over their corner. It was Max Baer, his blood-stained silk robe draped over his sweating shoulders. Gould glared at the fighter. Max ignored the manager, looked Jim Braddock in the eye.

"You beat me. No matter what they say."

Jim broke the stare, fumbled for the right words. Baer was gone before Jim had a chance to say them.

Pacing only a few feet away, Sporty Lewis missed the exchange. His eyes were on the judges, still locked in a huddle. Lewis slapped the cub reporter on the arm. "They're robbing him. Stealing Braddock's night."

Some of the fans—toughs from the Jersey docks— overheard Lewis's assessment. A plug-ugly brute with beefy arms etched with tattoos stepped forward.

"Make up your minds, ya bums," he barked at the judges. "We all know who won."

A thousand voices joined the chorus. The stamping feet rolled like thunder, shook the stands. At last, the judges solemnly handed Al Franzin, the Garden's announcer, a small, white card. Without glancing at it Franzin climbed over the ropes, moved to the microphone stand set up in the middle of the ring. The roar of the crowd faded. Thirty-five thousand people watched as the announcer held the card over his head.

"Ladies and gentlemen. I have your decision!" Franzin squinted as he studied the card. "The winner . . . and *new* heavyweight champion of the world . . ."

The rest of the ring announcer's words were lost in an explosion of noise as a roar like Niagara's echoed across Astoria's flats.

* * *

On the streets of Weehawken, North Bergen, Bloom-field, Wayne, and Newark, people poured from their houses. Horns honked, sirens blared. The hot June night was suddenly alive with a riotous celebration not seen since before the Crash.

In the smoky interior of Quincy's bar, Quincy him-self dispensed free beer to the boisterous crowd. Years of despair were wiped away. Faces creased and worn were suddenly young again. Laughter shook the roof, and hardened dockworkers sobbed like babies.

At his butcher shop, Sam placed a slab of beef on the chopping block and gleefully hacked away, con-vinced that if he sold enough meat, he could produce a hundred more champs just like James J. Braddock.

A blast of air stirred the candles in Father Rorick's church. The tall doors were flung wide, golden light spilled into the street as the devoted filed out of the church to join everyone else in an impromptu street party.

Sara Wilson remained inside. She held her baby girl in her arms, tears dewing her cheeks. At the altar, Fa-ther Rorick was unable to hide his satisfied smile. He turned his face toward heaven and gave thanks.

At their usual haunts, bookies sweated. At ten-to-one odds against Braddock, a flock of bettors who stuck with their favorite son were due big payoffs.

In a tiny shed inside the dockyard, Jake the foreman leaned his rail-thin form back in his chair and listened to the frantic announcer declare Jim Braddock the new champ, happy with the knowledge that tomorrow, one less lean, hungry face would be standing outside the gate, desperate for work.

It was a start, Jake thought. *One step at a time.*

On a quiet little residential block in Newark, Mae Braddock's cry cut the night, her children's excited shouts echoed down the block. In the midst of the hysteria, Rose Marie Braddock smiled up at her mother and with little-girl certainty declared, "It's the meat."

At ringside, the reporters were pushing and shoving to escape the mob and file their stories. Sporty Lewis sat alone. Seersucker suit rumpled, feet propped on his typewriter, he stared at the chaos in the ring without seeing it. With arms across his chest, a half smile frozen on his lips, he relived the fight—the miracle— in no hurry to lose the moment.

Around Sporty, fans surged forward in a mad rush to get a better look at the Cinderella Man. They wanted a chance to shake his hand, to pat his back, to take a little of his fairy-tale magic home with them tonight. But the ring was flanked by the Garden's security staff, who firmly pushed them back.

Boxing officials, the judges, and Jimmy Johnston climbed through the ropes to join Al Franzin in the center of the ring. Gould spied Johnston, and the paunchy little manager swept the big, stogie-chewing promoter up in a bear hug.

Flanked by the commission, by Joe Gould and Jimmy Johnston, Franzin made a victory announcement that was drowned in an ocean of cheers. Finally, Franzin lifted Braddock's fist over his head and stepped back.

In the center of the ring, bathed in golden light,

James J. Braddock stood with legs braced, arms lifted in victory. But as tears streamed down his battered face, as thousands of crazed fans shouted their adoration, Braddock's heart was somewhere else, across an island and two rivers, in a little New Jersey apartment, where his wife and three children waited for him to come home; because, in the end, long after all the photos were taken, the articles written, and winnings collected, Jim knew it was that simple fact and not much else that not only made him the heavyweight champion of the world, but the luckiest man in it.

EPILOGUE

. . . When Baer hit me on the chin with his Sunday punch and I took it, I'm the happiest guy in the world. Nobody knew what that fight meant to me. Money, security, education for my children, financial aid for my parents. If ever a guy went into the ring with something to fight for, I was the guy.

—James J. Braddock, 1935

JAMES J. BRADDOCK
HEAVYWEIGHT CHAMPION OF THE WORLD
JUNE 13, 1935–JUNE 22, 1937

And so it was, on June 13, 1935, James J. Braddock, at the age of 29, as a ten-to-one underdog, won the heavyweight championship of the world from Max Baer in a unanimous fifteen-round decision. The general response by press and public was to rule it one of the greatest upsets in boxing history. Most agreed that Baer, who was so confident he had told reporters he was afraid he might actually kill Braddock, was outfoxed and outboxed.

For two years, Braddock did not box again. Much backroom haggling was done over who would challenge him for the title. Finally, the fight was arranged. Jim would defend his crown against Joe Louis, the "Brown Bomber," one of the greatest boxers to ever enter the ring. On June 22, 1937, the two met in Chicago's White Sox Stadium.

By this time, Braddock had developed arthritis in the left side. The morning of the fight, his doctor gave him a shot in the arm so he could lift it, but Braddock found that he had very little strength in it during the fight. Still, he managed to knock Louis down in the very first round with an uppercut. By round four, however, Louis had gained the advantage.

According to Braddock, "After a couple of rounds I knew I was in there with a great fighter, and this is going to be a tough fight." The end came in the eighth round. "I fought as well as I'd ever done, but that Louis . . . oh, he was *good*! In the eighth I had nothing left, and when he hit me with that right I just lay there. . . . I could have stayed there for three weeks."

Joe Louis would go on to become one of the greatest heavyweight title holders in the history of boxing. His defeat of German Max Schmeling in one round June 22, 1938, at Yankee Stadium reverberated throughout the world, thwarting a powerful symbol of German dictator Adolph Hitler's contention of racial supremacy. Like Braddock, Joe Louis, a violin student turned pro boxer, would pay back all of the relief money he'd once accepted.

James J. Braddock would go on to fight one more match after Louis, in 1938, against the young Welsh boxer Tommy Farr, who'd gone fifteen full rounds against Joe Louis and was favored three to one going into the Braddock match. It was an exhilarating "comeback" victory for the aging Braddock, who'd yet again been rated an underdog climbing into the ring and hailed as an upset winner going out. Less than two weeks after that victorious match, however, when lucrative offers were still on the table, he announced his retirement from the sport, making the decision to go out a winner. Jim Braddock won fifty-one of eighty-five career bouts, twenty-six by KO; his record included three draws, two no contests, and seven no decisions; and boxing histories wrote about him in his epitaph as having gone down a fighting champion.

"I have won my last fight," Braddock announced to the press at the time, "and I think I could still beat most of the outstanding contenders for the heavyweight championship, but I have spent fifteen years in the game, and in fairness to everyone, but especially to my wife and children, I believe it is time for me to withdraw. . . . This is my farewell to boxing, a sport which owes me nothing and to which I owe everything—the many friends I have made, and the means with which I have been able to provide for my family."

After his boxing career ended, Jim maintained his friendship with Joe Gould, who had scored Jim a cagey deal. In return for granting Joe Louis the chance to claim the title from Braddock in 1937, Gould required that Louis's wealthy Chicago manager, Mike Jacobs, agree to pay Braddock 10 percent of his share of the heavyweight championship fights for a decade, should Louis win. The deal is said to be one of the shrewdest ever struck in boxing, because Joe Louis's supremacy (1937 to 1949, the longest in the sport's history) meant

Jacobs controlled the heavyweight title fights for more than ten years. It provided Jim and Mae Braddock with an annuity that helped secure their financial future.

He remained "Jersey Jim" till the day he died, residing in the same North Bergen home he and Mae had bought after he'd won the championship. For the rest of his life, Braddock was applauded, admired, and respected by friends, neighbors, and strangers on the New Jersey streets. He was inducted into the Ring Boxing Hall of Fame in 1964, the Hudson County Hall of Fame in 1991, and the International Boxing Hall of Fame in 2001. As for any last words, they rightfully belong to James J. Braddock himself, who gave up his crown with the same gracious humility with which he'd worn it.

"Here's the situation as far as that goes," Braddock said in his 1972 interview with Peter Heller, two years before he passed away in his North Bergen home, "having the championship and then losing it. You always got to figure you're not the best man in the world, there might be somebody better. That's the way it was. That's the way boxing is. The champion don't always stand up. There's always somebody coming up to take him. That's a part of life."

JAMES J. BRADDOCK
JUNE 7, 1906–NOVEMBER 29, 1974

And so Braddock won the big title, and in the time he has held it, he has endeared himself to the American public by his unchanging modesty, his affability, and his sturdy character. His devotion to his wife and family . . . and withal his attitude as champion of the world that he will fight anybody regardless of color, or creed, has made him the most popular champion in the history of the game.

—Damon Runyon,
foreword from *Relief to Royalty*,
James J. Braddock's authorized biography, 1936

BIBLIOGRAPHY AND POSTSCRIPT

The screenplay for *Cinderella Man*, by Cliff Hollingsworth and Akiva Goldsman, is based on the life of James J. Braddock. However, certain characters, scenes and locations have been changed or combined for dramatic purposes in both the screenplay and this prose adaptation.

In the writing of this novel, the author also consulted source material beyond the screenplay, including contemporary sources such as newspaper and magazine articles, and books written long after the events, such as *An Illustrated History of Boxing* (sixth revised and updated edition) by Nat Fleischer and Sam Andre, with Dan Rafael, Citadel Press, 2001; *In This Corner: Forty-two World Champions Tell Their Stories*, by Peter Heller (expanded edition with Introduction by Muhammad Ali), De Capo Press, 1994; and *Hard Times: An Oral History of the Great Depression* by Studs Terkel, Random House, 1970.

Most invaluable to the creation of this text was the authorized biography *Relief to Royalty: The Story of James J. Braddock, World's Heavyweight Champion* by Lud (real name Ludwig Shabazian), sports editor for the *Hudson Dispatch* of Union City, New Jersey. Published in 1936 with a foreword by Damon Runyon, the book is currently out of print.